TEMPORARY PERFECTIONS

TEMPORARY PERFECTIONS

GIANRICO CAROFIGLIO

translated by Antony Shugaar

Rizzoli
ex libris

First published in the United States of America in 2011
by Rizzoli Ex Libris, an imprint of
Rizzoli International Publications, Inc.
300 Park Avenue South
New York, NY 10010
www.rizzoliusa.com

Copyright © 2010 Gianrico Carofiglio
First Italian edition Sellerio editore via Siracusa 50 Palermo,
January 2010
This edition published by arrangement with Rosaria Carpinelli
Consulenze Editoriali srl

The characters, events, and situations depicted in this novel are
entirely imaginary.

2011 2012 2013 2014 / 10 9 8 7 6 5 4 3 2 1

Distributed in the U.S. trade by Random House, New York

Printed in the United States of America

ISBN-13: 978-0-8478-3630-4

Library of Congress Catalog Control Number: 2011930247

1.

It all began with an innocent phone call from an old college classmate.

Sabino Fornelli is a civil lawyer. If one of his clients runs into criminal problems, Sabino calls and gives me the case. Then he washes his hands of it. Like many civil lawyers, he thinks of the criminal court system as a dangerous and disreputable place. He tries to steer clear of it.

One March afternoon, while I was absorbed in an appeal I was scheduled to argue the following day before the Court of Cassation, I received a call from Sabino Fornelli. We hadn't spoken in months.

"Ciao, Guerrieri, how are you?"

"Fine, how about you?"

"Same as ever. My son's doing a semester abroad, in the U.S."

"Great. Wonderful idea, that'll be a memorable experience."

"It's been a memorable experience for me, certainly. My wife's been driving me crazy since the day he left. She's been worried sick about him."

We went back and forth for a few more minutes, exchanging the usual platitudes, and then he got to the point of his call: Two clients of his wanted to see me about a sensitive and urgent matter. He spoke the words "sensitive and urgent" in a hushed voice that struck me as slightly ridiculous. The most serious case Fornelli had referred to me so far was a dramatic little affair involving obscenities and insults, a beating, and a breaking-and-entering charge.

Basically, given our past history, I couldn't take it too seriously when Sabino Fornelli called any case he sent my way "sensitive and urgent."

"I'm going to Rome tomorrow, Sabino, and I don't know what time I'll be back. The next day is Saturday." I glanced quickly at my appointment book. "Ask them to stop by late on Monday, some time after eight. What's the case?"

He didn't speak for a moment.

"Fine, some time after eight. I'm going to come, too. We'll tell you all about it in person. That'll be easier."

Now it was my turn not to speak for a moment. Fornelli had never come to my office with any of his referrals. I was about to ask him why he was doing it this time, and why he couldn't tell me anything over the phone, but something stopped me. Instead, I just said that it was fine and I'd expect them in my office at 8:30 on Monday. Then we both hung up.

I sat there for a minute, wondering what this was about. I couldn't think of an explanation, so I went back to my appeal.

2.

I like appearing before the Court of Cassation in Rome. It's Italy's highest court, and the judges are almost always well informed. They rarely fall asleep during hearings, and the chief magistrates, with the occasional exception, are courteous, even when they're ordering you to keep it short and not to waste the court's time.

The Court of Cassation is different from the criminal courts and especially the appellate courts. When you appear before the Court of Cassation, you feel you're in an orderly world, part of a justice system that works. That's just a feeling, of course, because the world is *not* orderly and justice is *not* served. Still, it's a nice feeling to have, and I'm usually in a good mood when I have to argue a case before the Court of Cassation, even though it means I have to get up earlier than usual.

It was a beautiful day, chilly and bright. The airplane took off and landed on time, defying the prevailing pessimistic expectations about air travel.

During the taxi ride from the airport to the courthouse, I had an unusual experience. The cab was just pulling away from the terminal when I noticed a dozen or so paperbacks piled on the passenger seat. I'm always curious to see which books people have in their homes, so I was even more curious about these books, found unexpectedly in the front seat of a cab. I glanced at the covers. There were a couple of mass-market detective novels, but also Simenon's *Red Lights*, Fenoglio's *A Private Affair*, and even a book of poetry by García Lorca.

"What are you doing with those books?"

"I read them, between fares."

Fair enough—a stupid question deserves a short answer. What does anyone do with books but read them?

"I asked because it's a little . . . unusual to see books in a taxi, especially so many of them."

"That's not true, actually. Lots of cab drivers like to read."

He spoke an almost unaccented Italian, and he seemed to choose his words deliberately. He handled his words with caution, as if they were delicate—even slightly dangerous—objects. As if they were razor sharp.

"I'm sure you're right. But you have a whole library up there."

"That's because I like to read several books at once. I switch depending on my mood. So I bring a lot of books with me, and then I forget to take home the ones I finish, and before you know it I've got a whole pile of them."

"I like to read several books at once, too. What are you reading now?"

"A Simenon novel. One reason I like it is that part of it takes place in a car, and I spend all my time in a car. That helps me appreciate it. Also, some García Lorca poems. I really like poetry, but it's pretty challenging. And when I'm tired, I read that one." He pointed at one of the mass-market mysteries. He named neither the title nor the author of the last book, and rightly so, I thought. I felt as if there were a complete aesthetic—precise, incisive, and well-defined—in the way he had discussed, and tacitly classified, his current reading list. I liked that. I tried to get a look at his face, from the elusive glances I caught of his profile as he drove and from his reflection in the rearview mirror. He was about thirty-five and pale, with a hint of shyness to his eyes.

"How did you become such an avid reader?"

"You won't believe me if I tell you."

"Try me."

"Until I was twenty-eight, I'd never picked up a book in my life outside of school. And I had a speech defect: I stuttered. I had a very bad stutter. You know, a stutter can ruin your life."

I nodded. Then I realized he couldn't see me.

"Yes, I can imagine. But you speak perfectly," I said. As I said it, though, I thought of his cautious way of speaking, the way he handled the words with care.

"After a while, I couldn't take it anymore. I went to see a speech therapist, and I took a course to get rid of my stutter. During the course we read books aloud."

"And that's how you got started?"

"Yes, that's how I discovered books. I finished the course, but I kept on reading. People say everything happens for a reason. Maybe I stuttered because I was meant to discover books. I don't know. But now my life is completely different from the way it used to be. I can't even remember how I used to spend my days."

"Well, that's a great story. I wish something like that would happen to me."

"What do you mean? Don't you like to read?"

"No, no, I love it. It's probably my favorite thing. What

I meant was I wish my life would change in some fantastic way like yours did."

"Oh, I see," he said. We were quiet as the car sped along the bus-and-taxi lane of the Via Ostiense.

We made it all the way to Piazza Cavour without hitting traffic once. My friend the book-reading cabbie stopped the car, turned off the ignition, and turned around to look at me. I thought he was about to tell me how much I owed him. I reached for my wallet.

"I'm reminded of a Paul Valéry quote."

"Yes?"

"It goes something like, 'The best way to make your dreams come true is to wake up.'"

We sat there for a few seconds, looking at one another. There was something more complex than shyness in the man's eyes. It was as if he were accustomed to fear, and he had disciplined himself to control that fear, in the knowledge that it would always be with him, waiting. I think my eyes displayed astonishment. I tried to remember if I'd ever read anything by Valéry. I wasn't sure.

"I thought that line might help you, considering what you just said. About change. I don't know if other people feel this way, but I like to share the things I read. When I repeat a line that I've read, or an idea, or a verse, I sort of feel a little as if I were the author. I love that."

He said the last few words almost as if he were apologizing. As if he had realized that he might have been a little pushy. I hastened to reassure him.

"Thanks very much. I've done the same thing since I was a boy. But I don't think I could have described it so clearly and so well."

Before I got out of the car, I shook hands with him. As I

was heading off for my appointment, I knew I would rather have stayed there, talking about books and other things. I was at least an hour early. I knew every detail of the case, and there was no need to go over my papers, so I decided to go for a walk. I crossed the Tiber, making my way over the Ponte Cavour. The river water was greenish yellow, glittering with quicksilver flashes of light, a delight to behold. There weren't many people around, only the occasional muffled sounds of cars and faint voices—background noises. I had the powerful and wonderfully irrational impression that this almost complete silence had been imposed for my own personal enjoyment. Someone said that moments of happiness take us by surprise and sometimes—often—go completely unnoticed. We only realize that we were happy afterward, which is pretty stupid. As I was walking toward the Ara Pacis, a memory from many years ago came to me.

I was studying for my exams with two friends, shortly before I was to graduate. In fact, the three of us had become friends because we studied together, wrote our theses at the same time, and graduated in the same class. These are things that create a bond, at least for a while, in certain cases. We were actually very different and had little in common, starting with our plans for the future. That is, they had plans for the future, while I didn't. They had decided to study law because they wanted to become magistrates, without a shadow of a doubt, with relentless determination. I had enrolled to study law because I didn't know what else to do.

I had mixed feelings about their determination. Part of me looked down on it. I thought my friends had narrow outlooks and predictable aspirations. But another part of me envied them their unambiguous plans, their clear vision of a desirable future. It was something I didn't really understand, something I failed to grasp, and which seemed to offer comfort. An antidote to the lurking anxiety that tinged my unfocused vision of the world.

Right after graduating, without even taking a real vacation, they immediately applied themselves seriously to studying for the magistrates exam. I applied myself seriously to wasting time. I spent my days as an intern in a civil law firm, a waste of time, and I fantasized about taking courses at foreign universities, though what kind of courses they might be remained vague. I was considering enrolling in the department of literature. I was pondering the idea of writing a novel that would change both my life and the lives of its large audience of readers, though luckily I never wrote a single page. In other words, I had my feet firmly on the ground and a head filled with clear ideas.

Because of these clear ideas, when the magistrates examination was announced, I decided on the spur of the moment that I would apply to take the test, too. When I told Andrea and Sergio, we shared a moment of odd, slightly embarrassing silence. Then they asked me what on earth I was thinking, since they knew perfectly well that I hadn't cracked a book since the day I'd received my degree. I told them I planned to study for the three months leading up to the written exam and give it a shot. Maybe, while I studied for that exam, I'd figure out what I wanted to do with my life.

I really did try to study during those few months, secretly cherishing the hope of a stroke of luck, a shortcut, a magical solution. The lazy man's dream.

Then, one February morning, in the middle of the stupid decade of the 1980s, Andrea Colaianni, Sergio Carofiglio, and Guido Guerrieri set off in Andrea's father's old Alfa

Romeo. They headed to Rome to take a battery of written examinations for the position of entry-level magistrate in the Italian judiciary.

I remember bits and pieces of that trip to Rome, an assortment of images—gas stations, an espresso and a cigarette and a piss, half an hour of impressively hard rain high in the Apennines—but the only memory I have of the whole episode is a feeling of lightness, an absence of responsibility. I had studied a little, but I hadn't really made an investment, not the way my friends had. I had nothing to lose, and if I failed to pass, as was all too likely, no one could call me a failure.

"Why are you doing this, anyway, Guerrieri?" Andrea asked me again as we drove, after turning down the car stereo. We were listening to a mix tape I'd made for the trip; songs like "Have You Ever Seen the Rain?," "I Don't Want to Talk About It," "Love Letters in the Sand," "Like a Rolling Stone," and "Time Passages." When Andrea asked me that question, I believe Billy Joel was playing "Piano Man."

"I don't really know. It's a shot in the dark, a game, whatever. Of course, even if I luck out, I don't think I'll see being a magistrate as my mission in life. I don't have your burning ambition."

It was the kind of thing that drove Andrea crazy, because it was right on target.

"What the fuck does that mean? What does burning ambition mean? Who has a mission in life? This is the kind of work I want to do. It interests me, and I think I'll enjoy it." He stopped and corrected himself immediately, to keep from jinxing himself. "I *would* enjoy it. And it would be a chance to do something useful."

"Same for me. I think the only way you can change

society, change the world, is from the inside. I believe that if you work as a magistrate—if you do a good job, of course— you can help change the world. Cleanse it of corruption, crime, and rot," Sergio said.

It was his words that stuck in my memory, and when I think back on them I feel something ambiguous, a mixture of tenderness and horror, at how those naïve aspirations were swallowed whole by the voracious crevasses of life.

I was about to deliver a rebuttal, but then I thought I really had no right. I was an interloper in their dreams. So I shrugged and turned up the sound on the tape deck, just as Billy Joel's voice faded and the opening guitar riff of Creedence Clearwater Revival's "Have You Ever Seen the Rain?" played. Outside, a massive thunderstorm had just ended.

The civil service test involved three written examinations: civil law, criminal law, and administrative law. The order in which the tests were administered was assigned randomly each year.

That year, the first exam was on administrative law. That was a subject I knew absolutely nothing about, and so I withdrew from the civil service exam after three hours, renouncing my secret and irrational hopes. The sliding door that leads to the world of adulthood wasn't destined to open for me just then, so I went to sit in the waiting room. I would remain in that waiting room for quite some time to come.

There have been times, in the years since, when I've wondered what my life would have been like if, by some fluke, I had passed that exam.

I would have left Bari. I might have become a different person, and I might never have returned home. That's what happened to Andrea Colaianni, who passed the exam; he moved far away and became a prosecuting magistrate, but in time he was forced to rein in his dreams of changing the world, for real, on his own.

Sergio Carofiglio didn't pass. He wanted to become a magistrate even more than Colaianni did, if that was possible, but he failed the written exams. He sat for the exams a second time, and then even a third, the maximum number the law allowed. We were no longer close by the time I heard that he had failed the third and final time, but I stopped to think about the devastating feelings of defeat and failure he must have experienced. Then he met a girl whose father was a manufacturer from the Veneto region, got married, and went to live somewhere around Rovigo, where he worked for his father-in-law and drowned his bitterness and broken dreams in the northern fog. Or maybe that's just how I imagined it; maybe he's actually rich and happy. Maybe not becoming a magistrate was the best thing that ever happened to him.

I stayed in Rome, after withdrawing from the civil service exam. My room in the *pensione* was paid up for three nights, that is, for the entire period of the written examinations. And so, while my friends were struggling with criminal law and civil law, I enjoyed, to my own surprise, the most wonderful Roman holiday of my life. With nothing I had to do and nowhere I had to be, I strolled for hours, bought half-price books, stretched out comfortably on the park benches in Villa Borghese, read, and even wrote. I wrote horrifying poems that, fortunately, have been lost over the years. On the Spanish Steps, I made friends with two overweight American girls. We went out for pizza together, but I politely declined an invitation to continue the evening back in their apartment, because I thought I'd glimpsed a conspiratorial glance passing between them. Reckoning that they tipped the scales at one hundred seventy-five to two hundred pounds each, I decided that, as the saying goes, to trust is good, but not to trust is better.

The world was teeming with endless possibilities in that warm and unexpected Roman February, as I teetered between the no-longer of my life as a child and the not-yet of my life as a man. It was a brief, euphoric, temporary moment in time. It was wonderful to stand, poised, in that moment. And only what is temporary can be perfect.

I remembered these things during the course of an hour that, by some strange alchemy, seemed as timeless and sweet as the days I had enjoyed twenty years earlier. I had the irrational, exhilarating sensation that the tape was about to rewind, and that I was about to be offered a new beginning. I felt a shiver, a vibration. It was beautiful.

Then it dawned on me that it was ten o'clock, and I realized that if I didn't get moving I'd be late. I turned and walked briskly back toward Piazza dei Tribunali.

3.

When you argue before the Court of Cassation, the first thing you do is rent a black robe.

The dress code of Italy's highest court requires that all lawyers wear a black robe, but—except for lawyers who practice in Rome—almost no one actually owns one. And so you have to rent one, as if you were acting in a play or attending a Carnival masquerade party.

As usual, there was a short line at the robe rental room. I looked around in search of familiar faces, but there was no one I knew. Instead, standing in line ahead of me was a guy who was, to judge from his appearance, the product of repeated, passionate couplings between close blood relatives. His eyebrows were very bushy and jet black. His hair was dyed an unnatural blond with red highlights. He had a jaw that jutted out in front of him, and he was wearing a forest green jacket that looked vaguely Tyrolean in style. I imagined his mug shot in the newspaper under the headline "Police Break Up Ring of Child Molesters," or proudly posing on a political campaign poster alongside a virulently racist slogan.

I took my rented robe and forced myself to refrain from sniffing it; doing so would have resulted in suffering a queasy sense of disgust for the rest of the morning. As usual, I mused for a few seconds about how many lawyers had worn it before me and the stories they could tell. Then, also as usual, I told myself to quit indulging in clichés, and I walked toward the court chambers.

My case was one of the first. A mere half hour after the hearing began, it was my turn.

It only took the reporting advocate a few minutes to summarize the history of the case, explaining the reasoning behind the guilty verdict and then the grounds for my appeal.

The defendant was the youngest son of a well-known and respected professional in Bari. At the time of his arrest, nearly eight years earlier, he was twenty-one years old, attending law school without much to show for it. He was much more successful as a cocaine dealer. Anyone in certain circles who occasionally wanted or needed some coke—and sometimes other substances—knew his name and number. As a dealer, he was careful, punctual, and reliable. He made home deliveries, so his wealthy customers weren't obliged to do anything as vulgar as traveling around the city in search of a drug dealer.

At a certain point, when everyone knew his name and what he was up to, the Carabinieri noticed him, too. They tapped his cell phones and followed him for a few weeks and then, when the time was right, they searched his apartment and garage. It was in the garage that they found almost half a kilo of excellent Venezuelan cocaine. At first, he tried to defend himself by saying that the drugs weren't his, that everyone else in the building had access to his garage, and that the coke could have belonged to anyone. Then they confronted him with the recordings of the phone calls, and at last he decided, on the advice of his lawyer—me—to avail himself of his right to remain silent. It was a classic case—any further statements could have been used against him.

After a few months of preventive detention he was placed under house arrest, and a little more than a year after his initial arrest he was released, with the requirement that he remain a resident of the area and show up regularly to sign a register. The trial proceeded at the usual slow pace, and the defense theory, all other chatter aside, was based on a claim that the phone taps were not legitimate evidence. If that objection had been accepted, the prosecution would have had a much weaker case.

I had raised the issue of the legality of the phone taps in the first criminal trial. But the objection had been dismissed, and the court had sentenced my client to ten years' imprisonment and a huge fine. I had raised the issue of the lawfulness of the recordings in our first appeal. The appeals court had once again dismissed the argument, but at least the sentence had been reduced.

I appealed to the Court of Cassation based on the illegality of those phone taps, and that morning I was there in my final attempt to keep my client—who had in the meantime found a real job and a girlfriend and was now the father of a young child—from serving a substantial prison sentence, even after various amnesties, early releases, and so on. In supreme court sessions, normally there's no audience. The chambers have an abstract solemnity, and—most important—the discussion involves only points of law: The kinds of brutal facts discussed in criminal trials are nowhere to be found in the hushed environment of the supreme court.

In other words, you might expect the outcome and the setting to be devoid of the emotional edge typical of standard criminal trials.

That's not true, though, for one very simple reason.

When a case is appealed to the highest court, you're very close to the end of the judicial process. One of the possible outcomes of an appeal is for the court to deny the appeal. And if the Court of Cassation denies an appeal in a case involving a prison sentence, it's likely that your client's next step will be to surrender to the prison system and begin serving his time.

That means a case before this court is hardly an abstract exercise; the seriousness of the outcome transforms the rarefied atmosphere of the chambers and the hearing into a dramatic foreshadowing of things that are anything but rarefied, and frequently frightening.

The advocate general called for the dismissal of my appeal. He spoke briefly, but it was evident that he had studied the facts of the case, which isn't always true. He made a strong argument against the basis of my appeal, and I thought that if I had been one of the justices, I would have found him persuasive and I would have ruled against the appellant.

Then the chief justice addressed me, saying, "Counselor, the panel of judges has read your appeal as well as your brief. Your point of view has been set forth quite clearly. Therefore, in oral argument, I'd ask you to stick to the fundamental aspects of the law or to matters that were not treated in the appeal or the brief."

Very courteous and very clear. Please be quick, refrain from repeating the things we already know, and above all, don't waste the court's time.

"Thank you, sir. I'll try to be concise."

I was quite concise. I went back over the reasons why I believed those wiretaps should be excluded as evidence, and the verdict should be overturned, and in a little more than five minutes, I was done. The chief justice thanked me for having kept my promise to be brief, courteously told me I was free to go, and called the next case. The decision would be announced that afternoon. In the Court of Cassation, the judges hear oral arguments for all the appeals first, and then they retire for deliberations. They emerge, sometimes quite late in the day, and read all the decisions, one after the other. Usually, they read them to an empty courtroom because no one wants to wait for hours and hours in the hallways, surrounded by unsettling marble statues, amidst the echo of lost footsteps. For lawyers, especially those like me who are only in town for the day, this is how it works: You ask one of the clerks to inform you of the decision in your case, and you hand him a folded sheet of paper with your cell phone number written on it, folded around a twenty Euro bill.

Then you leave the court building, and from that moment on, every time your cell phone rings, your stomach lurches, because it might be the clerk, calling to inform you of the verdict in a chilly, bureaucratic tone.

It happened while I was in the airport; the plane was already boarding, and I was about to turn off my phone.

"Counselor Guerrieri?"

"Yes?"

"The court's verdict on your appeal is in. The appeal was denied, court costs to be paid by the appellant. Good evening."

"Good evening," I said, though only my cell phone heard me—the clerk had already hung up, and was already phoning someone else to dispense his own personal verdict for a (modest) fee.

On the plane, I tried to read, but couldn't. I thought about having to tell my client that in just a few days he would be walking into a prison and staying there for many years. The prospect of that conversation put me in a grim mood of sadness mixed with a brooding sense of humiliation.

I know. He was a drug dealer, a criminal, and if they hadn't caught him, he might have gone on selling drugs and profiting from them. But in the years between his arrest and the verdict, he'd become another person. It struck me as intolerable that the past should just leap up, in the form of a cruel, clear-cut verdict, and wreak havoc like that.

I thought it was a travesty for this to happen so many years after the fact, and it seemed even more senseless because there was no one to blame.

With these thoughts racing through my mind, I dropped off into a troubled sleep. When I opened my eyes again, the lights of the city were looming close.

4.

When I got home I called my client and did my best to ignore the heavy silence that slowly solidified between us, once I'd given him the news. I tried to ignore the human life that was being torn to pieces in that silence. I hung up and thought that I was getting too old for this kind of work.

Then I attempted to throw together a dinner out of what I had in my fridge, but instead I basically drained almost an entire bottle of 29-proof Primitivo wine. I slept only fitfully and the whole weekend was a slow, dull, exhausting trudge. On Saturday I went to the movies, but I picked the wrong film, and I exited into a relentless drizzle. It rained all day and was still raining on Sunday, which I spent at home, reading, but I picked the wrong books, too. The highlight of the day was watching a couple of *Happy Days* reruns on a satellite channel.

When I got up on Monday morning and looked out my window, I saw some rays of sun poking through the remaining clouds. I was happy the weekend was over.

I spent the whole morning at the courthouse, dealing with insignificant hearings and running around to various clerks' offices.

In the afternoon I went over to the office. My new

office. I'd been working there for more than four months, but every time I pushed open the heavy burglar-proof door the architect had insisted on installing, I felt the same sense of bewilderment. And each time I asked myself the same thing: Where the hell am I? And then: Why on earth did I leave my old, small, comfortable office to move into this alien, antiseptic place, reeking of plastic, leather, and wood?

In reality, there had been a number of excellent reasons for the move. First of all, Maria Teresa had finally earned her law degree and asked to continue on at the firm, moving up from secretary to apprentice lawyer. I hired a gentleman in his sixties, named Pasquale Macina, to take over Maria Teresa's secretarial duties. He had worked for many years for an elderly colleague of mine who had recently passed away.

Around the same time, a law professor friend of mine asked me to hire his daughter. She had finished school and passed the bar, but she wanted to become a criminal lawyer. She'd practiced civil law in her father's office, and it wasn't to her taste.

Consuelo had been adopted from Peru. She has a dark, chubby face, with cheeks that at first sight give her a faintly comical appearance—she looks a little like a hamster. If you meet her gaze at certain times, however, you realize that *funny* is not the right word at all, to describe her. When Consuelo's dark eyes stop smiling, they transmit a very straightforward message: The only way to get me to stop fighting is to kill me.

I hired her, which meant that in just a few months, the law firm grew from a staff of two to a crowd of four, shoe-horned into a work space that had been small to begin with, but which then was completely untenable.

So I looked for a new office. I found a large apartment in

the old part of town, very nice indeed, but it would have to be completely renovated, from top to bottom. I liked doing renovations more or less as much as I liked going to the proctologist. I found an architect who considered himself an artist and didn't want to bother listening to the trivial opinions of his client or waste time quibbling over such silly questions as the cost of materials or furniture, or his own fee.

The work took three long months. I should have been satisfied, but I just couldn't get used to the new space. I couldn't see myself as the kind of professional who had this kind of office. Before I had an office like mine, if I walked into an office like mine, I always assumed the owner was a clueless asshole. Now I was the clueless asshole, and I was having a hard time getting used to it.

I shut the heavy armored door, said good afternoon to Pasquale, said good afternoon to Maria Teresa, said good afternoon to Consuelo, and went to hide in my office. I turned on my computer, and in a few seconds the screen displayed my calendar with the appointments for that afternoon, three of them. The first was with a surveying engineer who worked for the city zoning office and had the unfortunate habit of demanding tips in order to move projects off his desk. Technically, this is known as extortion, and it's a pretty serious crime. The financial police had conducted a search of the engineer's office, and now he was in a state of complete panic, convinced—not without reason—that a warrant would be issued for his arrest any minute. The second appointment was with the wife of an old client of mine, a professional burglar, who had been arrested for what seemed like the thousandth time. My last appointment of the day was with my fellow lawyer Sabino Fornelli and his clients, to discuss the case that he had been unwilling to tell me about over the phone.

I met with the surveying engineer and then the burglar's wife, with Consuelo in attendance. Every time I introduce her, my clients look a little baffled.

"This is my colleague, Consuelo Favia, who will be handling this case with me."

Colleague?

Every client's face asks the same question. So I spell it out for them, saying, "*Counselor* Consuelo Favia, a lawyer who's been working with me for several months now. We'll be handling your case together."

Their astonishment is understandable, and it's not racism, per se. It's just that in Bari, and in Italy in general, people still don't expect a young woman with dark brown skin and Andean features to be a lawyer.

The surveying engineer wore a watch that he could never have afforded on his salary and a charcoal gray suit over a black t-shirt, like a playboy running out the clock, and he was on the verge of a nervous breakdown. He kept saying that he hadn't done anything wrong, that at the very most he'd accepted a few tips and small gifts. They were given spontaneously, he insisted. Come on, who turns down a gift? Was he to be arrested for that? He wasn't going to be arrested, was he?

Now, I want to point out here that I despise criminals like this surveying engineer. I defend them because that's how I earn my living, but frankly, if it were up to me, I'd be happy to throw them all into a big comfortable prison cell and arrange to lose the key permanently. After letting him ramble on for twenty minutes or so, I was obliged to resist the urge to encourage his fear rather than offering words of reassurance. I told him that before I could express an opinion, we would need to examine the search-and-seizure warrant, and that we might need to contest it before the special arraignment court. Then we could decide whether to request a meeting with the prosecutor. I suggested that he avoid having any potentially compromising conversations over the phone or in the offices that the financial police had searched; they could easily have been bugged. Finally, Consuelo coolly informed him that we'd be in touch in a few days' time, and that in the meantime he should speak to the secretary on his way out to pay our retainer.

I love her when she absolves me of the unpleasant responsibility of talking about money with my clients.

The burglar's wife, Signora Carlone, was much less agitated. Talking with a criminal lawyer about her husband's latest legal problems wasn't a new experience for her, even though this case was much more serious than usual. A police investigative team had been looking into a worrisome epidemic of break-ins and had wiretapped a number of phones, followed suspects, and taken fingerprints in the apartments of the victims. In the end, they'd arrested Signore Carlone and five of his friends, who were now charged with multiple counts of aggravated theft, running a burglary ring, and criminal conspiracy. Carlone had a lengthy criminal record (which made for especially dull reading, because he'd committed the same crime, burglary, over and over), so when his wife asked about the only thing that mattered to her—when she could expect her husband to be released from jail—we told her that it wouldn't happen soon, and we weren't certain it would happen at all. For now, we could contest the court order for preventive detention before the special arraignment court, but, I informed Signora Carlone, it would be better not to get our hopes up, because if even half of what was written in the court order was supported by the files of the investigation, he would remain in jail.

After Signora Carlone left, I asked Consuelo to study the documents that the surveying engineer and the burglar's wife had brought in and to prepare two draft appeals to the special arraignment court.

"May I say something, Guido?"

Consuelo always approaches a subject that she knows or suspects will lead to an argument with those words. She's not actually asking permission. It's a conversational tic, her way of announcing that she's about to say something I might not like.

"You may."

"I don't like clients like—"

"Like our surveying engineer. I know. I don't really like them myself."

"Then why do we take their business?"

"Because we're criminal lawyers. Or perhaps I should say: I'm a criminal lawyer. You might be done before you even get started if you worry about this sort of thing."

"Are we obligated to take all the clients who come to us?"

"No, we have no obligation to take everyone. And in fact, we don't take child molesters, rapists, or Mafiosi. But if we start refusing to take the case of some respectable public servant who accepted a bribe or extorted money from the citizenry, then we might as well limit ourselves to arguing parking tickets."

I was trying for light sarcasm, but a slight note of exasperation crept into my voice. It bothered me that deep down I agreed with her, and I hated being forced to play the part that I liked least in that conversation.

"But if you don't want to handle the appeal for that clown with the Rolex, I'll handle it."

She shook her head and gathered up the files, and then she stuck out her tongue at me. Before I could react, she turned on her heel and left the room. The little scene aroused an unexpected feeling in me. It gave me a sense of family, of domestic warmth, of well-being mixed with splinters of nostalgia. The people who worked alongside me in my law office were my substitute family, the family I no longer had. For a few seconds, I was on the verge of tears. Then I rubbed my eyes, though I wasn't actually crying, and told myself that I ought to at least try to lose my mind a little at a time, not in one fell swoop. Back to work.

At 8:30, as Maria Teresa, Pasquale, and Consuelo were leaving for the evening, Sabino Fornelli arrived with his clients and their mysterious case.

5.

Fornelli's clients were a man and a woman, husband and wife. I guessed that each was about ten years my senior. A few days later, I would read their personal information in the court records and discover that we were almost exactly the same age.

Of the two, the husband made the stronger impression on me. His gaze was vacant, his shoulders stooped, his clothes hanging off his frame. When I shook hands with him, I felt as if I'd picked up an unhappy invertebrate creature.

The wife, who was nicely dressed, looked more normal. But on closer inspection, there was something unhealthy about her gaze, the aftermath of an injury to her soul. When they came into my office, it was like a gust of damp, chilly wind came in, too.

We introduced ourselves in this vaguely uneasy atmosphere, which remained in place throughout our conversation.

"Signore and Signora Ferraro have been my clients for many years. Tonino, Antonio," and here he gestured toward the husband, perhaps concerned that I might assume that the wife was named Tonino, "owns a few furniture and kitchen supply stores, here in Bari and in the province. Rosaria was a gym teacher, but she retired from teaching a few years ago, and now she works with him managing the stores. They have two children."

At that point, he stopped talking and sat for a minute in silence. I looked at him, then over to Antonio, aka Tonino, then at Rosaria. Then I looked back at him with a friendly but quizzical smile that morphed into a grimace. From the street outside, I heard a clash of sheet metal, and figured that there'd been a fender bender. Fornelli went on.

"They have a daughter, their older child, and a son who's younger, sixteen years old. His name is Nicola, and he goes to the science high school. Their daughter, Manuela, is twenty-two, and she's at the university in Rome—the LUISS."

He paused, as if to catch his breath and gather his strength.

"Manuela disappeared six months ago."

I don't know why I blinked my eyes shut at those words, but when, in the darkness behind my eyelids, I saw globes of blinding light, I opened them again immediately.

"Disappeared? What do you mean, disappeared?"

Truly a brilliant question, I thought to myself a second later. *What do you mean, disappeared?* Maybe he meant during a magician's stage show. You're really at your best tonight, Guerrieri.

The father looked at me. There was an indescribable expression on his face; a few facial muscles twitched, as if he were about to speak, but he said nothing. I had the distinct impression that he was simply unable to speak. As I looked at him, the words of an old song by Francesco De Gregori floated into my mind: "*Do you by any chance know a girl from Rome whose face looks like a collapsing dam?*" The face of Signore Ferraro, furniture salesman and desperate father, looked like a collapsing dam.

It was the wife who finally spoke.

"Manuela disappeared in September. She'd spent the weekend with friends who have a group of *trulli* in the countryside between Cisternino and Ostuni. On Sunday afternoon, a young woman gave her a ride to the train station in Ostuni. No one's heard from her or seen her since."

I nodded. I didn't know what to say. I ought to have expressed my sympathy, my understanding, but what do you say to two parents grieving over the disappearance of their daughter? Oh, I'm so sorry to hear that, but don't get too upset, this sort of thing happens. You'll see, before you know it, your daughter will show up, life will go on as before, and this will all seem like a bad dream.

A bad dream? I thought to myself that if a grownup has been missing for a long time—and six months is *definitely* a long time—either something bad has happened, or he or she has run away. Sure, it's possible she's lost her memory, maybe she's wandering around confused and eventually will be found and brought home. Sometimes that happens to the elderly. Manuela, though, was not elderly. But why were they meeting with a lawyer? What did I have to do with this? Why had they come to see me? I wondered when I'd be able to ask that question without seeming callous.

"I imagine the police, or the Carabinieri, have questioned her friend, right?"

"Of course. The Carabinieri handled the investigation. We have copies of all the documents. I'll bring them to your office," Fornelli said.

Why would he need to bring me copies of the documents? I shifted in my chair the way I do when I don't understand what's going on and I feel uncomfortable.

"Anyway, here's the story in brief. Manuela didn't have a

car; she went to the *trulli* with a group of friends. She was supposed to come home Sunday afternoon, but she hadn't managed to find anyone who was coming back directly to Bari, so she accepted a ride to the station in Ostuni so she could take the train."

"Do we know whether she got on a train?"

"We think so, but we don't know for sure. We do know she bought a ticket."

"How do you know she bought a ticket?"

"The Carabinieri talked to the ticket clerk. They showed him her photograph, and he remembered selling Manuela a ticket."

That's unusual, I thought to myself. Ticket clerks, like anyone else who works with the public, barely glance at their customers. They hardly see their faces, and if they do they forget them immediately. It's understandable: They see so many faces every day that they can't possibly remember them all, unless there's something special about them. Fornelli sensed what I was thinking and provided the answer before I could even ask the question.

"Manuela is a very pretty girl, and I believe that's why the ticket clerk remembered her."

"And you said it was impossible to know whether she got on the train."

"They couldn't establish that with any certainty. The Carabinieri talked to the conductors on all the afternoon trains. Only one thought he might have seen a young woman who resembled Manuela, but he was much less confident than the ticket clerk. Let's say that it's likely she got on a train—you'll see the statements later—but we can't be sure of it."

"When did they realize their daughter had disappeared?"

"Tonino and Rosaria have a beach house at Castellaneta

Marina. They were there with Nicola. Manuela spent a few days with them and then left. She said she was going to spend the weekend at her friends' *trulli*. From there, she phoned them to say that she was leaving for Rome Sunday night by train, or by car if she managed to find a ride. The following week, she was supposed to go to the university, I believe either for a meeting with a professor or to go to the registrar's office."

"She was supposed to meet with a professor," the mother said.

"Yes, that's right. Anyway, they realized that she was missing on Monday. Tonino and Rosaria came home to Bari on Sunday night. She didn't call the next morning, but that was pretty normal. Rosaria tried to call her in the afternoon, but got a recording saying Manuela's cell phone was out of range."

The mother broke in again, while the father sat in silence.

"I tried to call her two or three times, but the phone was still out of range. Then I sent her a text message, telling her to call me, but she didn't. That's when I started getting worried. I called her all afternoon, but her phone was turned off. So I called Nicoletta, the friend she lived with in Rome, and she told me that Manuela never showed up."

"Do you think she was ever home in Bari?"

Fornelli answered me, because Rosaria was breathing hard, as if she'd climbed several flights of stairs.

"The concierge lives in the building, and she keeps an eye on things even on Sundays; she never saw her. And there was no sign she'd been home.

"After they talked to Nicoletta they called a few other friends of Manuela's, but nobody knew anything. Only that she'd been at the *trulli* and that she left on Sunday afternoon. At that point, they called the Carabinieri—it was nighttime by then—but they said there was nothing they could do. If Manuela had been a minor, then they could have started a search, but Manuela is an adult, so she's free to come and go as she pleases, to turn off her cell phone if she wants to, and so on."

"And the Carabinieri told them to come in early the next day to make an official missing persons report."

"Yes. At that point, they tried calling the police, but the answer was more or less the same. So they called me. Tonino wanted to get in the car and drive to Rome, but I talked him out of it. What could he do in Rome? Where could he go? They'd already spoken to Manuela's roommate, who told them that she hadn't been there. And nothing proved she'd left for Rome anyway. The opposite, actually. So we spent the night calling every one of Manuela's friends whose number we could find, but we turned up nothing."

For a few moments I had a clear, suffocating, intolerable perception of the anguish that must have saturated that night, with the frantic phone calls and the lurking, unnameable fear. I had an urge—absurd but powerful—to jump up and run away from my own office, just to get away from that sense of anguish. And I really did escape, for a few seconds: I was mentally gone, as if I'd allowed myself to be dragged to safety in some other place that was less oppressive. As a result, I missed part of Fornelli's account. I remember becoming aware of his voice again through my dazed fog when he was already halfway through the story he was telling.

". . . and at that point they realized there was a serious problem, and they opened an investigation. They interviewed a lot of people. They requested Manuela's cell phone records and her ATM transactions, and they examined her computer. They were thorough, but in all these months not a thing has turned up, and we don't know any more today than we did the first day."

Why were they telling me all this? Perhaps the time had come to ask.

"I'm very sorry. Is there some way I can be of help?"

The woman looked at my colleague. The husband also turned slowly and looked at him, with that devastated face that looked like it was about to fall apart. Fornelli looked at them for a few seconds, then turned to speak to me.

"A few days ago, I went in to talk to the assistant district attorney who has the case."

"Who is it?"

"A guy named Carella who's been here only a short time."

"Yes, he just got here. He came from Sicily, I think."

"What do you make of him?"

"I don't know him well yet, but I'd say he's a respectable attorney. He's a little dull, perhaps, but I think he earns his keep."

Fornelli grimaced, almost imperceptibly and certainly involuntarily, and then continued.

"When I went to see him, to review the situation, he told me he was getting ready to request that the case be closed. Almost six months have gone by, he told me, and he has no evidence that would justify extending the investigation."

"What did you say?"

"I tried to tell him that he can't just close a case like that. He responded that if I had any other leads to suggest, I was welcome to do so, and he'd take my request under consideration. Unless I brought something else to his attention, though, he'd have to request the case be archived. Of course, that doesn't mean they couldn't reopen the case if something new came up."

"So," I said, as I began to guess why they'd come to see me.

"On my recommendation, Tonino and Rosaria would like to hire you to study the file and identify any further lines of investigation that we can suggest to the prosecutor, to keep him from closing the case."

"Your confidence in me is flattering, but that's a job for an investigator, not a lawyer."

"We don't feel comfortable going directly to a private investigator. You're a criminal lawyer, and you're a good one. You've seen plenty of files. You know what goes into an investigation. Money is the least of our concerns. In fact, money isn't a concern at all. We'll spend whatever's necessary, for you and for a private investigator, if you decide you want to work with one."

Except I had no fee schedule for that kind of professional service. The official guild fee list doesn't include "investigative consultation to locate missing persons." That unhappy thought came to mind immediately and made me feel uncomfortable. In my discomfort I looked around, and I happened to meet the gaze of the father. That's when it dawned on me that he was probably on medication. Psychiatric drugs. Maybe they were causing his vacant expression. I felt even more uncomfortable. I decided that I should thank them courteously but decline the offer. It would be wrong to feed their hopes and take their money. But I didn't know how to say it.

I felt like the hard-boiled detective character in one of those cheap mystery novels. A down-on-his-luck private investigator who receives a visit from a client, insists he can't take the case—just to give the story a little rhythm, to add an element of suspense—and then changes his mind and goes for it. And of course, he always solves the mystery.

But there was nothing to solve in this case. Maybe they'd never know what happened to their daughter, or maybe they would, but I certainly wasn't the right person to get them the information they wanted.

I spoke almost without realizing it and without complete control of my words. As often happens, I said something entirely different from what I was thinking.

"I don't want you to get your hopes up. In all likelihood—almost certainly—the district attorney's office and the Carabinieri have already done everything possible. If there have been gross oversights, we can think about doing some further investigating and file some writs of insufficient evidence, but, I repeat, don't get your hopes up. You said you have a complete copy of the file?"

"Yes, I'll bring it tomorrow."

"All right, but there's no reason for you to come in. You can have one of your assistants drop it off."

Fornelli awkwardly pulled out an envelope and handed it to me.

"Thank you, Guido. This is an advance on your expenses. Tonino and Rosaria want you to accept it. We feel sure you can do something for us. Thank you."

But of course, I thought to myself. I'll solve the mystery, between a shot of whiskey and a vigorous fistfight. I felt like Nick Belane, Charles Bukowski's bizarre private investigator, and there was nothing funny about it.

I walked them to the door and then returned to my room, passing through the dark, empty outer office. For a moment I was uneasy, scared the way I'd been as a child.

I sat at my desk and looked at the envelope, still where Fornelli had put it. I opened it up and pulled out a check. It bore a ridiculously high number. For a moment, my vanity was flattered, but that was cancelled out by discomfort.

I decided I had to return it, but immediately afterward I realized that for the Ferraros—and perhaps for Fornelli as well—paying me was a way of soothing their anguish. It gave them the illusion that the payment would inevitably be followed by some concrete useful action. If I returned the check, it would be proof that there really was nothing left to do, and I would have deprived them of even that last, tiny, temporary sense of relief.

I couldn't do it. Not right away, at least.

I couldn't manage to get the face of Signore Antonio Ferraro, aka Tonino, out of my head. Evidently, the loss of his first-born daughter had caused him to lose his mind.

I searched for that old song on YouTube. I found a live recording, and I put my feet up on the desk and half-closed my eyes as the opening chords played.

Now he lives in Atlantis with a hatful of memories,
And the face of someone who understands.

Exactly.

6.

In the street, the air was chilly, especially because of the northwest mistral wind.

I didn't want to go home. I had no desire to hole up in the solitude that sometimes hangs a little too heavy in my apartment. I needed to shake off the grim mood of that meeting before going to sleep. And, secondarily, I needed a nourishing meal and a comforting drink. So I decided to go to the Chelsea Hotel.

Not the famous red-brick hotel in Manhattan's Chelsea neighborhood, but a club—in Bari's San Girolamo neighborhood—that I had stumbled upon a few weeks earlier. It had become my favorite place to go in the evening when I didn't want to stay in.

Since moving my practice to my new office, I'd developed a habit of taking long walks late at night in unfamiliar sections of the city. I'd leave work after ten o'clock, as I had that evening. I'd wolf down a sandwich, a slice of pizza, or some sushi, and then I'd start walking, with the brisk step of someone who has places to go and no time to waste. Actually, I had nowhere to go, though I was probably searching for something.

These walks gave me a workout when I didn't feel like

training with a punching bag, but more importantly they gave me a chance to explore the city and my solitude. Every so often, I stopped to think how little social interaction I had since Margherita had left, and even more so since she'd written me that she wouldn't be coming back.

I missed the life I used to have—or rather, I missed the *lives* I used to have. Lives that were more or less normal. When I was married to Sara and when I was with Margherita. But it was a gentle emotion, painless. Or perhaps I should say there was a tolerable amount of pain.

There were times when I wished I could meet someone I liked as much as I had once liked them, but I realized that wasn't realistic. The thought made me a little sad, but that too was generally quite tolerable. And when that sadness welled up, at times verging dangerously on self-pity, I told myself not to complain. I had my work, sports, the occasional trip on my own. I went out, occasionally, with courteous, distant friends. And then there were my books. Sure, there was something missing. But I was one of those kids who took it to heart when they told me I shouldn't complain because children in Africa were starving.

A few weeks earlier I had left my office about ten o'clock at night, after it had rained all day. I bought a green-tea yogurt at the corner store that stays open late, and I started eating as I walked north.

I love eating on the street. Given the right conditions— those nighttime walks, for one—it brings back memories of being a child. Intact crystal-clear memories with no regret attached to them. Sometimes I feel a kind of euphoria, as if time had short-circuited and I had become the boy I once was, with an abundance of first experiences still ahead of me. It's an illusion, but it's not bad, as illusions go.

I skirted the endless fencing around the harbor and stayed on Viale Vittorio Veneto, alongside the bicycle path. After all that rain, the city looked as if it had been varnished with a shiny black lacquer. No bicycles, no pedestrians, not many cars. It was a scene out of *Blade Runner*, and this feeling only grew stronger when I turned onto the empty blue-black streets that sprawl in all directions behind the Fiera del Levante, a giant industrial complex that has been abandoned for decades, and the former public slaughterhouse, which has been converted into a national library. Its courtyards look like something out of a Giorgio de Chirico painting. There are no cafés, restaurants, or stores in that part of town. Only machine shops, depots, empty warehouses, garages, dead smokestacks, the courtyards of factories that have been shut down for decades, full of weeds, stray dogs, owls, and furtive urban foxes.

The sense of unease that emanates from those places feels good to me, oddly enough. It seems to drain my own personal unease, drawing it into its own dark vortex. It's as if the vague fear of an external danger frees me from my fear of internal danger, which is darker and harder to control. After I take these walks in deserted, spectral places, I sleep like a baby, and I usually wake up in a good mood, too.

I was in the middle of the no-man's land along the boundary between the Libertà neighborhood and the San Girolamo neighborhood when, down a side street, I saw a blue-and-red sign that looked like a neon sign from the 1950s glowing in the damp, slightly grimy dark.

It was a bar, and it seemed to have been dropped among

the industrial warehouses, the machine shops, and the darkness from a faraway place and a time long ago.

The sign read CHELSEA HOTEL NO. 2, the title of one of my favorite songs. A dim green light came from inside, through thick, green ground-glass windows.

I walked in and took a look around. There was a nice smell in the air: food, cleanliness, and spices. It smelled warm, dry, and comfortable, the way some houses do.

The club was furnished in an American mid-century modern style that matched the neon sign; the furniture seemed to be arranged quite casually. But as I looked around, I realized that there was nothing random about the place. Someone who knew what he—or she—was doing and who enjoyed that kind of work had spent a lot of time on it. The walls were covered with film posters. Some of the older posters looked original—and expensive.

The music was at an acceptable volume—I hate loud music, with a few rare exceptions—and there were a lot of people, considering the late hour. Something else was in the air, something I managed to put my finger on only as I was sitting down at the bar, perched on a high wood-and-leather stool.

The Chelsea Hotel No. 2 was a gay bar. As that epiphany hit me, I remembered someone explaining to me years before that Chelsea was New York's most crowded and effervescent gay neighborhood. And so—I said to myself in a mental whisper—the name of this club, in which I was sitting, so deliberately American, was neither random nor (solely) born of a love for Leonard Cohen's music.

At one table, two young women were holding hands, talking intently, and occasionally kissing. They reminded me of the two Giovannas, friends of Margherita's, martial arts enthusiasts and sky divers. In fact, for a couple of seconds, I wondered if it was them, but then it dawned on me that the two Giovannas were probably not the only two lesbians in the whole city.

The other tables were occupied mostly, in fact almost exclusively, by men.

Suddenly, I felt as if I had been tossed into the famous scene in the movie *Police Academy* in which the two stupid cadets wind up in a gay leather bar and find themselves slow dancing with mustachioed, muscle-bound men wearing Nazi trooper hats and black leather. I wondered how many of them I'd be able to knock down before I was outnumbered and I succumbed to the inevitable.

Okay, I'm exaggerating. The situation was totally normal. The music wasn't by the Village People (while I was thinking those things, "Dance Me to the End of Love" was playing, quietly and respectably, in the background), and nobody was wearing black leather or anything remotely S&M looking.

That said, however, my being here might prove to be awkward. I could imagine running into someone I knew—perhaps a fellow lawyer, or a magistrate—and wondered how I'd explain that I'd ended up here due to my habit of taking long walks late at night in the more run-down sections of the city.

I tried to remember all the gay lawyers and judges I knew. I came up with five, and noted to my relief that none of them were in the club.

Then, immediately after this mental screening process, I decided I must be losing my mind. Sure, this was a slightly unusual situation, but it still wasn't a normal reason for me to look around with a worried and vaguely furtive expression, as if the sign outside read Stonewall Lambda Gay and Lesbian Activist Headquarters, or something like that.

While I was planning a nonchalant exit—from that place and from my own tortured thoughts—a voice drowned out the notes of Leonard Cohen and abolished the possibility that my visit to the Chelsea Hotel No. 2 might pass unobserved.

"Counselor Guerrieri!" I turned to my right, blushing and wondering how I could explain my presence in the club to the person behind that voice, whoever it might be.

Nadia. Nadia, but I couldn't remember her last name.

She'd been my client, four or five years earlier.

She was a former model, a former porn actress, and a former high-end escort, and she had been arrested for organizing and running a business providing very beautiful and very expensive escorts all over the city. I had succeeded in getting her acquitted in an unexpected way—on what those outside the profession might call a technicality. I discovered a vice of form, an irregularity in the wiretapping. The prosecution's case crumbled like a cracker.

I have a very clear image of Nadia during the trial. She wore a charcoal-gray suit, a white blouse, very discreet makeup. She looked like anything but a prostitute. The fact that she didn't fit any of the clichés of her profession had become increasingly clear to me every time I saw her—first in jail, immediately after her arrest, later at my office, and, for the last time, in the courtroom.

That evening, however, she was wearing a pair of faded jeans and a tight white t-shirt. She seemed—I'm not sure how this was possible—both older and younger and, despite her casual dress, she was just as elegant as the last time I'd seen her. I tried to remember if I'd noticed how pretty she was when she was my client.

"Hey there," I said, and then I realized how flip it sounded. "I mean, hello, good evening. I'm sorry, I didn't mean to be rude, but, well, I'm surprised to see you."

"And I'm surprised to see you here. Welcome to my club."

I straightened up and tried to speak properly. "Your club? This is your place of business?"

"And you didn't offend me at all. I like to think we know each other well."

"Oh, of course. We needn't stand on ceremony."

"What are you doing in this part of town?" She said it with a smile and, I seemed to detect, a hint of amused mischief. The real question, tacit but not all that tacit: So you're gay? Now I understand why you behaved so properly when I was your client and didn't try to take advantage of the situation.

No. I'm. Not. Gay. I just happened to walk into the place, because I like to take long walks late at night through the far-flung sections of the city, because I like to walk where there aren't any crowds. No, I didn't come here to see who I could pick up, and yes, yes, I realize that it might seem hard to believe, but I assure you that I was just taking an aimless walk. I saw the light in the dark street, and I stepped inside, but I did *not* know that this was a, well, I didn't know what kind of club it was, not that I'm prejudiced in any way. Let me make this clear: I've always been liberal. I'm open-minded, and I have lots of friends who are homosexuals.

Well, okay, maybe not lots, but one or two. Anyway, let me repeat: I'm. Not. Gay.

But that's not what I said. I just shrugged and put on an expression that, I think, could have meant anything. And which therefore meant nothing. And which was therefore the right expression for that situation.

"Well, I was just out walking. I saw the sign, and I was curious, so I thought I'd step inside and take a look. Nice place you have here."

She smiled.

"Are you gay? You certainly didn't strike me as gay when I was your client."

I was happy that she asked. It simplified things. I told her that, no, I wasn't gay and then I told her about my late-night walks, and she thought it sounded perfectly normal, and I felt a surge of gratitude that she said that. Then she offered me a little glass of delicious rum—a brand I'd never heard of in my life. Then she offered me another, and when I looked at my watch, I realized it was really late. She made me promise to come back, even if I wasn't gay. There were other straight customers—not many, she added, but a few— and it was a quiet, relaxed place. The food was good and they often had live music, and she said she'd like it if I came back. She looked me in the eye when she said that, with a natural manner that I liked very much. So I promised, and as I said it, I knew it was a promise I would keep.

After that, I became a regular at the Chelsea Hotel. I liked being able to sit by myself without feeling alone. I felt comfortable there, and it was a generally happy and fairly intimate environment. It reminded me of something that I couldn't quite pin down.

One of the first times that I went there, while I was waiting for my order to arrive and I was sitting alone at my table, a young man stopped right in front of me and asked if he could sit down.

"Now, be civil," I said to myself as I gestured to indicate

that, of course, he was welcome to sit down. He shook my hand—he had a firm grip—and told me that his name was Oliviero. After a brief chatty exchange, Oliviero stared into my eyes and told me that he liked mature men. I thought, but didn't say, *Who are you calling mature?* I was trying to come up with a polite way to let him know that things aren't always as they seem. Just then, Nadia arrived with my order.

"Guido isn't gay, Oliviero."

He gave her a dramatic sneer. Then he looked at me, with disappointment stamped on his face.

"What a pity. But it's never too late. I had a boyfriend—much older than you—who didn't figure out he was gay until he was forty-four. How old are you?"

"Forty-five," I said, with a slightly excessive burst of enthusiasm. Then I specified that I doubted there were any radical changes in view, as far as my sexual orientation was concerned. Still, Oliviero was welcome to drink a glass of wine with me.

It turned out Oliviero didn't drink. A short while later he left with a puzzled expression on his face. And that was the only time that a man tried to pick me up at the Chelsea Hotel.

I rode there on my bicycle, I listened to music and sometimes discovered things I'd never heard before, I ate, I conversed with Nadia, I drank excellent liquor, and I went home feeling pretty relaxed. Not a bad thing in hard times.

That evening, when I left my office after my meeting with Fornelli and the Ferraros, I decided that it was a perfect night to go see Nadia. So I got out my bike, and fifteen minutes later I was there. But when I turned the corner and saw the sign was turned off and the security shutter pulled down, I remembered that the place was closed Monday nights.

Wrong evening, I said to myself as I turned back toward the center of town and home. I could tell I wasn't going to have an easy time getting to sleep.

7.

The next morning, Fornelli called to express his gratitude again.

"Guido, I can't thank you enough. Believe me, I understood what you were trying to tell us yesterday. I know this is a last-ditch effort that probably won't lead to anything. I know this isn't the kind of work you do."

"It's okay, Sabino, don't worry about it."

"When the prosecutor told me that he was planning to close the case, the only thing I could think to do was to call you. Those poor people are both just ravaged by grief. He's worse off than she is, as you probably noticed."

"Is he taking some kind of medication?"

He was silent for a moment.

"Yes, he's drugged to the gills. But it doesn't seem to have any effect, except to make him sleepy. He was—" Fornelli realized the grim implication of his use of the past tense, and quickly stopped himself. "He is very fond of his daughter, and all this has just crushed him. The mother is stronger. She's ready to fight. I haven't seen her shed a tear since the girl disappeared."

"I didn't ask yesterday whether you tried to get in touch with that TV show about missing persons."

"*Chi l'ha visto?* Yes, they included a short segment about Manuela's disappearance in a couple of episodes, and they put her in their database. But it didn't do a lot of good. You'll see in the file that there's a statement by a nutcase who called the Carabinieri after watching the show. He said that he'd seen her working as a prostitute on the outskirts of Foggia."

"Did the Carabinieri look into it?"

"Yes, they did. And they realized almost immediately that this guy systematically calls police stations and Carabinieri barracks all over Italy to report sightings of dozens of missing people. Six or seven other people called in to say that they thought they'd seen a girl who looked like Manuela at the Ventimiglia train station, in Bologna, in Brescia dressed as a gypsy, in a small town near Crotone, and some other place that I can't remember. All of them were interviewed and reports were filed, but nothing solid emerged. The Carabinieri explained to me that every time a missing person is discussed on television, they receive a bunch of phone calls from people who claim to have information but actually know nothing at all. They may not all be pathological liars, technically speaking, but they do it to get attention."

I let this new information sink in, and realized that at this point I was curious to take a look at the file.

"All right, Sabino, let me take a look at the documents. I'll see if there are grounds to consider a new investigation, and maybe to hire a private investigator. But if I don't see anything, if I decide there's no point in looking into it any further, you're going to have to take back that check."

"Just deposit it for now. We'll talk again after you've had a chance to examine the documents. And reading a file is work, in any case."

I was about to say that I'd take the money when I'd earned it. I was going to say it in a courteous yet firm tone of voice, one that would not allow him to answer. Then it struck me as a pretentious cliché. So I just told him to send me the documents as soon as possible. He said that I'd have a complete copy of the entire file that afternoon, and that was the end of our conversation.

To whatever extent possible, it's best to avoid pretentious clichés, I thought.

That afternoon, someone from Fornelli's law office came and handed Pasquale a sizable stack of files. Pasquale carried them into my office and reminded me that in about half an hour we had a meeting with the building commissioner from a small town in the surrounding province; our client had received a formal notification that he was under judicial investigation for malfeasance and illegal approval of subdivisions. For all I knew, the building commissioner was a perfectly law-abiding person, but in some small towns politics takes the form of anonymous accusations and complaints with the public prosecutor's office.

I let the half hour slide by as I leafed through the file without really focusing on it. More than anything else, I felt it. Those photocopies had an aura that planted a deep and terrible sense of unease in me. I thought about the girl's parents and about how I would have experienced something as horrifying as the death of a daughter. I tried to imagine it, but I couldn't. It was so staggering that my imagination failed to provide me with a specific depiction of it. I could barely guess at the nature and scope of that horror.

Why would a normal young woman, with a normal life and a normal family, vanish from one moment to the next, without warning, without giving a sign, without leaving the slightest trace?

Was it possible that she had simply left of her own free will and was so heartless as to abandon her family to its anguish and despair? I decided that wasn't possible.

If she hadn't left of her own free will, two possibilities remained. Either someone had kidnapped her—but why?— or someone had killed her, intentionally or accidentally, and then arranged to conceal her body.

Those were some brilliant ideas, I thought. Signore and Signora Ferraro and my colleague Fornelli had certainly made the right decision when they hired a latter-day Auguste Dupin like myself.

The big question, though, was this: What could I do? Even if I read the file and managed to find a shortcoming in the investigation, what would the next step be? In spite of my conversation with Fornelli, I had absolutely no intention of hiring a private investigator. There must have been good investigators around, but I'd never been lucky enough to meet one. I had had only two experiences with detective agencies, and they had both been disasters. I'd sworn I'd never make that mistake again.

Moreover, the notion that I might start investigating the matter myself was crazy, crazy but dangerously enticing.

The only serious option, if I did manage to identify a plausible clue of any kind, was to request a meeting with the prosecutor and—very tactfully, because such people were quick to take offense—suggest that he investigate a little further before closing the case once and for all.

When the building commissioner arrived, I was in the

throes of this sort of speculation. Luckily, I now had to think about him and his problems with the law, which distracted me from my tortured logic.

He seemed pretty upset. He was a high school teacher. This was the first time he'd held government office, and this was also his first brush with the law. He was afraid he might be arrested any minute.

I asked him to explain the situation in general terms. I took a quick look at the official notice he'd received and read through a few other documents he'd brought with him. In the end, I told him he could relax: As far as I could tell, there was really no serious evidence of wrongdoing on his part.

He seemed dubious, but relieved. He thanked me and we said our good-byes; I promised to meet with the prosecutor and inform him that my client was entirely willing to come in for an interview and felt sure he could clear up his role in the matter.

One by one, my colleagues—oh, how I dislike that word—came into my office to say good night before going home. This ceremony always makes me feel like a doddering old fool.

When I was finally alone, I called down to the Japanese take-out place a couple of blocks from my office and ordered a truly outsized meal of sushi, sashimi, temaki, uramaki, and a soybean salad. When the woman taking my order over the phone asked if I wanted something to drink, I hesitated for just a moment, then asked for a well-chilled bottle of white wine as well.

"Chopsticks and glasses for two, I imagine," the young woman said.

"Of course, for two," I answered.

8.

~

Forty-five minutes later, I was clearing a jumbled mess of plastic trays, little bottles, chopsticks, empty packets, and napkins off my desk. When I finished, I poured myself another glass of Gewürztraminer, stuck the plastic cork back into the bottle—I hate those plastic corks, but I have to admit that I haven't had any corked wine since they were invented—and put it in the fridge. Every step performed slowly and very carefully. That's how I always do things when I am preparing myself to begin a new task that makes me anxious. I do everything I can to delay the moment when I'll have to begin, and I have to say, I'm pretty creative about it.

They call it a pathological tendency to procrastinate.

Apparently, this is a syndrome that is typical of insecure individuals who lack self-esteem; they continually put off disagreeable tasks in order to avoid being faced with their own shortcomings, fears, and limitations. I read something along those lines once, when I was leafing through a book called *How to Stop Procrastinating and Start Living*. It was a self-help book that explained the syndrome's causes and then suggested about two hundred pages of crazy exercises to be used—I'm quoting verbatim—"to rid yourself of this disease of will and live a full, productive life, free of frustrations."

I thought to myself that I wasn't all that eager to have such a productive life, that self-help books that tell you how to change your life give me hives, and that a certain amount of frustration really didn't bother me. So I put the book back on the shelf where I'd found it—as usual I was in a bookstore reading for free—and I bought an Alan Bennett book and went home.

After clearing away every trace of my Japanese dinner, after drinking a little more wine, after checking in vain for new e-mail, I realized the time had come.

I decided to read the file in the chronological order in which the authorities conducted their investigations, beginning with the event in question and moving forward from there. That's not usually how I go through a file.

If I'm examining a file in which a warrant has been issued and my client is in jail, or under house arrest, the first thing I do is to read the court order for the warrant, which is the last document in the judicial proceedings. If I know the judge who wrote it, I immediately form an opinion about whether it's a serious matter or not. After the judicial order, I read the other documents, working backward from last to first. I do the same thing if I've been hired after a trial verdict has been handed down, meaning first I read the court order that I'm being hired to appeal, and then I read everything else.

But in the case of the missing Manuela Ferraro, I thought it would be best to retrace the investigation as it developed, through the documents, doing my best to intuit whatever I could about the story behind those documents.

It was what's called a "Form 44 file," in reference to the papers filed in cases with unknown defendants. Printed on the cover were the name of the missing person, the date of her disappearance, and the classification of the crime— Article 605 of the Italian Penal Code, abduction. This is the only crime heading that can be invoked when a person disappears and there is no evidence to support other, more specific theories.

The first document in the file was the report from the Carabinieri—signed by Inspector Navarra, a non-commissioned officer I knew and respected—informing the prosecutor's office of the existence of the missing persons report filed by the parents and the transcripts of the investigation's early interviews.

I began with the statement of the young woman who had taken Manuela to the train station. Anita Salvemini— that was her name—had also been a guest at the *trulli* where Manuela spent the weekend. She'd given Manuela a ride because she was going to Ostuni to meet some friends, but that was the first and only time they'd met.

During the twenty minutes of the short car trip from the *trulli* to the train station, they chatted about inconsequential matters. Manuela told her she was studying law in Rome and said she planned to return to Rome by train later that evening or the next morning.

No, Anita didn't know whether Manuela was planning to meet someone at the Bari train station, nor did she know if Manuela was seeing anyone, had a boyfriend, and so on.

No, Manuela hadn't seemed worried to her. Moreover, she hadn't really observed her carefully for the obvious reason that she—Anita—was driving the car, and she therefore needed to keep her eyes on the road.

No, she didn't recall Manuela making or receiving any calls during the car trip between the *trulli* and the Ostuni train station. Manuela may have taken her cell phone out of her purse at some point. Maybe she got a text, or sent one, but Anita couldn't really say with any certainty.

No, she couldn't remember exactly how Manuela was dressed that afternoon. She'd definitely had a large dark-colored bag with her, and a smaller purse, and she thought she might have been wearing jeans and a light-colored t-shirt.

No, she couldn't remember the exact time of their departure from the *trulli*, nor could she remember exactly when they arrived at the train station and she said good-bye to Manuela. They probably left a little after four, which would mean they got there around 4:30.

No, she couldn't say exactly when Manuela's train was scheduled to depart. Probably shortly after they arrived at Ostuni, but that was a guess, because she had no memory of having talked about it.

No, she had nothing more to add.

Read, approved, and signed.

After that deposition came the statements of the three friends—two young women and a young man—who'd been at the *trulli* with Manuela. These three statements were short and said basically the same thing: They'd planned to return to Bari on Sunday night. Then, because there was a party, the three friends had decided to stay until Monday. Manuela still wanted to go home on Sunday, as they had originally planned. She told them not to worry, because she'd found a ride to Ostuni, and she planned to catch a train there.

The end.

Then came the statement of the ticket clerk Fornelli had mentioned. The clerk recognized Manuela, though he didn't know what time she'd come to his window to buy her ticket.

From the report, it appeared that the Carabinieri had checked the schedule for trains departing the station of Ostuni. Manuela could have taken either a Eurostar, an express, or one of two locals between 5:02 P.M. and 6:58 P.M.

The Carabinieri had been very thorough and had interviewed the conductors on all those trains: There were ten or so statements—all identical, nearly all useless.

The conductors were each shown a photograph of the girl, and they answered that they couldn't remember ever having seen her.

Only one, the conductor on the 6:50 train, said that Manuela's face was familiar. He thought he'd seen that girl before, but he wasn't sure if it had been on Sunday afternoon or some other time.

There followed a series of transcripts of the statements of the other young people who'd spent the weekend at the *trulli*. None of the statements was even remotely useful. Only one thing caught my attention: The Carabinieri asked everyone whether narcotics had been used over the weekend. Everyone interviewed ruled that out, but no one had been able—or willing—to say whether Manuela ever used drugs, even occasionally.

Then there was the sketchy information obtained from two of Manuela's friends who were also students in Rome: Nicoletta Abbrescia—the girl who shared an apartment with Manuela—and Caterina Pontrandolfi.

The Carabinieri had asked them about drugs, too. Both

admitted that Manuela might have smoked a joint every now and then, but said she never used anything stronger. Between the lines of the bureaucratic language, there were glimpses of embarrassment and perhaps even reticence, but that was probably normal and understandable, since the conversation was, after all, with the Carabinieri.

But the most interesting part of their depositions concerned a certain Michele Cantalupi, Manuela's most recent boyfriend. Both young women described a troubled relationship, marked by frequent fights, that came to a stormy end that included verbal and even physical violence.

The Carabinieri reported that in the days immediately following Manuela's disappearance they had not been able to track down Cantalupi. His parents told them that their son was on vacation, out of the country. The detectives were puzzled by their responses (in the report, they wrote that the parents' attitude had seemed somewhat evasive), and they requested authorization to pull the records for Cantalupi's cell phone, as well as those for Manuela's cell phone and her ATM records. They wanted to see with whom they'd been in contact most recently and more importantly to determine whether Cantalupi really had been out of the country for several days.

One week later, in another long report, the Carabinieri detailed a number of further steps that had been taken in the investigation. First, they had conducted an interview with Michele Cantalupi, who had returned from his vacation in the meantime. Cantalupi confirmed that he had been Manuela's boyfriend for nearly a year; he confirmed that the relationship had ended badly, but he pointed out that it was all over many months prior to her disappearance, and that in fact they'd been on much better terms lately.

The relationship had ended for a variety of reasons, and Manuela was the one who decided to end it. He admitted that there had been fights, some of them violent. He also admitted that on occasion those fights had taken place in the presence of friends. No, there had never been any assault, no punches thrown. He was informed that one of Manuela's girlfriends said that during a fight, in her presence, slaps had been exchanged. He admitted that there had in fact been a slap, but said that it had been Manuela who slapped him, not the other way around. He admitted that he shoved her and said she reacted by slapping him. That was the end of it, and that was also the only time there had been any form of physical conflict. No, he didn't have another girlfriend now. No, he didn't know whether Manuela was seeing someone else in Rome. He admitted that he had asked her, but she told him it was none of his business. Yes, they had met once, they'd had a cup of coffee together and chatted a while. This was in downtown Bari, in early August. No, there had been no conflict. They had said good-bye amicably.

I found the transcript puzzling. Reading between the lines of the police report, you could see Cantalupi trying to make it all sound normal and peaceful, when, perhaps, it wasn't completely peaceful, at least not according to Manuela's girlfriends.

On the other hand, the cell phone records seemed to rule out Michele Cantalupi's involvement in Manuela's disappearance. First of all, it was clear that for several days, his phone had been routed through foreign cell networks, so he really had been out of the country. Second, there was no contact—that Sunday or in the days before that—between Manuela and her ex-boyfriend.

Manuela's cell phone didn't seem to get a lot of use. The cell phone records covered the week prior to her disappearance: only a few calls and a few text messages, all to girlfriends or to her mother. None of the numbers belonged to anyone outside of her small circle of friends. Nothing unusual, except perhaps for how few calls and messages there were. Taken alone, however, that was not particularly significant.

That Sunday, Manuela had received only two phone calls, and she had exchanged text messages, again, with her mother and with a girlfriend. The last sign of life in the phone records was a text message she sent to her mother in the afternoon. After that, nothing. The cell phone went dead for good.

Her friend was interviewed by the Carabinieri, but she'd been unable to supply any useful information. She'd called Manuela to say hello, since she had to go back to Rome and they hadn't had a chance to get together in the previous few days. She had no idea what Manuela was planning to do that evening, how she would be getting back to Rome, much less what might have happened to her.

The ATM records provided nothing useful, since the last withdrawal had been made in Bari on the Friday before she disappeared.

In the days that followed, a number of photographs of Manuela, with a description of the clothing she was probably wearing that afternoon, were published in local newspapers and shown on the television program *Chi l'ha visto?*. Some of those photographs were in the file. I looked at them for a long time, searching for a secret, or at least an idea of some kind. Of course, I found nothing, and the only brilliant conclusion that I managed to draw from my examination was that Manuela was—or had been—a very attractive young woman.

After the photographs were published, as Fornelli had told me and as always seems to happen with disappearances, a number of people—nearly all of them of good candidates for psychiatric treatment—had phoned in and claimed to have seen the missing girl.

The third report showed the effects that publishing the photographs had on an array of mentally unbalanced individuals. There were a dozen or so statements sent from Carabinieri stations all over Italy. They were all declarations from people who claimed, in varying tones of confidence, which in turn correlated exactly to how precarious their mental health was, that they had seen Manuela.

There was the pathological liar Fornelli had mentioned to me who claimed he'd seen Manuela working as a prostitute on the outskirts of Foggia. Then there was a woman who noticed Manuela wandering absentmindedly through the aisles of a superstore in Bologna. There was a guy who swore he'd seen her in Brescia, flanked by two suspicious-looking men who spoke some Eastern European language. They had shoved Manuela into a car, which tore away, tires screeching.

The Carabinieri noted that none of these statements appeared to possess even a shred of credibility. As I read, I thought to myself that I had rarely agreed so wholeheartedly with a police document.

Also in the file were a number of anonymous letters that had been sent directly to the district attorney's office. They spoke, variously, of the white slave trade, international conspiracies, Turkish and Israeli intelligence agencies, satanic cults and black masses. I forced myself to read them all, from start to finish, and I emerged from that experience exhausted, dispirited, and with absolutely nothing to show for it.

Manuela had been sucked silently into a vacant and terrifying vacuum on a late-summer Sunday, and I could think of nothing more that might be done to keep alive the desperate hopes of her parents.

I walked over to the fridge and poured myself another glass of wine. I looked back over the few notes I'd jotted down and decided they were useless.

My nerves were on edge, and I seemed unable to control my thoughts. I wondered what the private investigators and police detectives from some of the many American crime novels I'd read over the years would have done in my situation. For instance, I tried to imagine what Matthew Scudder, or Harry Bosch, or Steve Carella would do if he were assigned to this case.

The question was ridiculous, and yet, paradoxically, it helped me focus my thoughts.

The investigator in a crime novel, without exception, would begin by talking to the policeman who conducted the investigation. They would ask him what ideas he might have developed, independently of what he'd written in his reports. Then they would contact the people who'd already been questioned and try to extract some detail that they'd overlooked, or forgotten, or failed to mention, or that simply hadn't made it into the report.

It was just then that I realized something. A couple of hours earlier, I had assumed that when I read the file, I wouldn't find any new clues. And in fact, reading the file had only confirmed my suspicions. But I also assumed that I would then report my findings to Fornelli and the Ferraros, return their check, and get myself out of an assignment that I had neither the skills nor the resources to take on. It would be the only right and reasonable course of action. But in that two-hour period, for reasons I could only vaguely guess at and that I didn't want to examine too closely, I had changed my mind.

I told myself I'd give it a try. Nothing more. And the first thing I'd do would be to talk to the non-commissioned officer who had supervised the investigation, Inspector Navarra. I knew him. We were friends, and he would certainly be willing to tell me what he thought of the case, aside from what he'd written in his reports. Then I'd decide what to do next, what else to try.

As I walked out onto the street, with a studied gesture I pulled up the collar of my raincoat, even though there was no reason to do so.

People who read too much often do things that are completely unnecessary.

9.

On my way home, I decided to put in half an hour on my punching bag. The idea, as always, made me slightly giddy. I think it might be interesting for a skilled psychologist to spend some time studying my relationship with the heavy bag. Obviously, I punch it a lot. But before I get started, in the pauses between rounds, and especially afterward, perhaps while drinking a cold beer or a glass of wine, I talk to it.

This began when Margherita left for New York, and it got more serious when she wrote to say that she wasn't planning to come back to Italy. That letter—a genuine letter on paper, not an e-mail—certified what I already knew: It was over between us, and she now had another life, in another city, in another world. That left me with the crumbs of our old life, in our old city, in our old world. In the months that followed, what I talked about most of all to him—to the punching bag, I mean—was Margherita and the other women I've loved. Three in all.

"You know, friend, what strikes me as especially sad?"
"—"

"I no longer remember the devastating feeling that I experienced, albeit differently, with Tiziana, Margherita, and Sara. I just can't seem to remember it. I know I felt it, but I have to work to convince myself of that, because I have no memory of it. It's gone."

Mister Bag swung from side to side, and I understood he wanted an explanation. I probably hadn't described it well. What did I mean when I said that I couldn't remember that devastating feeling?

"Maybe you know that song by Fabrizio De André, 'The Song of Lost Love.' You remember that verse that goes, 'Nothing's left but a few halfhearted caresses and a little tenderness'?

"—"

"Okay, you don't know it. Well, you might not recognize the words, but you've definitely heard the song. There was a time when I played it a lot. Yeah, I know, it's a little pathetic. After all, you're the only one I talk to about it. Anyway, I want to tell you something, but you have to promise to keep it to yourself."

"—"

"You're right, sorry. No one can keep a secret like you. You know how sometimes I feel like crying?"

"—"

"Sure, I'll tell you why. Because I actually feel the need to talk about it. I feel like crying when I realize that the memory of the women I loved doesn't make me suffer. The worst it does is give me a sort of vague, feeble, distant sadness. It's so nothing. It's like a puddle of stagnant water."

"—"

"Okay, I admit, that's not much of a metaphor. And you're right, I get lost in my own thoughts and don't do a good job of explaining things. The reason I feel like crying is that everything seems drab, silent. Even my pain. My so-called emotional life is like a silent movie. I know that you're not exactly the kind of guy who delves into subtleties, but I'm sad, and I feel like crying, because I can't manage to get in touch with that sadness. That healthy sadness, the kind that makes your temples throb, that makes you feel alive. Not this flabby, miserable, soft thing. You understand?"

By this point in the conversation, Mister Bag was completely motionless. The last bit of swing from the punches he had so obligingly absorbed from his clearly unbalanced friend—me—had worn off, and he hung there, perfectly still. As if what I was telling him were so upsetting that it froze him. He was thinking, but it wasn't his style to offer answers, opinions, or advice.

Still, believe it or not, after those conversations, so rife with psychiatric pathology—and after throwing a lot of punches, of course—I always felt better, and sometimes I even felt perfectly fine.

To tell the truth, Mister Bag is the perfect therapist. He listens and never interrupts. He never judges (at the very most, he might swing a little), and he never charges a fee. Plus, the transference problem is minimal: I feel a certain tenderness for him, but without any sexual implications. That's why I'd never dream of replacing him. When he splits where I've been hitting particularly hard or insistently, I repair him with a length of duct tape. I really appreciate how it makes him look like a battle-scarred warrior, and I think that he's grateful to me for not tossing him out and replacing him with some shiny new bag that has no significance.

I walked into the apartment, loosening my tie, and the first thing I did was put on a CD that I had burned for myself with twenty or so songs of all kinds. Two minutes later, I had taken off my trousers and shirt (still wearing my boxers, just to be clear), taped up my hands, and put on my gloves, and I was punching the bag.

I went for a first round of mild jabs, just a warm-up session. Light combinations of three or four punches with both hands, without follow-through. Jab, straight, left hook. Right hook, left hook, uppercut. Jab, jab, straight right. And so on, for the first three minutes, getting warmed up. Between rounds, I exchanged a few words with Mister Bag, but to tell the truth, that evening neither of us really felt much like talking. When I started the second round, I began putting a little more energy into my punches. The shuffle feature on my CD player brought up the intermezzo from *Cavalleria Rusticana*, which made me feel a lot like Robert De Niro in *Raging Bull*.

Sometimes when I'm punching the heavy bag with the right music and the right level of focus, unexpected memories pop out of nowhere. Doors swing open to show me scenes, sounds, noises, voices, and even smells that I'd long forgotten.

That evening, while I was pummeling Mister Bag, who patiently let me work on him, I remembered, as if I were screening a movie in my mind, my first fight as an amateur boxer, welterweight, classification novice.

I was just sixteen, tall, skinny, and scared to death. My opponent was shorter and more muscular than I was, with an acne-scarred face and the expression of a murderer. Or at least, that's what he looked like to me. I had decided to become a boxer precisely to help me overcome my fear of guys like him. In the interminable minutes before the bout began, I thought—among many other things—that clearly the treatment wasn't working. My legs were shaking, my breathing was labored, and I felt as if my arms were paralyzed. I thought I'd never be able to raise my arms to defend myself, much less to throw a punch. The terror became so intense that I even considered faking illness—falling to the floor and pretending to faint—just to keep from having to fight.

But when the bell rang, I stood up and walked out to fight. And that's when a strange thing happened.

His fists didn't hurt me. They pummeled my helmet and especially my body, since he was shorter than I was, and he was doing everything he could to make up for it. With every punch he threw, he exhaled with a guttural grunt, as if he were trying to deliver the final haymaker. But his punches were slow, feeble, and harmless—and they didn't hurt. I kept moving around him, trying to take advantage of my reach, and I kept tapping him with my left.

In the third round, he got mad. Maybe his trainer told him he was losing the match, or maybe he figured it out on his own. In any case, when the bell rang he lunged at me furiously, frantically windmilling his arms. My right-cross counter-punch shot out and caught him in the head, without my quite realizing what I'd done. I still can't remember it exactly. What I do remember—or more likely what I think I remember—is a sort of film still, an image from the moment a fraction of a second after the punch connected and before he dropped to the canvas, in just as sprawling and disorderly a fashion as he had come windmilling and lunging toward me in the first place.

In amateur boxing, it's a rare thing to knock down your opponent, and a knockout is even rarer. It's an event, and everyone knows it. When I saw my opponent flat on his back, a rush of heat and savage joy rose from my hips all the way to the nape of my neck.

The referee ordered me into my corner, and he began the count. The other guy got to his feet almost immediately, raising both gloves to show that he could continue the fight. And in fact, the fight resumed, but it was already over. At that point, I had an unbeatable lead, and if my acne-scarred opponent wanted to win, he was going to have to knock me out for the full count. He wasn't up to that. I kept on circling around him, easily staying out of reach of his lunges and attacks, which were increasingly feeble and frantic, and I kept tapping him with my left until the bell rang, ending the round and the match.

That night, I didn't get a wink of sleep. I was still a child and that was why I knew, as I would at few other times in my life, what it meant to feel like a man.

I stopped punching. I stood there, face-to-face with Mister Bag, trying to regain control of my breathing, feeling the violent throbbing in my temples, as a desperate, fondness for the man-child I'd been, lying awake in the darkness, wrapped in my blanket, looking forward to what was yet to come, swept over me.

When the swaying of the bag and my own breathing slowed, I shook myself out of that trance.

Nico and the Velvet Underground were singing "I'll Be Your Mirror."

"Okay, Mister Bag, I'm going to go take a shower and then I'm going to sleep. I hope. Anyway, it's always a pleasure to spend a little time with you."

He nodded, swinging, understanding. He loved me, too, in spite of everything.

10.

Inspector Navarra is a likable guy. He doesn't particularly look like a policeman, and he looks even less like a military man. He has the face of a slightly overweight kid. He's certainly not someone you'd imagine kicking in doors, gun in hand, to round up a ring of drug dealers, or interrogating suspects and slapping them around. His wife is an engineer who works as a researcher at National Research Council. He met her in college when he was studying engineering himself. Then he took the civil service exam to become a non-commissioned Carabinieri officer, passed, and stopped his university studies. He has three children, a dog, a hint of melancholy in his eyes, and a hobby that he loves: making paper airplanes.

That sounds like a hobby for little kids, like a way of passing the time in a doctor's waiting room.

But not the way he does it. For every plane he builds, he spends days developing rough sketches, and then refining the blueprints, and then building prototypes and smoothing the rough edges, until the airplane flies just the way he wants. And when I say "flies," I mean it in the truest sense of the word. Long, soaring flights, incredibly long, as if there were an engine and a pilot in the plane, or as if the plane were alive. As a way of thanking me for some legal advice I once gave his sister, he gave me one of his airplanes.

I still have it, and I have to say it's one of the few objects with which I'd really hate to part.

I had Navarra's cell phone number, so the following morning I gave him a call.

"Inspector Navarra, it's Counselor Guerrieri."

"Hello, counselor, how are you doing? Do you still have the paper plane I gave you?"

"Of course I do. From time to time I look at it and wonder how you manage to create something like that out of pieces of paper."

"Is there something I can help you with?" he asked.

"Yes, there is. I'd like to talk to you for half an hour. Could we meet somewhere?"

"What's it about?"

"The disappearance of Manuela Ferraro. Her parents came to see me a few days ago and I've read the file. I'd like to discuss it with you if you have a minute."

"Are you going to court today?"

"I don't have any hearings, but if you're going to be in court, we could meet there."

"If you're coming just to talk to me, then don't go to the trouble. Let's do it this way: I'll go to my hearing, I'll ask if I can testify first thing, and when I'm done I'll give you a call and then I'll drop by your office."

I told him I didn't want to impose on him; he replied that it was a pleasure for him to come and see me. He said that he liked me, which he couldn't say for most of my colleagues, and that, in his opinion, I should have been a prosecutor. He liked the way I had argued on behalf of the plaintiff in a trial for usury for which he'd conducted the police investigations. He said that if it had been up to the prosecutor, the bastard who was on trial would have gotten off scot-free. If the judges sentenced that band of loan sharks to hard prison time, it was to my credit, he said. It would be a pleasure to come see me, he said again.

He called me earlier than I expected. His trial had been adjourned because of a failure to serve certain papers, so he'd been able to free himself up almost immediately. Twenty minutes later, he was sitting across from me.

"Weren't you in a different office until recently?"

"Yes, we moved four months ago."

"It looks sort of American. Nice. I'd like to make some changes, too. But it's not so easy if you're a Carabiniere. You've got a fixed income, and you can't predict your schedule. I was thinking of going back to college."

"You'd like to study engineering again?"

He looked at me in astonishment.

"Good memory. But no, not engineering. I don't think I could get up to speed, especially in my spare time. I was thinking of literature, or philosophy. But maybe that's a pipe dream. It's just that once you pass age forty, you start to ask yourself some hard questions about the meaning of what you're doing, and especially about time passing, which it seems to do more and more quickly."

"A while ago I read a good book by a Dutch psychologist. It's called *Why Life Speeds Up As You Get Older*, and it talks about that very phenomenon. It's really interesting."

"Just hearing the title makes me anxious. There are times when I feel like I'm losing my balance and falling over. It's not a pleasant feeling."

I knew what he was talking about. In fact, it's *not* a pleasant feeling. We sat in silence, with those words hanging in the air.

"All right, let's forget about time rushing by and my

midlife crisis. You said on the phone that you're looking into the disappearance of Manuela Ferraro."

"Yes. As I told you, her parents came to see me, accompanied by an old civil law colleague of mine. They asked me to examine the file and see if I could find any grounds for further investigation. Last night I read through the documents, and of course the first thing I noticed was that you were in charge of the investigation."

He nodded, and said nothing. So I continued.

"I want to know what you think about her disappearance, aside from what you wrote in your reports."

I refrained from asking him explicitly if he thought further investigation was merited. Even a well-balanced and intelligent person like Navarra can be touchy about certain things. I figured something might emerge if we just talked it over casually.

"It's never easy to form any solid theory in a missing persons case. In my experience—and I think statistics back me up on this—once a certain amount of time has gone by the percentage of positive outcomes in missing persons cases is very low."

He stopped as if he'd just thought of something important.

"You know that Detective Tancredi is a first-class specialist in this type of investigation, right? He's built up an incredible body of experience with missing children. I think you know him, don't you?"

"Yes, Tancredi and I are friends."

"Well, if you're a friend of Tancredi's, I'd ask his opinion. I won't be offended. In any case, aside from what happens in general, you want to know if I have any ideas of my own, above and beyond what's written in the reports."

"That would be helpful, in fact."

Navarra pressed his lips together. He scratched the back of his neck. He rocked his head gently from side to side, as if he were weighing the wisdom of confiding in me what he really thought. Then he must have come down on the side of taking the risk.

"If I had been able to dedicate a lot more time to this case . . . no, let's say if I had been able to dedicate all my time to this case, I would have looked into that young woman's life in Rome. I had the impression that her two friends—Abbrescia and Pontrandolfi—weren't telling me everything they knew, that they were covering up something, but I don't know what. Let me be clear: the first target of my investigation was Cantalupi, Manuela's ex-boyfriend. He's a spoiled brat, a conceited and overindulged little playboy who just makes you want to slap him silly. But according to the phone records he was actually in Croatia when Manuela disappeared, and he didn't come back to Italy until four or five days later. In other words, unless we're willing to consider the possibility of teleportation, there was no way he could have been in contact with the girl when she went missing."

"The fact that Cantalupi was in Croatia is proven only by the cell phone records."

He looked at me with a smile.

"Believe me, I wasn't happy to give up the idea that this guy was somehow involved in the girl's disappearance. And I thought the same thing you're thinking—though I hope you don't mind my saying that it's kind of crazy: Someone else could have used the phone. But the cell phone records show calls made to his phone from his home, so they must have been made by his parents. Anyway, since I didn't like the guy, I went ahead and did some informal checking on my own. I talked to the captain of the boat that he took. I'm afraid there's no doubt about it. On the days in question, that little shit was on the other side of the Adriatic Sea."

While he was talking, I decided the theory that Cantalupi had given his cell phone to someone else in Croatia so that he could establish an alibi in advance before hurrying back to Italy to kidnap or murder his ex-girlfriend was silly. Why would he bother? I felt foolish having thought of it, even though a seasoned professional investigator like Navarra had entertained the same thought.

"But you were saying about her two friends?"

"Right, her two friends. Let me start by saying that I always try to be very cautious about my instincts on whether a witness or a suspect is reliable or sincere. You know a good way to tell if an investigator is a fool?"

"No, tell me. It might come in handy."

"Ask him if he can tell when someone's lying. The ones who say they can tell, who think it's impossible to trick them with a lie, are the biggest fools around. They're the ones a skilled liar can wrap around his little finger with the greatest ease and enjoyment."

"I know a couple of prosecutors who claim that they know immediately if a defendant or a witness is lying. And in fact they're the biggest idiots in the district attorney's office."

"They're probably the same ones I'm thinking of. Anyway, that was a bit of a digression, but I'm trying to say that I take my impressions about the truthfulness of someone I'm interviewing with a grain of salt. That doesn't mean that I ignore my instincts entirely. I think of the interview as an opening and try to explore more deeply."

At that point I asked him if he would like a coffee or

anything else. He said, yes, please, he had just been thinking how much he'd enjoy a cappuccino. I called the café
downstairs, ordered two cappuccinos, then looked over at
Navarra.

"So?"

"So, I had the impression that something wasn't quite
right when I talked to the two young women."

"What wasn't right, in particular?"

"That there were things they didn't tell me. Let me
give you an example. At a certain point, I asked Nicoletta,
Manuela's roommate in Rome, and then the other one, if
Manuela used narcotics."

"Yes, I read that in the statement. Both of them said no,
as far as they were aware, except for the occasional joint."

"Right, but the thing was *how* they said it. There was
something about the answers both of them gave to that
question that didn't convince me entirely. I followed up on
that line of questioning a little bit, and both of them shut
down. I had nothing concrete to work with, so I had to drop
the matter. But I was left with a very distinct impression
that they hadn't told me everything they knew. And the one
who seemed most uncomfortable was Nicoletta Abbrescia."

"So did you talk to your superiors or to the prosecutor
about your concerns?"

"Sure I did. And by the way," he added, as if he'd just
remembered that he was giving me confidential details
about an investigation that was officially still open, "the
conversation we're having right now never happened."

"It never happened. So what did your superiors and the
prosecutor have to say about it?"

"My captain shrugged it off. And all things considered, I can see why. What were we supposed to do with

my suspicions in the absence of any concrete evidence? I tried suggesting that we follow the two girls for a couple of days. He looked at me as if I'd just morphed into the creature from *Alien*. He asked me where I wanted to act out this American detective movie. In Rome, obviously. And was I supposed to authorize my own mission to Rome? And while I was at it, would I be paying for it out of my own special reserve fund, since they'd just cut the budget for fueling our patrol cars? So I suggested tapping their phones, requesting their call records. And he told me to talk to the prosecutor about it."

"So what did you do?"

"I went to the district attorney's office and talked to the magistrate in charge of the investigation."

"And what did the magistrate say?"

"He was pretty nice about it, all things considered. He asked me whether I was planning to justify a wiretap request by writing that Inspector Navarra is doubtful about the truthfulness of two people who have information about what happened. He asked me if I had any idea what the judge would likely respond. I told him that, yes, I could imagine, and we dropped the matter, meaning that I never even submitted a written request. Obviously."

Just then, the delivery boy arrived, carrying our cappuccinos on a tray. Navarra held his cup with both hands when he drank, like a child. There was some milk left on his upper lip. He wiped it off carefully with a couple of paper napkins, the way a person might who knows what happens when you drink a cappuccino, and who therefore takes appropriate steps. Calmly and deliberately.

I really liked his simple, precise sequence of actions. All he did was wipe a little cappuccino foam off his lips, but I thought I'd like to be the kind of person whose actions are so careful and conscious.

Navarra crumpled up the napkins and then resumed speaking.

"So, in short, we did what we could. We're so over-worked, we have mountains of files on our desks, and we have to work our way through them. Among other things, technically, we don't even have a crime report. I mean, the young woman . . ."

"Of course, of course. The young woman is no longer a minor, there's no explicit evidence that her disappearance is directly linked to a crime, there is no way of ruling out the possibility that she simply wanted to get away from every-thing, and so on."

"And so on. It's unlikely, but she might have had a reason for leaving. She might not have wanted to be found."

I looked him in the eye. He returned my gaze, then shrugged.

"Okay, okay, I don't believe it either. But there was noth-ing more I could do. Unless, like I told you, I devoted myself to this case full time. And since I couldn't do that, I was forced to close the case and work on other things. But maybe you can manage to uncover something I missed."

He said it without a hint of sarcasm, at least as far as I could tell. But the idea struck both of us as fairly unlikely.

"So what do you plan to do?" he asked, as he pushed his chair back.

"You know better than I do that my chances are very slim. If you couldn't find anything, I doubt very much I'll be able to."

"Don't be so sure of that. Investigations work in mysteri-ous ways. Sometimes, you do everything right, by the book, and you don't find a damned thing. And then, when you've finally set your mind at ease that there's nothing else to be done, something random happens and you're handed the solution, all wrapped up and tied with a bow. With this kind of work, more than any other, there is no technique or planning or experience that's half as important as a piece of dumb luck. And you might just have that piece of luck this time."

I shrugged and shook my head, but I liked what he'd said. He'd encouraged me. I was an absolute beginner as far as investigating went, but where strokes of dumb luck were concerned, I'd always done all right.

"I think I'll try to talk with Manuela's two girlfriends, the ones who go to school in Rome. And I'll talk to the guy you like so much, the ex-boyfriend. I don't know whether it's worth trying to talk to the girl who gave her a ride from the *trulli* to the train station in Ostuni."

"Anita Salvemini. I'd definitely have a conversation with her."

"Why?"

"It will almost certainly be a waste of time. But sometimes, very rarely, it happens that a person, interviewed again at a different time, maybe in a slightly less stressful setting, is able to remember details she forgot or overlooked the first time. It may happen that a shred of memory surfaces, and that it turns out to be the one detail that allows you to unravel the whole ball of wool. It doesn't happen often, but it wouldn't cost you anything to try talking to that young woman again."

"Do you have any other advice for me?"

"The handbooks suggest proceeding in two phases when interviewing a witness. In the first phase, you should let the witness talk freely, without interruption, and you should speak only to make it clear that you're paying attention to what he says. Then, when he's done with this uninterrupted account, you should ask a series of specific questions, to clarify in greater depth. At the end, always leave the door open. You should tell the witness that in the hours or days that follow your interview, he is likely to remember some further detail. That detail may seem unimportant to him, and he will be tempted to keep it to himself. You can't let that happen. You might find the key to the case in those seemingly insignificant details."

"So?"

"So you should tell the witness that if anything else comes to mind—*anything*—he needs to call us. It's important because it encourages him to provide you with any information he might have, but it also reinforces the witness's sense of responsibility. If a witness feels responsible, he'll keep an open and active mind, and that's crucial to gathering new information."

"With your interests and expertise, maybe you should study psychology, not literature."

"Yeah, I've thought of that. But like I told you, whenever I think of going back to college, a minute later it strikes me as a stupid idea, at age forty-three, with no prospect of doing anything useful with that degree. And there's a whole series of thoughts that follows, none of them particularly agreeable."

Then, after sitting for a few seconds with a rapt, slightly faraway expression on his face, he said it was time for him to get back to the Carabinieri barracks.

"Do you think the girl's still alive?"

He hesitated for a moment, before answering. Then he shook his head.

"No, I don't think so. I don't have the slightest idea what could have happened to her, but I doubt she's still alive."

That was exactly what I thought. That was what I had thought from the very beginning, but it was still hard to hear him say it. His expression showed that he knew that and was sorry about it, but there was nothing he could do.

"If you need anything else, call me. And of course, if you find anything, call me."

Of course. I'll solve the mystery, generously hand over the guilty party, and then fade back into the shadows. It's what we always do, we solitary heroes.

"One day I'd like to watch you launch your paper airplanes."

He smiled.

"I'll invite you, one day."

11.

That afternoon I called Tancredi. It took three or four tries for the call to go through, and when it rang it sounded as if I were calling overseas.

"Guido. So, you're still alive."

"Alive, yeah, pretty much. How are you doing? You're not out of the country, are you?"

"You don't miss a thing, do you? Sharp as a tack. I'm fine, and I'm in Virginia."

"Virginia? You mean Virginia in the United States?"

"Yes, that Virginia."

"This call is costing you a fortune then. We'll talk another time. By the way, what time is it there?"

"It's eleven. We're on our coffee break. And don't worry, I can still afford a few long distance calls. Anyway, nobody else has called me from Italy, so, for lack of anyone better, you'll have to do."

"What are you doing in Virginia?"

"I'm at the FBI Academy. I'm taking a special international police course. Questioning techniques and criminal profiling."

"A course in what?"

"Techniques for identifying criminals and techniques for questioning witnesses and suspects."

"Are they teaching you, or are you teaching them?"

"They're teaching me, believe me. It's a whole other world. You'd find it interesting from a lawyer's perspective, too. What are you calling about?"

"I wanted to ask you something, but it's nothing urgent."

"Go ahead."

"No, really, it's not something I can talk about on an international call. Anyway, it isn't urgent," I lied. "When do you get back?"

"In three weeks."

"When you're back, give me a call. I'll tell you all about it in person."

"Are you sure you don't want to tell me now?"

"Yeah, I'm sure. Thanks, Carmelo. Enjoy your trip. Give me a call when you get back."

"I'll do that. I'm having a great time. I wish you could see my classmates. The one I like best is a Christian Turk who found out I'm from Bari. Ever since I told him, he keeps saying that we Baresi—and as you know, I'm not from Bari originally—stole the bones of Saint Nicholas of Myra from the Turks and should give them back. And let me tell you, you're not allowed to smoke a damn cigar anywhere, except maybe in a garbage dump. Anyway, I've got to go. Ciao, Guido, I'll call you when I get back."

We hung up, and when I thought about Tancredi, thousands of miles away, I felt lonely. To ward off that sensation, I decided to do something useful, or at least practical. I called Fornelli.

The way a person answers the phone—at least when he doesn't know who's calling, and Fornelli obviously didn't recognize my number—tells you some deep truths about him. Fornelli's voice, with its strong Bari accent, was quiet and bland.

"Hi, Sabino, it's Guido."

His voice got a little more lively. It took on a shape, and even a little bit of color.

"Hey, Guido."

"Hi, Sabino."

"Have you had a chance to read the file?"

I told him that I'd read the file. I didn't tell him about my conversation with Navarra, since I'd promised I'd keep it to myself.

"What do you think? Do you think there's anything left to try?"

"In all honesty, I doubt there's much of a chance of finding anything new beyond what the Carabinieri found in their investigation. Still, there are a few things to check out, just to go beyond any shadow of a doubt."

"That's great. What exactly did you have in mind?"

Now he sounded very different from the slightly depressed gentleman who had answered the phone moments before. He sounded almost excited. Stay calm, I told him in my mind. Nothing's going to come of this. Don't get your hopes up, and above all, watch what you say to those poor parents.

"I thought I'd talk with Manuela's ex-boyfriend, her two friends in Rome, and maybe the girl who drove her to the station the day she disappeared."

I told him I'd need some help getting in touch with these people. He said, sure, he'd take care of it. He would call Manuela's mother right away—the father, as I'd seen, was in no shape to help us—and ask her to get in touch with those young people. He'd let me know right away what the story was. He knew he'd done the right thing when he contacted me, he said at the end, with an incongruous note of cheerfulness in his voice. Then he plunged back into the murky space he'd occupied before answering the phone.

I thought maybe now I could get to work.

Lawyer work, that is. I was through playing at being an investigator for now. The next day I would be in court for one of the most surreal trials of my so-called career. I called Consuelo, who'd been studying the file for me, and told her to come into my office to bring me up to speed.

12.

My client was twenty-five, and he was charged with mass murder.

Put in those terms, the act sounds pretty impressive. It summons up tragic images, the bitter odor of gunpowder, ravaged corpses, screams, blood, shattered limbs, and ambulances with wailing sirens rushing to the scene.

But if you read the official charges and the file from the initial investigation, things looked different. The charges stated that Nicola Costantino was accused of the crime described in and punished under Article 422, Paragraph Two of the penal code because, with the intent of killing himself, he also committed acts liable to endanger the public safety, specifically opening the gas line in his home with the intent of filling the air with gas and causing an explosion with the potential to destroy the entire apartment building. Only the intervention of the Carabinieri stopped this wholesale destruction from taking place.

Nicola Costantino, long under medical care for psychiatric issues, tried to commit suicide by gas. He was alone in the apartment. He locked himself in the kitchen, drank half a bottle of rum, and downed a powerful dose of tranquilizers, and then he turned on the gas without lighting the burners. A neighbor with a sensitive nose almost immediately smelled that something wasn't right and called the Carabinieri. The paramilitary police—"promptly arriving at the site," as the report noted—knocked down the front door and threw open the windows. They found the young man unconscious on the floor but, miraculously, still in and of this world. In other words, they saved his life. But, after checking with the magistrate on duty at the time, they also arrested him. On charges of mass murder.

If you consult a handbook of Italian criminal law, you will find that no one need die in order for charges of the crime of mass murder to be brought. There just needs to have been a clear and present danger, provided that the act or acts in question were carried out specifically to kill.

The classic case studied in the classroom is one in which a terrorist places a highly explosive device in a public place. The bomb fails to go off, let's say because the police bomb squad intervenes, or because it malfunctions, but the terrorist can still be tried for mass murder because it was his intention to kill an indeterminate number of people, and his actions were designed to bring about that result.

My client's story was—how can I put this?—slightly different. Nicola Costantino was no terrorist; he was just a scrawny young man, mentally disturbed and irremediably prone to failure. He had decided to kill himself, and he'd failed at that, too. This proved mostly that his ineptitude extended to the field of self-destructive behavior.

There is no doubt that by doing something as stupid as turning on the gas, he had endangered everyone else in his apartment building; there is likewise no doubt that his idiotic actions were not a reflection of his intent to kill anyone except himself.

This was the very basic argument I had tried to make to

the prosecuting attorney and the special arraignment court in an attempt to persuade them that the crime of mass murder wasn't justified in this case, and that there was therefore no legal basis for holding my client in prison.

I hadn't persuaded them. In rejecting the appeal, the judges wrote that "all that is required to justify a charge of mass murder is that someone should have had the intention of killing anyone, which would, of course, include the intention of killing only himself."

That argument was powerfully paradoxical.

Hadn't Costantino in fact threatened the public safety with his attempt—unsuccessful only because of the timely intervention of the authorities—to kill himself? If so, then he was clearly guilty of the crime of mass murder, which in his case rose to the required threshold with respect to all factors, both objective and subjective.

And since the nature of the defendant's acts and his evidently unstable personality (this was the one point on which I tended to agree with the judges) could reasonably suggest the likelihood of a recidivistic repetition of the same kind of behavior—in other words, he was liable to do it again—the court was bound to confirm the order of preventive detention, in its most trenchant form: prison.

I was preparing my Court of Cassation appeal of this half-baked interpretation of Italian criminal law when my clients' parents came to see me. They seemed slightly embarrassed, but after some initial hesitation, they managed to convey, with much hemming and hawing, that they didn't want me to appeal the court's verdict.

"Why not?" I asked, nonplussed.

The man and woman looked at one another, as if trying to decide which of the two should answer.

"If it's a matter of my fee," I said, trying to remember how much I'd told them the appeal would cost, "don't worry about it, you can pay me when you have the money."

The father answered.

"No, thank you, counselor. It's not about the money. It's just that Nicola seems to be doing so much better in prison. Both the guards and the other inmates treat him well. He's socializing. He's made friends, and when we go to visit him, he seems almost happy. Honestly, we haven't seen him in such good spirits in years."

I wasn't sure I'd heard them right. The father shrugged.

"Let's leave him in jail for a few more months," added the mother, with an expression that seemed to blend a sense of guilt with a sense of relief, and even a touch of cheerfulness.

"When they finally bring him to trial, we're sure you'll manage to win an acquittal. They'll release him from prison, and we can help him rebuild his life. But for now, maybe we should leave him in jail for a while, since he seems to be doing so well. It's as if he were in a treatment facility," the father concluded, with the relieved expression of someone who has just completed a challenging task.

I was about to say that Nicola was legally an adult and therefore, for reasons of professional ethics, I would have to ask how he felt about this novel solution.

Instead, I thought it over for a few seconds and, in a decision I would prefer the ethics committee of the bar association not know about, said nothing. I only held out both hands, palms up, in a gesture of surrender to the inevitable.

Now, months later, it was time for the preliminary hearing.

———————

That morning, prior to my hearing, there was a social security fraud trial with dozens of defendants. The hall—the largest hearing room in the building—was teeming with defendants and their lawyers, and it had all the dignified sobriety of the Marrakech souk. There was every reason to suppose that this would take some time. Since I didn't know how else to pass the time, I pulled my iPod out of my briefcase and set it on shuffle.

Suddenly, as if by magic, the scene was transformed into a spectacle of deranged, mythical, senseless beauty.

Unbeknownst to them, lawyers, defendants, the judge, court clerks, and police officers were all dancing to the syncopated rhythm of rock 'n' roll, in an extravaganza staged just for me.

Lawyers standing up and declaiming, saying things I couldn't hear, defendants conferring amongst themselves, the judge dictating a statement: a sort of collective movement that, thanks to the music, seemed to take on meaning and necessity.

The best part of my private musical came when a colleague of mine whose most distinctive professional quality has always been his implacable scorn for the proper use of the subjunctive, stood up and addressed the judge, gesticulating vigorously, in perfect time—at least, that's how it appeared to me—to the voice of Freddie Mercury singing "Don't Stop Me Now."

Sometimes being a lawyer isn't bad at all, I thought, as I settled back, stretched out my legs under the bench in front of me, and enjoyed the show.

———————

After the initial hearing in the social security fraud trial, the courtroom emptied out and I put away my earbuds. It was our turn. The only people left in the room were the judge, the court clerk, me, Consuelo—who had arrived after making the rounds of the various clerks' offices—the prosecuting attorney, my client, and the two prison guards who had brought him to court and who continued to keep a close eye on him. You never knew—he might take it into his head to turn on the gas and murder an entire courtroom full of people.

After briskly dispensing with the initial formalities, the judge asked if there were any requests. I stood up and said that Signore Costantino wished to be questioned. The defendant had only been questioned once, when he was arraigned, two days after his arrest, I reasoned. At that time he hadn't been perfectly lucid, to put it mildly.

The judge dictated a brief order for the stenographer to enter into the record, and then ordered the two prison guards to bring the defendant before him. Then, he asked the prosecutor to begin.

"Have you read the charges in the indictment?" the prosecutor asked Nicola. Nicola looked at him in bewilderment, as if he couldn't understand the purpose of such an idiotic question. Then he saw me nod my head and got that he was expected to answer.

"Yes, of course."

"Did you do the things that are written in the formal charges?"

"I turned on the gas because I wanted to end it all. But I certainly didn't want to kill people. Later, when I got my head on straight, I realized I could have caused a disaster."

"Do you mean to say that you realized you had put into effect a chain of events capable of threatening public safety?"

I was about to object, but I thought better of it. An objection would be pointless, since the question was pointless. My client, who was not, as I have mentioned, the sharpest tool in the shed, sounded fairly reasonable as he responded. The prosecutor asked a few more questions, then said he was finished.

"Would you care to proceed, Counselor Guerrieri?" the judge asked.

"Thank you, your honor. I have very few questions to ask because, as you know perfectly well, the key to this trial has more to do with the law than the facts." I paused, and I thought I detected an almost imperceptible nod of approval from the judge. This isn't always a good thing, but the judge that day was well-informed and also intelligent, so that slight tilt of his head struck me as a promising sign.

"Signore Costantino, it is a well-established fact that you turned on the gas and that it was your intention to commit suicide. We need not cover that ground again. But I'd like to ask you something else: When you turned on the gas, was it your intention to kill anyone else?"

"No, of course not."

"At the moment when you turned on the gas, did it occur to you, did you imagine that your action might result in the death of other people besides yourself?"

"No, no, I just wanted to go to sleep and end it all. I told you I was out of my mind. I was on medication."

"Do you mean that you were taking pharmaceuticals?"

"Yes, antidepressants."

"You said that it was only afterward that you realized the consequences your actions might have had. Is that right?"

"Yes, many days later, when I was beginning to recover. In prison."

"Thank you. I have no further questions."

"Very good. If there are no further questions, I would say that we can proceed to summation," said the judge.

The prosecutor stood up and once again ran through his innovative interpretation of the definition of mass murder. The crime required the intention of killing, without any specific indication of who might be the victim of that intention. Costantino, when he opened the gas, intended to kill himself and implicitly accepted the risk of killing other people. This was sufficient basis for trying and convicting him. For mass murder.

Then it was my turn.

"Please indulge me, Your Honor, if I go on a little longer than is usually allowed in a preliminary hearing for the ritual, and often pointless, request for an acquittal. Because this is certainly one of those cases with potential for acquittal, even at this early juncture, without wading through the lengthy process of a full criminal trial. To tell the truth, the idea of hauling a defendant before a criminal court for a gas leak, albeit an intentional one, is paradoxical, if not verging on the outright grotesque."

The judge picked up a pen and wrote something. I made a mental note, thinking that it might be a good sign, though judges are unpredictable creatures. I continued.

"There is no question that this trial should be resolved on the point of law, the interpretation of criminal law, given that the facts are unquestioned. Indeed, an unhappy young man struggling with depression attempts suicide. The Carabinieri heroically intervene, rescue the young man, and avert a potential tragedy. The question that this trial must answer is the following: Did the behavior of this young man involve all the elements of the crime of mass murder? A crime, let us remember, that is punishable by imprisonment for a term of no fewer than fifteen years."

I spoke for about ten minutes in all. I did my best to convey a fairly straightforward concept: The crime of mass murder can be said to have taken place—even if no one dies—only in a case in which the defendant acted with the intent of killing an unspecified number of people, because it is a crime against public safety. To put it simply, if someone tries to kill himself, he's not trying to commit mass murder. And so if no one dies, quite simply, no crime has been committed.

I found that I was having a hard time explaining something so self-evident. Perhaps it was too self-evident to be argued effectively. When I was done, I was dissatisfied with my efforts, and I was convinced that the judge was about to order my client to stand trial.

Instead, the judge rapidly wrote something down, stood up, and read aloud: There were no grounds for subjecting Nicola Costantino to a criminal trial because the acts of which he was accused did not constitute a crime. The defendant should therefore be released immediately, unless he was in custody for any other cause.

That was the sudden and abrupt end of the hearing, and the judge had already vanished into chambers when I walked over to the young man to inform him that he had been acquitted and that, in a few hours—the time required to process his release from prison—he would be a free man.

"Congratulations. I was sure that they'd order him to stand trial, to avoid the responsibility of making the decision themselves and save themselves the trouble of having to write the opinion," said Consuelo as we left the court-room.

"Yeah, I didn't have high hopes for an acquittal either."

"And now?"

"What do you mean, and now?"

"Will his parents be happier that Nicola has been acquitted, or more concerned about what might happen now that he's coming home?"

That was exactly what I was wondering just then. And of course, I had no answer to the question.

13.

I had said good-bye to Consuelo and was just stepping into a wine bar to get a bite to eat when Fornelli called. He said that he had spoken with Manuela's mother, and that she in turn had called the two girlfriends and the ex-boyfriend. Through other friends of her daughter, she had also contacted Anita Salvemini, the young woman who had given Manuela a ride to the Ostuni train station. She'd explained to all of them that we were making an effort to find out what had happened to her daughter, and she asked them if they'd agree to talk to me. They'd all said yes, except for Abbrescia.

"Why not Abbrescia?"

I heard a brief hesitation at the other end of the line.

"She told Manuela's mother that she was in Rome. She said for the next few weeks she's very busy with classes and exams and she's not sure when she'll be back in Bari."

There was another hesitation, and then Fornelli went on.

"To tell you the truth, Signora Ferraro thought the girl seemed uncomfortable. That she wasn't particularly happy about the phone call, and even less interested in the idea of talking to you. Talking to a lawyer, in other words."

"Can you get her phone number?"

"Sure. Anyway, all the others said they would be willing to come talk to you in your office. Even today, if you have time."

I told him to hold on for a second, took a quick look at the appointment book I carried in my briefcase, and saw that I had only a couple of meetings scheduled in the early part of the afternoon.

"Okay. There are three of them, so let's ask them to come in one after the other, an hour apart. Let's say at six, seven, and eight o'clock. That way I'll have all the time I need to talk with each of them. Could you call them and schedule the meetings?"

"Of course, I'll take care of it. Unless you hear back from me within an hour or so, assume it's all confirmed."

The first one to show up, a few minutes past six, was Anita Salvemini.

She was a short, stocky young woman, dressed in cargo pants and a brown leather jacket. She had a face that was chubby but determined; when we shook hands, she had the grip of a man. All told, she struck me as trustworthy.

"Let me start by thanking you for agreeing to come in. I believe that Signora Ferraro already explained why I wanted to talk with you."

"Yes, she told me that you're doing some kind of investigation into Manuela's disappearance."

Before I could catch myself, a sensation of intensely pure and completely idiotic vanity swept through me. If I was doing "some kind of investigation," then you might say I was some kind of investigator.

Or perhaps—I thought, as I regained control—it might be more accurate to say I was some kind of asshole.

"Let's just say that we're going over the documents from the investigation that the Carabinieri did to see whether, perhaps, they might have missed some minor detail that might suggest a new theory about what happened to Manuela."

"You're a lawyer, though, right?"

"Yes, I'm a lawyer."

"I didn't think that lawyers did . . . well, that lawyers did that kind of thing. Like a private investigator, right?"

"Yes and no. It depends on the circumstances. What are you studying, Anita?"

"I'm about to graduate with a degree in communications."

"Ah. Are you planning to be a journalist?"

"No, I'd like to open a bookstore, though it's a tough business. I think I'll get a master's degree, and then I'll work in a bookstore chain for a few years. Maybe somewhere outside of Italy. Someplace like Barnes & Noble, or Borders."

There's no faster way to win me over than to say you want to be a bookseller. When I was a boy, I sometimes thought I'd like to run a bookstore. It was mainly because I had a romantic and completely unrealistic idea of what that job entailed; in my vision, it would consist mostly of spending my days reading any book I wanted for free. Oh, from time to time, I'd have to stop reading to wait on someone, but customers wouldn't hang around, probably because they wouldn't want to interrupt me. I figured that if I were a bookseller, or perhaps a librarian, I would have lots of time to write my novels, especially on long spring afternoons, when the sun's rays would slant in low through the shop windows—something along the line of City Lights Books—landing on the tables, the bookshelves, and, of course, the books.

"Good idea. When I was a kid, I thought it would be nice to run a bookstore. To get back to your question: You're right, as a rule investigations are done for the defense by private detectives, but in this specific case, Manuela's family wanted a lawyer to do it—someone with expertise in the judicial process."

I spoke as if this were something I did all the time. She nodded her head, and her expression suggested she was happy with the answer I'd given her. To be exact: happy that she'd asked the question and happy with the way I'd answered her, treating her respectfully. I thought this was a good starting point, and decided to ask her to tell me her story.

"All right, let me start by asking you to tell me what you remember about that Sunday afternoon."

"I told the Carabinieri everything I remember."

"No, sorry. Don't think about what you told the Carabinieri. In fact, I'd like you to try to forget everything you said in the Carabinieri station, when and how the interview was conducted—everything. As far as you are able, I'd like you to tell me what happened as if it were the first time, thinking visually if you can. Which is to say: tell me about going to the *trulli*, why you went, who you knew there. Whatever pops into your head. Just let go of the story you told the Carabinieri."

I wasn't doing some cop act. I'd studied these techniques while preparing to do crucial questioning in the courtroom during a trial.

Once we've told a story about something that happened—especially if we have told that story in a formal context, before a judge or to a detective, with a written, signed statement—and we are asked to tell it again, we tend to reiterate the first narrative rather than evoking direct memories of the actual experience. This mechanism only becomes more firmly cemented with each successive repetition and, in the end, what happens is that we no longer remember the actual events, but instead our account of the events. Naturally, this mechanism makes it increasingly difficult to recover details that we overlooked the first time. Details that may seem insignificant, but can prove to be crucial. In order to succeed in recovering these details, it is necessary to release the person being questioned from the memory of the earlier account, to bring the person back to the actual memory of the events experienced. But of course that doesn't always work.

I didn't go into this whole explanation with Anita, but she seemed to understand that there was a certain logic behind my request. So she sat in silence for a few moments, as if she were concentrating before doing what I'd asked. Then she began.

"I didn't know Manuela, that is, I only met her that weekend at the *trulli*."

"Had you been to the *trulli* before?"

"Yeah, lots of times. It's an odd place. All sorts of people wind up there. Maybe you've been there, at some point."

I told her that I'd never been, and she explained to me that it was a large compound of *trulli* that a group of friends rents and where lots of people come out to spend time, all summer long. There was enough room, if everyone squeezed in, for maybe thirty people to sleep there. There were parties and all kinds of happenings every night. It was a sort of commune for well-to-do young people, generally left-wing young people, on the radical-chic side of things.

"That Sunday afternoon, I had to go to Ostuni to meet a girlfriend and Manuela asked if I'd give her a ride. She had to get back to Bari and the people she'd come with wanted to stay at the *trulli* that night."

"Do you remember who came with Manuela?"

"I remember their faces. I don't know their names."

The names of the young people were in the file. Their statements had been so insignificant that I hadn't even bothered to include them in the list of people to interview.

"Before you tell me about the car ride that Sunday afternoon, I'd like you to talk to me about life at the *trulli*."

"What do you mean?"

"What was going on, exactly? People coming, people leaving, if you noticed any unusual people, for instance, who might have been talking to Manuela. I don't know, someone drinking, maybe someone smoking a joint."

I felt a little awkward as I pronounced that last phrase. I said "smoking a joint" because it struck me that using legal terminology such as, "Did you observe the consumption of narcotics?" would just interfere with our ability to communicate. Instead, I realized that I'd spoken as if I were a grownup clumsily trying to talk hip like the kids, and it made me deeply uncomfortable. In any case, I thought I saw a momentary evasiveness come into Anita's gaze, a sudden loss of eye contact, as if the question about whether joints were being smoked upset her a little. But it was a passing moment, and I told myself that maybe there was nothing to it.

At the *trulli*, life began late in the morning, though a small group woke up very early, did tai chi, and then went to the beach when there was still virtually no one else there. Around one o'clock, at lunch, some drank espresso and cappuccinos while others sipped their first aperitifs—a Spritz or a Negroni, generally speaking, she told me, as if the information were crucial. Big, informal meals of pasta, drinking, music, people coming and going. Down to the beach in the afternoon, where they'd stay until sunset, happy hour on the beach, with music and more Negronis and Spritzes, then back to the *trulli* or to a restaurant for dinner in one of the surrounding towns: Cisternino, Martina Franca, Alberobello, Locorotondo, Ceglie, or, of course, Ostuni.

These were rituals I knew all too well, because I had taken part in them myself until just a few years ago. And yet, listening as this young woman—twenty years younger than I—described them, they seemed a world away. It wasn't a pleasant sensation.

"You said that you were a fairly frequent guest at those *trulli*."

"Yes."

"Did you notice anyone in particular, that weekend? Or was it different in some way from what usually happened?"

"No, I don't think so. There were some English kids, but nothing happened that seemed out of the ordinary."

"Naturally, at a certain point, a few people smoked pot, right?"

As I expected (and for that matter, as had just happened), the mention of marijuana made her uneasy.

"I'm not sure . . . I mean, maybe, but . . ."

"Listen, Anita. Let me explain something to you, before we go any further. Something important. I'm not with the police, and I'm not with the district attorney."

I paused to make sure she understood what I was saying.

"That means that it's not my job to investigate crimes and prosecute the people who commit them. I don't care in the slightest if people at the *trulli* smoked themselves silly, got drunk, or ingested substances of some kind. Or, rather, I care only if that information can help me find out something about Manuela's disappearance. You have nothing to worry about. This conversation is, and will remain, completely confidential. For that matter, there's probably no connection between someone smoking a little grass and Manuela's disappearance. But I'm feeling my way in the dark here, and the slightest scrap of information could be helpful, in theory. The only way I can know that is if I'm able to evaluate the information for myself. Is that clear?"

Anita didn't say anything right away. She scratched an eyebrow, then smoothed it with her middle finger. She heaved a sigh.

"There were some drugs out there."

"What kind of drugs?" I asked cautiously, afraid that at this point in the conversation any questions I asked might cause her to stop talking, instead of encouraging her to say more.

"I only saw joints. But I think there were other drugs."

"Cocaine?"

"You promised me this conversation would be confidential."

"Absolutely confidential. You don't have a thing to worry about. No one will ever know you told me any of this."

"Cocaine, yes. And some acid. But like I said, I never saw it, I never touched it."

I felt a triumphant thrill of excitement—as if the objective of my investigation had been to discover whether in the *trulli* of the village of Saint Such-and-Such there were a bunch of bored kids who were ingesting various grades of psychotropic substances, and therefore my mission was accomplished.

"Do you know whether Manuela ever used drugs?"

"No, absolutely not."

"No, you mean that she didn't use narcotics, or no, you don't know whether she did?"

"No, I don't know. We met for the first time Saturday night, even though we'd probably crossed paths earlier, at the beach at Torre Canne, but at the *trulli*, too, or in Bari. I'd seen her face before, but we met, we spoke for the first time that Saturday night."

"How did Manuela happen to ask you for a ride?"

"The evening . . . well really, the night before, when the party was already over and those who weren't sleeping at the *trulli* had already left, there were five or six of us left talking, one or two were smoking cigarettes. It was our last conversation before going to sleep. It was past three, a good bit past three. At some point, Manuela asked if anyone was going back to Bari the next afternoon, because she needed a ride."

"And nobody was going back to Bari?"

"No one who was still awake. I said I needed to go to Ostuni on Sunday afternoon. If she wanted, I'd be glad to give her a ride to the station, and from there she could catch a train to Bari."

"And Manuela accepted immediately."

"She said that if she hadn't found a ride all the way back to Bari by then, she'd come with me."

"And evidently she couldn't find a ride?"

"We ran into each other the next morning, around noon. There were definitely people going back to Bari that night, but late. She wanted to get back early, in the afternoon, so she told me she'd come with me to Ostuni and then she'd catch a train."

"Did she say she *had* to get back in the afternoon? Did she have something to do, something that meant she had to get back before evening?"

"She didn't say that."

"But you had the impression that was it."

"Yes, it did seem as if there was some specific reason she needed to get back before evening."

"But she didn't tell you what the reason was?"

"No. We agreed to meet around four o'clock and then she headed off. I don't know what she did between then and when we met up for the drive."

I nodded, doing my best to think if I had any other possible questions, before continuing on to her account of the drive from the *trulli* to Ostuni. I couldn't think of anything.

"All right. Shall we talk about what happened after that, in the afternoon?"

"Sure, though there really isn't much to say. She had a bag and she was wearing jeans and a t-shirt. We got in the car, we talked about this and that."

"What did you talk about?"

"First of all, we didn't talk much, because for most of the drive, she was fooling around with her cell phone. . . ."

"You said, 'fooling around.' Did she talk to someone or receive texts or what?"

"I already told the Carabinieri that I don't think she talked to anyone. Probably she was texting. At a certain point, the phone made a sound, and I thought it might be a message."

"Why did you think it might have been a message?"

"Because I believe it only made a single sound. That is, I don't think the cell phone went on ringing. Like an alert. It may have been a strange sound, but I can't explain exactly what I mean by that. I just remember something . . . unusual, that's all."

I was about to ask more, and then I realized that pressing her on this point was ridiculous. I had Manuela's phone records, so there was no point trying to push Salvemini to recover her shreds of memory. Completely unnecessary. Manuela's communications, that afternoon, would be listed in detail on her phone records.

"Okay. You said that you didn't talk much. But what did you talk about?"

"Nothing important. 'What are you studying? What did you do this summer?' That kind of thing, but certainly nothing important."

"How long did it take you to get to the station in Ostuni?"

"About twenty minutes. That time on a Sunday afternoon, everyone's still at the beach, so there's no traffic."

"Did Manuela make any particular impression on you?"

Anita didn't answer right away. She made the same motion she had before—by now, it struck me as a nervous tic of some kind—scratching her eyebrow and then smoothing it with her middle finger.

"Any particular impression? I couldn't say. Maybe she seemed, how to put it, kind of high-strung."

"You mean that she seemed irritable in the car?"

"No, it wasn't that. The night before, and the next morning, when we agreed to drive to Ostuni together, and in the car, too, she seemed to me . . . I don't know how to put this. She was just a little high-strung, I can't think of another word for it."

"Well, did she seem worried about something?"

"No, no. Not worried. It's just that she didn't strike me as an easygoing person."

"Could you describe any specific gesture that she made that might have given you that impression?"

Another pause to think.

"No. I couldn't indicate any specific gesture. But she was a little, how to put this . . . a little speedy, that's it."

I took a few seconds to make a mental note of this.

"How did you say good-bye?"

"What do you mean?"

"I mean, did you say, let's get together, let's have dinner sometime? I don't know, did you exchange phone numbers?"

"No, we just said good-bye, the way you do. Thanks, bye, and so on. We didn't exchange phone numbers."

"When did you find out that Manuela had disappeared?"

"A few days later, when the Carabinieri called me in for an interview."

I really couldn't think of anything else to ask. The fact that the drug use at the *trulli* had come out had given me a false sense of triumph, in part because no one had told the Carabinieri about it. In reality, though, aside from that detail—which really wasn't of any importance as far as I was concerned—nothing new had emerged. And of course that was frustrating. I had the feeling that I was trying to climb up a smooth glass wall.

I made one last attempt.

"While you were in the car together, did either of you mention the fact that stuff was circulating at the *trulli*, drugs, that is, as you mentioned before?"

"No, absolutely not."

"And you don't know whether Manuela used drugs."

"I told you, I don't know."

There really wasn't anything else to say. The time had come to say good-bye, and that's when I remembered the suggestion that Navarra had given me. I pulled one of my business cards out of my desk drawer, wrote my cell phone number on it, and handed it to her.

"It's possible, in fact it's very likely, that something else will come to mind—a detail, some minor thing that you've overlooked. That's the most normal thing in the world. If, and when, this happens, please call me. Call me here at my office, or on my cell phone. Call me even if you remember a detail that strikes you as irrelevant. Sometimes details that seem unimportant turn out to be key."

We stood up, but she continued looking at me, across the desk, as if she wanted to say something else, but couldn't think of the words, or was uncomfortable.

"Don't worry about the things you told me. Our conversation was completely confidential. It's as if you never said a thing."

Her expression relaxed. She half-smiled and told me that if anything else occurred to her, any detail at all, she'd certainly call me.

I shook her hand, I thanked her, and I walked her to the door.

14.

My next meeting was with Pontrandolfi. If she was punctual, she'd arrive in the next five minutes or so. I thought that I'd use my conversation with her to try to understand what kind of person Manuela was. Of course, that would be useful only if Manuela's disappearance had something to do with her past. Otherwise, if her disappearance was just a random event, there would be practically no chance whatsoever that I would be able to find out anything new.

While I was thinking this, the phone rang. Someone else picked up, and a few seconds later the phone blinked red, indicating an internal call. It was Pasquale.

"It's Counselor Schirani. He wants to speak to you."

Schirani is a dangerous cretin, and the fact that he wanted to speak to me was not particularly good news.

Somebody once said that all people are either intelligent or stupid, and either lazy or enterprising. There are lazy idiots, usually irrelevant and innocuous; then there are the intelligent and ambitious, who can be given important tasks to perform. The greatest achievements, in all fields, are nearly always the work of those intelligent and lazy. But one thing should be kept in mind: the most dangerous category, the people who are unfailingly responsible for the most appalling disasters, the ones you have to avoid at all costs, are enterprising idiots.

Schirani belonged to the last of the four categories. In fact, if there were an official parade for that group he would be up front, waving the flag. He was the ideal representative, the paragon of the category. He wore shirts with big collars and ties with overgrown knots. He understood nothing—and when I say nothing, I mean nothing—about the law, and he was convinced that he was a distinguished jurist, one who shouldn't be expected to waste his time with common lawyers. The few times we'd been on the same defense team—different defendants in a single trial—had been a nightmare. He gratuitously offended prosecutors and unfailingly annoyed judges. He was high-handed and abrasive with the witnesses.

In case I haven't been clear enough, I'll just say flat out that I couldn't stand him, and the last thing I wanted, right then and there, was to hear his voice.

"Pasquale, could you please tell him I'm in a meeting and I'll call him back as soon as I can?"

"That's what I told him. He insists that it's urgent, says he's calling on behalf of Michele Cantalupi."

"Fine, put him through," I said after mouthing a silent *fuck*.

"Guido?"

"Riccardo."

"Guido, what is the meaning of all this?"

"All what?"

"You order my client to come in for an interview in your office, without informing me, without so much as a word to me."

I took another deep breath, trying to repress the impulse to tell him to go fuck himself and slam the phone down.

"I presume you're referring to Michele Cantalupi."

"You presume correctly. Why have you ordered him to come to your office?"

I had to admit that I'd been surprised to hear that Cantalupi was willing to come and talk to me. Evidently, after saying he'd come in, it occurred to him that that might be a big mistake, and he decided to consult his lawyer. That is, none other than the asshole braying at me over the phone line right now.

"Well, to begin with, I didn't order him to come to my office. The mother of Manuela Ferraro, his former girl-friend—who, as you are no doubt aware, has been missing for months—asked him if he would be willing to come in and have a conversation with me. And, to make another thing perfectly clear, I only learned that Cantalupi is your client just now, from you."

"What are you up to?"

Oh, nothing. I was thinking about replacing the old punching bag I have in the living room of my apartment. I was wondering if you might be interested in the position? It's not bad, you just hang there all day doing nothing, then at night I get home, and I punch you, hard, for about an hour. That would be the fun part, making you swell up like a balloon.

"The girl's family has asked me to examine the file to make sure that the Carabinieri haven't overlooked any crucial details. I'm meeting with people who know Manuela well to see if there's any overlooked information or if I come up with any ideas that might help us understand what happened."

"So that you can try to screw my client?"

Third deep breath. Longer than the first two.

"Listen to me. No one is trying to screw your client. And how would I screw him, if I did want to? I'm only trying to reach out and talk to the people who were closest to Manuela, because her parents asked me to. These last interviews are their only remaining hope. Your client has nothing to fear."

"My client won't talk to you. I forbid him to."

"Listen. We need—"

"If you ever contact Cantalupi again, in two minutes this law office will file a complaint with the ethics committee of the bar association. I hope that I've made myself clear."

And he hung up, without giving me time to answer. There are few things in life more annoying than having an asshole hang up on you after he's managed to threaten you, without giving you a chance to return the courtesy or at least say something offensive. For a second or two I was tempted to call him back, just so I could tell him to go fuck himself and make myself feel better. I was still thinking about it when Pasquale called to say that Signorina Pontrandolfi was here and ask if he should send her in.

I told him to send her in, and thought to myself that she'd shown up just in time to keep me from doing something stupid that I'd have regretted.

15.

I had expected Pontrandolfi to be short, skinny, and small-framed. Maybe because, before that evening, I'd always associated the name Caterina with a fragile and delicate model of femininity.

The young woman who walked into my office a few minutes after seven that evening swept away once and for all that personal stereotype of mine, probably based on the world of Italian pop music.

Caterina Pontrandolfi was almost my height. She had a slightly broad nose, big lips, and resembled certain photographs of a young Marianne Faithfull. She looked like she might play water polo—one of those young women you wouldn't want to have take a swing at you. The flimsy and very feminine outfit—perhaps a little too flimsy, considering the season—that she wore under a denim jacket clashed pleasantly with her powerful swimmer's physique.

"Please come in, Signorina Pontrandolfi." While I was uttering that word—Signorina—I felt like an idiot.

"The word *signorina* reminds me of a couple of old maids who used to keep company with my grandmother. At my house, they were called *le signorine*, so to me a *signorina* is an old spinster. Do me a favor, if you don't mind; would you please use the informal? Otherwise you'll just make me feel awkward."

I doubted it would really be all that easy to make her feel awkward. I was about to say fine, I'll use the informal *tu*, but she should address me with the same informality, and so on and so forth, following the usual script people use in these situations. Then it dawned on me that—according to the name, address, and date of birth in the Carabinieri report— she was twenty-three years old. I was forty-five. I was a lawyer exercising my professional duties, and—technically speaking—I could have been her father.

I realized that I was stuck. I didn't know what to say. To tell her that I preferred to use the formal would be obnoxious and ridiculous. To tell her, okay, let's use the informal (and maybe we can go to the university café together and get a couple of Smurf-berry blue ice cream cones) would be inappropriate. So I made the best of a bad situation: I addressed her with the informal *tu* and let her continue to address me with the formal *lei*.

"All right, then. Thanks for agreeing to come in. I believe that Manuela's mother . . . explained the reason for this meeting to you."

"Yes. She told me you're trying to determine whether the investigation into Manuela's disappearance was conducted properly, and whether it's possible to do any further investigating."

"Yes, that's right. From what I was able to gather from reading the documents, you're one of Manuela's best friends."

"Yes, Manuela and I are very close."

"Tell me about her. Tell me what kind of person she is, how long you've known each other, what your friendship is like, and anything else that comes to mind. Even insignificant things, because I need to form a mental picture. I need ideas and unfortunately, right now, I'm short on ideas."

"Okay. Manuela and I met in Rome. Nicoletta introduced us. For a couple of years, more or less, they had been sharing an apartment in Rome. That is, Manuela went to live with Nicoletta, and moved out of the apartment where she'd been living before. I think she had some kind of trouble with her previous roommate."

"Nicoletta would be Nicoletta Abbrescia?"

"That's right. We went to high school together. She's a little younger than I am."

"Do you still live in Rome?"

"No. This is the first year I've fallen behind the normal academic schedule. In the spring, I had to move out of my apartment in Rome because the lease expired. I was supposed to go find another apartment in the fall, but then this thing happened with Manuela and . . . I don't know, I just didn't feel up to house hunting. So now I'm studying in Bari and then I'll go to Rome to take my exams."

I had the impression that there was a slight acceleration in the pace of her speech as she answered, as if the question made her nervous. She quickly broke into the syncopated flow of my thoughts.

"You're a criminal lawyer, aren't you?"

"Yes."

"I'm taking my degree in law and writing my thesis on criminal procedure, on special evidentiary hearings. I'd like to become a magistrate—maybe a prosecutor—or a criminal lawyer. Maybe after I get my degree you could take me on in your office as an intern."

"Why not?" I answered hesitantly, unsure how to respond.

"I'm cute. It would help your reputation if you showed up in court with me. Your colleagues would be jealous," she added.

"Well, there's no question about that."

"Okay, sorry. Sometimes I act like an idiot. I'm a little ditzy sometimes, and I forget about more serious matters. And we're here for a serious matter. What were you asking me?"

"What's Manuela like? I've seen photographs of her, but I still can't form a mental picture."

"Manuela is very attractive. She's not tall, she's a brunette—you can see that in the photos—she gets a dark tan in the summer. She's well put together. Nicoletta is a pretty girl, too, but she has a lot less personality. She's tall and thin. She worked as a model. When we get all dressed up and show up at a party or in a club, people—not just boys—turn and stare. We make a splash. They call us *Sex and the City*."

She met my eyes with a level gaze to see if I was duly impressed by this information. I did my best to ignore her.

"What's Manuela like, in terms of personality?"

"She's a determined young woman. If she wants something, she takes it. We're very similar in that way, Manuela and I."

As she said that, she looked me straight in the eye a few seconds longer than necessary.

I remembered what Anita had told me, about Manuela striking her as high-strung.

"Would you say that she's a relaxed person, or high-strung?"

"Relaxed. She keeps her cool in a tense situation. Definitely relaxed."

In that case, if Anita was correct when she sensed that Manuela was high-strung, there'd been something wrong that afternoon, even before she disappeared. It was a detail that might possibly be significant. Or else, they might just be two different people with two different points of view. In any case, I would need to come up with something more concrete.

"Obviously, you're aware that this is a confidential conversation?"

For the first time since she had walked into my office, she seemed to hesitate for an instant.

"Yes . . . that is . . . ."

"What I mean is that anything you tell me goes no further than this room. All I'm looking for is a shred of evidence, a flicker of light, something that helps me to understand."

"Okay . . . fine."

"I want you to tell me very honestly if you have any idea of what might have happened to Manuela."

"No. I have no idea. The Carabinieri asked me the same thing: Did I have any idea? But I really can't imagine what might have happened. I've racked my brains, like everyone else, but . . . ."

"Tell me what you've come up with. Your wildest guesses. You must have thought of something. Then maybe you discounted it, but you must have thought of something."

She looked at me. She'd become very serious. Up until then there had been something vaguely provocative flittering over and through her expression, as if, in some sense, she were playing a game. Now that subtle something was gone. She took a deep breath before she answered.

"I thought Manuela's disappearance might have something to do with Michele, her ex."

No question, that asshole was the perfect suspect, I thought to myself. It was a shame (but lucky for him) that he happened to be out of the country that day.

"But he was out of the country."

"Exactly."

"Why did you think of Michele?"

"What does that matter? He was out of the country, so he definitely couldn't have had anything to do with it."

"I'd appreciate it all the same if you'd tell me why you thought of him."

Caterina shook her head, as if she was sure that it was a mistake to talk about this topic. She took another deep breath. It was more audible this time, and she exhaled loudly, heaving a sigh. I was surprised to catch myself noticing how her breasts rose and fell, her clothing swelling with her vigorous respiration. Dirty old man.

"I never liked Michele. So that fact might prejudice me. Still . . ."

"Still?"

"Still, he's a real asshole."

"In what way?"

"In every way imaginable. He's violent, and if you ask me, he's stupid, too. After they broke up and the magic was gone, Manuela used to say he was crass and vulgar. She was right."

"But then why was Manuela dating him? Why were they together for so long? And by the way, how long did they see each other?"

"I couldn't say, exactly. When I met Manuela, they were

already dating. Then they broke up, or really Manuela broke up with him, more than a year ago. But he couldn't get over it. He badgered her for months. Imagine that: the great Michele Cantalupi, dumped by a schoolgirl."

"You still haven't told me what Manuela saw in this jerk. What am I missing here?"

"What you're missing here is that he's hot, so hot it burns. I mean, he makes Brad Pitt look homely."

I sat without speaking for a few seconds. I struck a pensive pose, as if the information on how hot Cantalupi was deserved some thought. In the end, I nodded gravely, as if I'd absorbed a challenging concept. Then I looked at her. She was sitting, composed, but occupying her space. I noticed a fine beading of sweat on her upper lip.

"And what does this gentleman do for a living?"

"Nothing. Nothing useful, anyway. He fucks anything that comes within range. He plays cards. He's working on *not* getting a degree in business, and, well, that's about it."

She'd stopped herself before saying something else. I noticed very clearly—she'd held back from saying more. There was something she'd decided not to tell me, something she didn't want to talk about. Or maybe she did want to, but, at the same time, she didn't. I needed to circle back around, but not right away.

"You said he's violent. Is that why you suspected he might have had something to do with Manuela's disappearance? Or was there something more specific?"

"No. Nothing specific. When I heard something had happened to Manuela but no one knew what it was, he was the first and only person who came to mind."

"When she broke up with him, he kept after her for a while, right?"

"Yes. He phoned her, wrote her letters, asked her to give him another chance. He even stalked her. He came down to Rome twice. Once he caused a huge scene in the street. They got physical. He hit her, and she hit him back, and then we separated them . . . ."

"Who's 'we'?"

"Me and two friends."

"How long did he keep after her?"

"For months. I can't remember exactly how many."

"I read the transcript of the statement that he made to the Carabinieri. He admitted that the end of their relationship had been pretty stormy, but he also said that things had gotten back on an even keel, and that after it was all over they were on friendly terms."

"I wouldn't say friendly. But it's true that he stopped calling her and coming around. Manuela said he'd probably just found another victim."

"Was that true?"

"I don't know. For that matter, I don't think Manuela knew either, and anyway she didn't give a damn."

"Earlier, when I asked you what Michele did for a living, you were about to say something else, and then you stopped yourself."

"When?"

"You were about to say something else, and you decided not to. Caterina, everything we say here is completely confidential, but I absolutely need to know everything. It may not have anything to do with Manuela's disappearance. In fact, it almost certainly has nothing do with it, but I need to know."

Now she seemed uncomfortable, as if the situation had gotten out of control and she was afraid of making a false move. She was wondering how to withdraw. I remembered what had come up in my conversation with Anita, about the drugs that were circulating at the *trulli*. I figured it was worth a shot; the worst thing that could happen was that she might tell me I was wrong.

"Caterina," I said, "is it something to do with drugs?"

She looked at me in astonishment.

"Then you already knew?"

Obviously, I didn't know. I felt the thrill of winning when you're bluffing in a poker game. I shrugged and acted indifferent. I said nothing; it was her turn.

"If you already know about it, then there's not much left to say. He loved cocaine, he always had plenty, and so . . ."

"Did he sell it, too?"

"No! That is, I don't know. I couldn't say for sure."

And then, hesitantly, after another pause. "But he always seemed to have plenty of it."

"Did the issue of drugs have something to do with why Manuela broke up with him?"

She shook her head forcefully, and I thought I glimpsed for just a fraction of a second a flash of despair, or something like it, in the way she did it. I told myself I needed to restrain my impulse to read too much into things.

"I assume there's no smoking in here, right?"

"I wouldn't have guessed you were a smoker. You look like an athlete."

"I only smoke a couple a day, well, three or four. After dinner, after a glass of wine. When I'm relaxing. But sometimes I need a cigarette when I'm feeling really tense. Like right now."

"Well, I'm sorry if I've made you tense. Go ahead and have a cigarette. You're allowed."

"No, it's not you making me tense. You've been very nice, in fact. It's just the whole situation, the . . . well, you know what I mean, right?"

She took out a brightly colored cigarette case, pulled out a cigarette, and lit it with an athletic gesture. I extracted an ashtray from a drawer and handed it to her.

"I *was* an athlete, in my day."

"In your day? What do you mean by that?"

"I was a good swimmer. I won a bunch of regional championships. I even won some national meets. That life is stressful, though. Training sessions twice a day, add that to full-time studying and you have no life. After a few years, I quit. And I never really looked back."

"I quit competitive sports, too, and I was about your age at the time."

Of course, there was absolutely no good reason for me to tell her that, other than my pathetic vanity.

"Which sport?" she asked, blowing a column of smoke out of the side of her mouth.

"Boxing."

"Boxing? You mean, like fighting, in the ring?"

"I fought for a few years. Amateur standing, of course. I won a regional title and silver at the national college championships."

What an idiot, I said to myself. You're flirting with a schoolgirl, as if you were her age. Cut it out, you moron.

"Cool. I like men who are men. I usually intimidate men, so I really like men who aren't easily intimidated. How old are you, Counselor?"

My wits blunted by my idiotic vanity, it took me a few

seconds to realize that she had successfully changed the subject away from my question, gaining precious minutes, and giving herself time to regroup.

"Let's forget about how old I am. We were talking about Cantalupi and how he was involved in narcotics. I was asking you whether, in your opinion, drugs had anything to do with Manuela and Michele's breakup."

"I don't know. I couldn't rule it out. I don't think it was any one thing. It was all of it. Manuela had figured out who that guy really was, and she didn't want to be with him anymore."

"Manuela . . . as far as you know, did she do coke with Michele? Or at least, had it happened at some time or other?"

She exhaled loudly. She shook her head. My impression was that she was telling herself that she'd made a mistake when she decided to come here, thinking that she'd be able to control the situation easily.

"What does that matter? What does Manuela's disappearance have to do with what she might have done with that asshole the year before?"

In all likelihood, she was right. Most likely it had nothing to do with anything, but I couldn't say that for certain without looking into it. Also, and especially, because *that asshole* was acting defensive, had refused to meet with me and, one way or another, had something to hide. I decided I needed to win Caterina's cooperation, bring her over to my side.

"Listen, Caterina. I have to assume that we're all just stumbling around in the dark in this thing. We have to try to figure out, feeling our way, what's there in the dark. No one can say, in advance, whether something is significant or not. That's why I need you to answer the question I just asked you."

I let a few seconds go by. She looked at me, scowling, and said nothing.

"I need to know, because Michele is refusing to meet with me. Which doesn't necessarily mean that he has anything to do with Manuela's disappearance, but I need to make an effort to look into this, at the very least."

"Michele refused to come in?"

"That's right. Manuela's mother called him, just as she called you. At first, he said he'd come in. In fact, he was supposed to come in right after you. Then, a short while ago, a lawyer called me, told me that Michele was his client, that he wouldn't be coming in to talk to me, and that if I tried to contact Michele again he would lodge a complaint with the ethics committee of the bar association. Does that surprise you?"

"Yes. Well, no, actually it doesn't."

"He probably has something to hide. That's the something that I have to find out, even if it's just to rule out that it has anything to do with Manuela's disappearance. Which is why I need all the information I can get."

"And what I'm about to tell you will stay between us?"

"Of course. Everything you tell me is covered by professional privilege." In reality, I was talking through my hat. Professional privilege is limited to information exchanged between a lawyer and a client. Caterina wasn't my client. Still, a reference to professional privilege is always impressive, and I thought it would reinforce my promise to keep what we said secret.

"Manuela did cocaine occasionally."

Before asking her anything else, I let her words hover in the air, then sink in and register between us.

"With Michele?"

"Yes. He let her try it the first time."

"Did she do it often, occasionally? A little, a lot? And did she keep on using it even after she stopped seeing him?"

"I don't know how often she used cocaine. And I don't know if she kept using it even after the two of them broke up."

I looked up at her, skeptically. My face must have communicated that I was having difficulty believing that answer. Skepticism that she wouldn't know something like that about a close friend.

"Okay, maybe she used occasionally, even after they broke up. But I didn't like it, so we didn't talk about it."

She thought for a few more seconds and then continued. "I was—I am—opposed to that stuff. I told her a couple of times, and she got mad, as if I were meddling in her business. Maybe she was right—everyone's free to do as they like. I don't like it either when someone tells me what I can or can't do. So I stopped telling her what I thought and she stopped talking about it, since she knew I didn't like it."

"Do you know if she'd been using it recently?"

"I don't know. I swear!"

She'd spoken with an exasperated tone, but she regained control almost immediately, and went on talking.

"Look, I'm helping you. And I'm not even sure how you got me onto this subject, which I had no intention of discussing. But the fact that I've been straight with you should convince you that I have no intention of hiding anything from you. You have to believe me."

"I believe you. But you might happen to overlook something, and that's why I'm pushing you."

"I don't know whether Manuela was taking drugs in the

months before she went missing. I don't know. If I did know I'd tell you. I've already told you a lot of things."

"Who could we ask?"

"I don't know. In the last few months I was in Bari and she was in Rome, and we didn't see as much of each other."

I wanted to ask her if she'd ever used cocaine with Manuela, but I couldn't bring myself to do it.

"What do you know about the place near Ostuni where Manuela spent the night between Saturday and Sunday?"

"Nothing in particular. I'd been there once, the year before, for a dinner party. It's a beautiful place, and there are always a bunch of nice people there, lots of activity. Manuela really liked it."

"Do you know the young woman Manuela stayed with?"

"Only to talk to."

I paused to process the information I had acquired. I wasn't taking notes. I figured the conversation would flow more naturally, and therefore be more useful, if I didn't have to stop to write. So I did my best to organize mentally the things that Caterina had told me. After she left, I'd quickly jot down some notes.

"Do you remember when you last saw Manuela?"

"Wednesday or Thursday. I can't remember exactly. I called her up, we met downtown, and we had a drink together before dinner."

"What did you talk about?"

"I don't remember. Nothing important."

"Was there any mention of Michele?"

"No."

"Did you notice anything unusual about her? I mean, I don't know, did she seem high-strung, upset, euphoric?"

"No. Manuela was perfectly normal. She might have said

something about having to go to Rome the following week. But I'm not even sure about that. It was a normal, ordinary conversation, like any other."

"Was Manuela seeing someone?"

"Do you mean, was she dating someone?"

"Yes."

"No. Earlier in the year, she'd gone out with a guy in Rome. But nothing serious. She definitely wasn't dating anyone in September."

"Do you know who the last guy she went out with in Rome was?"

"No. I remember a few months earlier she told me about this one guy who was calling her, and he'd taken her out to dinner, but she didn't especially like him. She agreed to go out with him just because she was bored."

"And you don't know this guy?"

"No, I've never met him. I don't even know his name."

"Maybe Nicoletta Abbrescia knows who he is."

"Yes, she might, if only because they lived in the same apartment."

"Nicoletta Abbrescia is in Rome, now, isn't she?"

"I think so. We haven't talked for a while."

"Why is that?"

"Since I left Rome, we've fallen out of touch. And she comes to Bari much less frequently than Manuela did. I'd say that since I moved back here, we might have seen each other three or four times."

"Since Manuela's disappearance, how often have you seen each other?"

"Never. We've talked on the phone, but we haven't seen each other."

"Why not?"

"I told you, we've fallen out of touch. And probably it was Manuela who kept us connected, in a way. Without Manuela, there was no reason to get together."

"But you talked on the phone."

"Sure, once or twice. She called me immediately when she heard Manuela had disappeared."

"When was that, exactly?"

"A couple of days afterward, I think. Manuela's parents had called her to ask if she'd seen Manuela, when they couldn't find her."

"And she didn't know anything."

"She didn't know anything."

"Did the two of you have any theories?"

She paused again, but only briefly. The subject had already been broached.

"Both of us thought of Michele, but then, of course, it turned out he wasn't in Italy at the time."

"What exactly did you say about it?"

"Nothing exactly. I don't know. 'Do you think Michele was involved?' And what he might have done. 'You don't think he could have kidnapped her, do you?'"

"So you talked about the possibility that he kidnapped her?"

"Not the possibility, really. We didn't know what to think, so we just said, 'You don't think he could have kidnapped her?' or something like that. But we were just talking."

"Who mentioned it first? You or Nicoletta?"

I realized that my voice was becoming insistent.

"It wasn't anything, really. It was just something we threw out there, just something to say, 'you don't think he could have kidnapped her?' We were just talking, since we didn't have any idea of what might have happened. I never really thought that he could actually have kidnapped her."

"But just a little while ago you said that when you first heard about Manuela's disappearance, the first thing you thought was that Michele might be involved."

She lit another cigarette, this time without asking permission.

"That's true. And it's true that we talked about kidnapping. But we just said it, I don't know. I can't actually imagine in practical terms how it would have happened. And anyway, it doesn't matter. It's impossible, because he wasn't even in Italy."

Now there was a note of exasperation in her voice, and I decided it was time to bring the session to a close. To keep from coming to a sudden end, and giving her the impression that I'd stopped because she'd lost her temper, I sat in silence for a few minutes, giving her time to finish her cigarette.

"All right, thanks very much. It's been very helpful to talk with you."

She looked at me and became visibly more relaxed. Now it appeared that she wanted to ask me a question.

"What are you going to do next?"

I gave her a look that was similar to the one she'd given me earlier. I wondered whether—and how—I should answer her question. I decided that maybe she could help me see into Manuela's world, that is, if it was true that the explanation of her disappearance was concealed there.

"That's a good question. I wonder the same thing. Of course, it would be interesting to be able to talk to Cantalupi, but that doesn't strike me as easy to arrange. I'd also like to talk to Nicoletta, in Rome if necessary. I just hope she'll be willing to talk to me."

"If you want, I can speak to Nicoletta about it."

I looked at her. Her offer surprised me.

"Well, if you did, it would be a help."

"I'm sorry I lost my temper, earlier. It happens to me in situations where I feel insecure. I don't like feeling insecure. Please forgive me."

"Don't worry about it. It was entirely understandable, and sometimes I can be a little pushy. I can see why you might get irritated."

"I'd like to help you. I'd like to do something to help find out what happened."

"If you could talk to Nicoletta and ask her to meet with me, that would be a big help. It really would."

"Fine. I'll call her and I'll let you know. Why don't you give me a cell phone number where I can reach you?"

I knew that she was asking for my cell phone number for a technical, practical reason. Still, for a brief moment, I experienced a dangerous thrill.

I pushed it out of my mind with some annoyance. I pulled out a business card, wrote my cell phone number on it with a pen, and handed it to her. The same thing I had done with Anita.

But it wasn't the same thing at all.

16.

Caterina left, and for the next hour I was caught up in meetings with Maria Teresa, Consuelo, and Pasquale, who came in one after another to present a variety of papers to sign or examine. Notifications of fees to be sent to the bar association, summonses and complaints served by courts all over the region of Puglia, the schedule for the following day, briefs for appeals drawn up by Consuelo and Maria Teresa, who were still learning the trade and, eager apprentices that they were, had successfully conveyed to me their intense anxiety.

Finally, I couldn't take it anymore. Pleading union rules, I told them it was long past normal quitting time. I insisted they go home, or go to see their sweethearts, or go wherever they felt like going. The important thing was that they go, and go immediately.

When I was alone at last, I tried to think through the events of that afternoon, from my meeting with Anita and the phone call from that asshole Schirani, up to my long conversation with Caterina.

Fifteen minutes of musing produced nothing, so I picked up a fat, brand-new legal pad and began jotting down on its blank pages everything that had emerged from my two meetings, as if I were writing a report for someone who hadn't been present. When I was done, I circled a few words in red ink and drew a double circle around the name Cantalupi every time it appeared in my notes, as if those red circles could make the answers emerge, or perhaps at least conjure some reasonable questions.

The only real working hypothesis—feeble though it was—involved Manuela's ex-boyfriend and the question of his use—and possible dealing—of narcotics.

I tried Googling Cantalupi's name, but I came up with nothing. Just to give it a shot, I Googled Manuela's name, too. There were a few hits, but none of the Manuela Ferraros were my Manuela Ferraro.

On my legal pad I wrote the following phrase: *investigate the world of drug dealing*, followed by a handsome question mark. I circled that note in red. I felt like an idiot. But then, immediately afterward, I did have an idea.

I rarely have clients from the world of organized crime, so I don't have much call to defend drug dealers. The few that I happen to take on as clients are generally lone operators, like the young man for whom I had gone to Rome a few days earlier to argue, unsuccessfully, the Court of Cassation appeal.

Among these clients, however, there was one—Damiano Quintavalle—who had continued to operate for years now because, even after he was caught, he always managed to emerge more or less unscathed. He was a smart young man, even likable, and most importantly for my purposes, he seemed to know a lot of people, in every walk of life, all over the city.

He was the only person I could reasonably contact to ask for help in discovering whether, and in what way, Michele

Cantalupi was involved with the world of drug dealing or with illegal activities of any sort. I decided I'd give him a call the next day and have a chat. I was feeling my way in the dark, I told myself, but it was better than doing nothing.

As I was deciding to call Quintavalle the following day, I found myself thinking about Caterina. I thought of her in a manner that was inappropriate, in view of the fact that—as I told myself over and over again with a certain masochistic emphasis—I could have been her father, or at least a young-ish uncle of hers.

Cut it out, Guerrieri. Get a grip: She's a schoolgirl. Ten years ago, she was thirteen years old, and you were already a grown—a fully grown—man. Fifteen years ago she was eight, and even then you were already a fully grown man. Twenty-two years ago she was just one year old and you'd just graduated from university. Twenty-four years ago you and your girlfriend Rossana spent nearly a month of horrible apprehension, thinking that you'd slipped up and were about to become twenty-year-old parents. That turned out to be a false alarm, but if it hadn't, you'd now have a son—or a daughter—Caterina's age.

At that point, I was caught in a maddening cycle. Since I couldn't go back in time twenty-four years, I decided the thing to do was to shift my point of view. I tried to remember how long it had been since I'd been with a girl that age.

The episode I managed to dredge up from my memory proved somewhat confusing. The last twenty-three-year-old with whom I'd had a fleeting and illicit sexual experience, over ten years earlier, was not exactly an inexperienced young girl. Quite the opposite. In fact, I realized as my recollections acquired greater—and increasingly unprintable—clarity, she showed a noteworthy willingness to push the envelope of conventional morality. In fact, she had been quite capable of providing me with instruction in a number of new forms of sexual experimentation.

I asked myself which category of twenty-three-year-olds Caterina was likely to belong to, and I imagined the answer. Now my thoughts were veering in a decidedly dangerous direction.

Time to get something to eat—I told myself—time to let those thoughts evaporate.

17.

It was cold out. The sky was filled with swollen, threatening clouds that looked as though they might burst into rain any minute. But I didn't feel like walking over to the garage, handing over my parking stub, asking them to bring up the car, and waiting for it to arrive, so I decided to run the risk of getting soaked and ride my bike.

When I walked into the Chelsea Hotel, piano music filled the air, along with the voice of Paolo Conte singing the opening of "Sotto le Stelle del Jazz."

The place was nearly empty, and there was a strange, agreeable sense of expectation in the air.

I sat down at a table not far from the entrance. Before long, Nadia emerged from the kitchen, spotted me, and came over to say hello.

"Tonight, Hans made a *tiella*—rice, mussels, and potatoes. Care to try it?"

Hans is Nadia's partner. He's a German cook and baker from Dresden. He looks like a former shot-putter who quit training and took up drinking beer instead. I don't know how he ended up in Bari, but I'd guess he's been here for a while, because he speaks fairly fluent dialect and he's learned the secrets of the local cuisine.

A *tiella* of rice, mussels, and potatoes is not too different from a *paella valenciana*, though any Barese will tell you it's much, much better. Here's how you make it: You take a cast-iron pan—or a *tiella*, as we call it—and layer it with rice, mussels, potatoes, zucchini, and chopped fresh tomatoes. Then you add the soaking water from the mussels, olive oil, black pepper, diced onions, and finely minced fresh parsley. Bake it in a hot oven for about fifty minutes. There's no guarantee it will be any good, though, unless your family goes back at least four generations in Bari.

"The last thing I'd want to do is offend Hans, if for no other reason than that I'd have to guess he weighs, what, at least two hundred seventy-five pounds, but I have my doubts about how good his *tiella* is."

"Yeah? Why don't you just try it and tell me what you think."

Nadia walked past my table as I was wolfing down the last forkfuls of my second dish of *tiella* and draining my second glass of Negroamaro. She gave me an ironic glance.

"So?"

I held out both hands, palms up, in a sign of surrender.

"So you were right. Only Old Marietta made a *tiella* this good."

"And who was Old Marietta?"

"Marietta was an old lady who kept house for us when I was a kid. She lived in the old town of Bari. Sometimes she'd bring us a sauce or homemade orecchiette. And her *tiella* was the stuff of legend. From now on, as far as I'm concerned, Hans is an honorary Old Marietta."

Nadia laughed, and in effect the idea of Hans-Marietta had its comic potential.

"Can I sit down with you? You're practically the only

customer tonight, and I doubt we're going to get anyone else in now that it's raining."

"Make yourself comfortable, of course. Is it raining? Great—I rode my bike here."

"If you're not in a hurry to get home, I'll drive you. I'd say that unless we get a rush of customers, we'll close at midnight. You can bring your bike inside and come back and get it when it's convenient."

"I'm in no hurry. And thanks, the idea of riding home in the pouring rain doesn't thrill me."

"Are you still hungry?"

"Hungry? I'm stuffed. If anything, I need a strong drink."

"Have you ever tried absinthe?"

"No. I haven't tried cocaine, peyote, or LSD either."

"Well, we don't serve peyote or any of that other stuff, but we do serve absinthe. Want to try some? It's legal."

I said sure, I'd like to try some, and she told Matilde—the bartender—to bring us absinthe for two. Matilde, who's no chatterbox, nodded almost imperceptibly, and a few minutes later she was standing at the table with a bottle of greenish liquid, a bowl of sugar cubes, and a carafe filled with water.

"What do we do with all this?" I asked.

"Are you familiar with pastis?"

"Yes."

"Same method. This is pure, very strong liquor, 136-proof. You dilute it with three to five parts water and, if you like, you add a sugar cube."

I followed her instructions, tasted it, and liked it.

Hell, I liked it a *lot*. I immediately poured myself another.

"Zola said that when you start pouring absinthe, you always wind up with drunken men and pregnant girls. Now I'm starting to see what he meant."

She nodded and gave me a mirthless smile.

"In any case, it's highly unlikely that the pregnant girl would be me."

She said it in a flat, neutral tone of voice, but it was instantly obvious that I had touched on a sore subject. I looked at her and said nothing. I carefully set the glass—which I'd just picked up to take another sip—down on the table.

"Two years ago, I was diagnosed with cancer, and they removed everything I'd need to become a pregnant girl. It's not like there was this long line of suitors asking to become the father of my son or daughter, but in any case, I'd say now the matter is settled once and for all."

Why on earth had I quoted Zola? No matter what, now that I thought about it, it had been an inappropriate thing to say, as well as embarrassingly vulgar. I really felt like a fool.

"I'm so sorry. Forgive me, it was a stupid thing to say."

"Relax. No need to apologize. If anything, I should apologize for bringing it up. There was no reason for me to dump all that on you, tell you about my personal problems, without fair warning."

I sat there with no idea what to say. She looked at her empty glass for a while. Then she decided that she felt like having another drink. She prepared a second glass of absinthe. Diluting it with three parts water, maybe less. She drank it slowly, methodically. When she'd finished her glass, she turned to me.

"Do you mind if we leave now? I feel like smoking a cigarette. Maybe we could go for a drive before heading home. Hans and Matilde can close up."

Five minutes later we were outside, in the rain.

Nadia had a compact minivan; I slipped into the front passenger seat quickly, without noticing the make or model. As Nadia was climbing in on her side, I thought I noticed something moving in the back of the car. I turned to look, and in the darkness I glimpsed a white gleam in the middle of an enormous dark mass. I looked closer, and realized that the white gleam was a pair of eyes, and that the eyes belonged to a black dog, the size of a young calf.

"Cute. What's his name, Nosferatu?"

She laughed.

"Pino, his name is Pino."

"Pino? As in Pino Noir the Killer Canine? Is that a name to give a beast of that size?"

She laughed again.

"I never would have thought it, but you're actually pretty nice. I always thought you were good at your job, reliable, even handsome, no question. But you never struck me as funny."

"No? Wait until you see me dance."

Third laugh. She put the car in gear and pulled out. I was looking straight ahead, but I knew that behind me, Pino Noir the Killer Canine was eyeing me, deciding whether to swallow me whole.

"What kind of dog is that?"

"The only officially recognized breed of Pugliese origin."

"And exactly what is this Pugliese breed? Demon hound of the Murgia highlands?"

"He's a Corso."

"Which means . . ."

" . . . which does not mean dog of Corsica. *Corso* comes from the Latin *cohors*, for courtyard or enclosure. The Corso dog is a descendant of the ancient Pugliese Molossian.

Pino's ancestors stood guard over the courtyards of the farms of Puglia, Basilicata, and Molise. Or else they fought bears and wild boars."

"I'm pretty sure that neither the bears nor the wild boars were thrilled at the prospect. So you like little lap dogs?"

"Ha ha. A friend of mine gave him to me. She trains and re-educates dogs."

"Re-educates dogs?"

"That's right. Pino was a fighting dog. The Carabinieri seized him, and many other dogs like him, when they broke up an illegal betting ring."

"Once I served as counsel in a trial for illegal dog fighting."

"You defended one of those bloodthirsty bastards that run dogfights?"

"No, I was representing the civil plaintiffs, an association for the prevention of cruelty to animals—they were assisting in the prosecution."

"Oh, that's a relief. I was thinking of letting Pino loose so you could argue your case with him directly."

"Are you sure that taking a fighting dog with you every-where you go is wise?"

"My friend Daniela re-educates these dogs. The courts assign custody to her—she runs a kennel—and she very patiently deprograms them. She turns them into compan-ion dogs."

"She *deprograms* them? That's what your friend does for a living?"

"She runs a kennel and a school for dogs: She trains them. Basic dog training—you know, sit, down, heel—or else trains dogs to work as guard dogs or for defense. And then she re-educates criminal dogs, which is what she calls them."

"*Criminal dog* strikes me as a very appropriate description of this canine piece of work."

"Pino is a very sweet, well-behaved dog. He wouldn't hurt a fly."

"Oh, I'm sure he's not especially interested in flies," I said, craning my neck to glance back at the big black monster, who continued to eye me as if I were a piece of raw steak.

We pulled up along the waterfront not far from my house. Nadia stopped on the roundabout near the Grand Hotel delle Nazioni and lowered her window. There was no wind, and it seemed as if the rain might be stopping. She lit a cigarette and smoked with such evident enjoyment that I regretted having quit. Then she started talking without looking at me.

"Maybe I put you in an uncomfortable situation tonight when I suggested leaving together. Maybe you're not all that eager to be seen around town with a former prostitute. And there is no such thing as former, in this world. Once a whore, always a whore."

"Say that again and I'll get out and walk."

She turned to look at me. She took a last drag on her cigarette and then tossed the butt out the window.

"So what I just said is bullshit?"

"I think it is."

She registered my answer. Then she pulled out another cigarette, but didn't light this one.

"The rain is stopping."

"Good. I don't like rain."

"You feel like taking a short walk? It would give Pino a chance to stretch his legs."

"As long as we don't give him a chance to stretch his jaws."

We got out of the car. Nadia opened the rear hatch and let Pino out. Unleashed, unmuzzled.

"You think it's a good idea to let him roam free like that, off the leash? I mean, I know they can do miracles these days with prosthetic devices and everything, but still, if he tears an old lady or a little kid limb from limb, there's going to be a lot of paperwork."

Nadia said nothing. Instead she whispered something to the dog that I was unable to hear. Whatever it was, once we started walking, the beast followed close behind us, sticking close to his mistress's left leg, as if he were on a tight, invisible leash.

His gait verged on the hypnotic; it was like watching a big cat prowl, rather than a dog out on a walk.

The dog's head, missing almost an entire ear, was the size of a small watermelon, and muscles taut as bungee cords rippled and sprang beneath his glistening black coat. Altogether, the dog conveyed a sense of lethal, well-disciplined power.

We walked a few hundred yards without speaking, as the last few drops splattered down and then it stopped raining entirely.

"So why did you name him Pino? That's not a very common name for a dog, especially not this kind of a dog."

"Daniela named him. She always gives human names to the dogs she re-educates. I think it makes her job easier, psychologically."

"How old is he?"

"Three. You know why I really like having this dog with me?"

"Tell me."

"He's a constant reminder that it's possible to change

and become something completely different than what you used to be."

I nodded. She stopped and the dog, obeying a silent command, sat expectantly at her side.

"You want to pet him?"

I was about to make another joke about how dangerous the dog was, but at the last minute I stopped myself and just said yes. She turned to Pino and told him that I was a friend, and I could have sworn the dog nodded in agreement.

"Before I pet him, I want you to know that I refuse to call him Pino. I understand your friend's ideas about naming dogs, but I really can't call him Pino."

"What would you rather call him?"

"Arthur Conan Doyle would have liked this fellow. I'll call him Baskerville, if you don't have any objections."

She shrugged and cocked an eyebrow, the way people do when dealing with someone a little odd.

I stepped over to the big dog and stroked his head, which felt like petting a small boulder. My open hand couldn't entirely cover it.

"Hi there, Baskerville. You're not as vicious as you look."

Pino/Baskerville looked up at me with a pair of eyes that were terrifying from a distance, but close up appeared to be filled with melancholy sweetness. I scratched behind his remaining ear, then slid my hand down toward his throat, soft and glistening. As I did, the dog closed his eyes and slowly lifted his muzzle, as if he were about to emit a doleful howl, offering up his throat to me, vulnerable and exposed.

And then, as a certain French gentleman once wrote, suddenly the memory revealed itself.

Raising his muzzle, offering his throat like that, was

something that my grandfather Guido's German shepherd, Marcuse, used to do, more than thirty years ago.

It's not like memories dissolve and disappear. They're all still there, hidden under a thin crust of consciousness. Even the memories we thought we'd lost forever. Sometimes they remain under the surface for an entire lifetime. Other times, something happens that makes them reappear.

A madeleine dipped in tea, or a huge dog with melancholy eyes that offers you his throat to be stroked, for example.

That dog's act of total, deeply moving trust summoned a tidal wave of memories that, as if following a very precise pattern, took no more than a few seconds to array themselves in a coherent and unified map of the long-ago past.

I am not usually able to conjure up memories from my childhood except as unrelated fragments, like so many indecipherable pieces of flotsam and jetsam, bobbing on the surface. But now everything was scuttling obediently into place as if performing some mysterious choreography of images, sounds, smell, names, and concrete objects. All together.

My old record player, ice cream bars, four-color-ink retractable ballpoint pens, Pippi Longstocking, Fruit of the Loom undershirts, "Crocodile Rock," *Il Corriere dei Ragazzi* magazine, Rin Tin Tin, Ivanhoe, the *Black Arrow* TV show, *E Le Stelle Stanno a Guardare* with Alberto Lupo, *Hit Parade*, *A Thousand and One Nights* with the theme song by the Nomadi, cartoon superheroes with the theme song by Lucio Dalla, *The Persuaders* with Tony Curtis and Roger Moore, a yellow-and-orange dirt bike with a banana seat, tabletop soccer, golden Saiwa cookies dipped in milk, four at a time, the smell of cotton candy at the Fiera del Levante, popsicles that left your tongue various colors, coils of rope licorice, Capitan Miki, Duck Avenger, Tex Willer, The Fantastic Four, Sandokan, Tarzan, tossing stink bombs into neighborhood shops and then running away as fast as your legs could carry you, spotting a green Prinz driving along was bad luck, Mafalda, Charlie Brown and the Little Red-Haired Girl, except she was real and didn't have red hair and never noticed me at all, soft putty erasers, playing soccer after school with a Super Santos soccer ball, the Mickey Mouse Club, pinball, foosball, the little boy who was just like us but who never had a chance to forget all these things because his father fell asleep while driving the family home from vacation in their Fiat 124, winter hats with earflaps, Lego, Monopoly, trading soccer cards, one television station, and then two and that was it, kids' shows, sticky paste, squares of pizza, milk delivery, the dim flickering light bulb in my grandparents' kitchen, those single textbooks that covered all of our subjects, plastic book bags, pencil cases, the smell of other kids, the smell of snacks, of Play-Doh, the silence on the playground as we lined up after recess, Lego and toy soldiers, Rossana sucking candies, Super-8 home movies, slides, birthday parties with fruit juice and mini-pizzas, Polaroids, soccer cards, the roller-skating rink in the pine woods, *Carosello* with its ten minutes of advertising disguised as entertainment, baked pasta at my grandparents' house on Sundays.

The light that filtered through my bedroom door, left slightly ajar, the noises in the house becoming more and more muffled, and last, always, my mother's light footsteps as I was dropping off to sleep.

18.

The street was deserted and glistening with rain.

I don't know how long my spell lasted, but it must have been a pretty long time, because at a certain point, in a worried voice, she asked me if I was all right.

"Fine, yes. Why, don't I look fine?"

"Fine? Well, it was a like a scene out of *The Exorcist*. You looked as if you were talking to someone—you were moving your lips, changing your expression—even though you never made a sound."

She stared at me for a few seconds. Then she asked, "You're not insane, are you?"

She smiled as she said it, but there was at least the shadow of a doubt in her eyes.

"It really looked like I was talking to someone?"

"Uh-huh," she said, nodding vigorously.

"When your dog lifted his head to let me stroke his throat, he reminded me of my grandfather's German shepherd, who used to do the same exact thing—with the same motion—many years ago."

"You know, even when he lets people pet him, he doesn't usually expose his throat like that. He likes you. It's pretty unusual."

"Well, when he did, it brought back this flood of memories from my childhood. Things I haven't thought of in thirty years. I'm not surprised to hear that I was talking to myself."

We started walking again, in the same formation: Nadia in the middle, Pino/Baskerville to her left, and me to her right. The smell of wet asphalt hung in the air.

"I can hardly remember anything from my childhood. I don't think it was particularly happy or unhappy, but that's only because I can't remember any moments of great sadness or great happiness. If I had sad or happy times, I've forgotten them. It's hard to explain. There are things that I know happened, and so I say I remember them, but I really don't remember anything. It's as if I know about the things that happened at that time in my life only because someone told me about them. It feels like I have memories of someone else's childhood," Nadia said.

"I know what you mean. Sometimes I'm not sure if something really happened or I dreamed it."

"That's it exactly. I think my mother threw a couple of birthday parties for me, but I couldn't tell you what happened at those parties, who came, or even what year it was. Sometimes it makes my head spin. It's too much."

"So, is there a part of your life that you remember more clearly?"

"Yes. I don't know if it's a good thing or a bad thing, but I remember becoming a working girl perfectly."

"When was that?" I asked, doing my best to preserve as neutral a tone of voice as possible. She ignored the question.

"You know, there's nothing tragic about the so-called life choices I made. It's pretty humdrum. More depressing than anything else."

I made a gesture with one hand, as if to wave something away. It was a small, involuntary gesture, but she saw it.

"Okay, I won't try to describe it. What I meant is that there aren't people or events that I can blame for what I became. My family, for instance."

"What did your parents do—or should I say, what do they do?"

"My father was an administrator in a middle school, and my mother was a housewife. They're both dead. I can't say that I had a great relationship with my parents. But they were probably no worse than the parents of lots of other girls who didn't grow up to be prostitutes. I have a sister who's a lot older than I am. She lives in Bologna. I haven't seen her in ages. Every once in a while we talk on the phone. We're polite and distant, like a couple of strangers. Which is, after all, exactly what we are."

I admired Nadia's straightforward honesty and the economy of words she used.

"Anyway, it all started when I was nineteen. I had graduated from high school with a bookkeeper's diploma, and I enrolled at the university to study business, but I immediately realized that I had no interest in continuing my studies. Or maybe I just wasn't interested in studying business, but it adds up to the same thing."

As she was talking, I sorted through my mental files for her date of birth, which I had read in the documents from the trial for which I had acted as her defense counsel. I don't know why, but I never forget anyone's age—even people I barely know or know only on a professional level.

I did some quick math in my head: When she was nineteen, I was twenty-four. What was I doing at age twenty-four? I had just received my college degree. I hadn't yet met

Sara, my ex-wife. My parents were still alive. Practically speaking, when Nadia was embarking on her adventures in the real world, though I was five years older than she, I was just an overgrown boy.

"I wanted to be independent. I wanted to get away from home. I hated my boring, ordinary family life. I couldn't stand that modest apartment, three bedrooms, a kitchen, and a bathroom, filled with objects in miserable taste and the smell of mothballs that wafted out of their bedroom. I couldn't stand their meaningless conversations and their pathetic prospects: pay the monthly installments on the car, find a little two-star *pensione* for our summer vacations, count the years until Dad can retire. I couldn't stand the calculations they performed to balance the family budget, warmed-over pasta for dinner, my big sister's hand-me-down clothes, the shiny oilskin tablecloth. But there was one thing I hated more than anything else."

"What was that?"

"My father drank a little wine, at lunch and at dinner. Just a little, but every day, twice a day. Of course, we couldn't afford expensive wine, so when we went to the grocery store, we always bought wine in cartons. There was always a carton of wine on the table, and I remember exactly how it went: My mother snipped the carton open with a pair of scissors; my father filled his glass halfway and then diluted the wine with water; at the end of the meal my mother pinched the mouth of the carton closed with a clothespin and put it away; then she put it back on the table for dinner. My God, I hated it. There are times when I relive it, and I can hardly breathe, just the way I could barely breathe then. Other times, I'm just overwhelmed by a suffocating sense of guilt."

"That's inevitable, I guess."

"Sure, I think so. Anyway, I was a good-looking girl, so I got a job with an agency that provided staff and services for conferences, political rallies, and other events. One day, one of the men organizing a convention for drug company representatives asked me out to dinner, after work. He was a gentleman of about fifty, very distinguished, very well-mannered. I accepted the invitation and arranged to meet him far from my house, because I was ashamed to have him see where we lived."

"Where did you live?"

"It was public housing, over near the church of the Redentore—you know, the Salesian church."

"Sure, I box right near there."

"You box? You mean you fight, in a ring?"

"Yes."

"You know you're not normal, right?"

"Come on, tell the story."

"He came to pick me up in a Ferrari Thema and took me to dinner at a well-known restaurant, one of the restaurants I used to dream about eating in. I remember it as if it were yesterday. I remember everything: the tablecloth, the silverware—real silver—the crystal glasses, the waiters treating me like a lady, even though I was just a kid. And I can still remember everything we ate and the wine we drank. It was a Brunello. It must have cost a fortune, and I can still taste and smell the flavor and aroma of that wine right here, right now, while I'm talking."

"Which restaurant was it?"

She told me the name, and I remembered it well. Twenty years earlier it had been one of the area's fanciest restaurants. It was just outside of Bari. I'd never gone there. I didn't go when I was a young man because I couldn't afford it, and I didn't go when I was an adult, because it had gone out of business, vanished into the void, like so many other things from that period.

"After dinner, he invited me to his place for a drink."

Her tone of voice was neutral. Still, you could sense tension and a climax arriving in the narrative. One of those stories with an ending you already know. An ending you don't particularly like, but there's nothing you can do to ward it off or change it.

"I thought he lived alone, and that he was taking me to his home. But in fact he was married, and he had a son about my age. He took me to a little apartment, a sort of pied-à-terre, and it all happened very naturally. When it was time to go, he gave me three hundred thousand lire."

She paused and looked at me for a few seconds before continuing in a tone of voice with an almost imperceptible note of challenge to it.

"And you know what? I really liked taking that money. I felt as if I was taking control of my life."

"It didn't make you uncomfortable?"

"Incredible as it might sound, no. I'd been with boys, I even had a boyfriend then. But this was different, and it all felt very natural. We hadn't talked about money beforehand, but, I can't say why, I just knew right away that he was hiring me, giving me a kind of assignment. It wasn't fun, but it wasn't repulsive either."

She paused again. I sat there, uncertain what to say, or for that matter what to think.

"After that night, I saw the gentleman in question a number of times. His name was Vito. I was sorry to hear that he died a few years ago. Going out with him wasn't exactly like being a whore. I mean, we'd get together and go out for dinner, and then we'd have sex, and then he'd give me a gift. I haven't been married myself, but I think that in many cases it works in the exact same way."

Her words hung in the damp air for a few seconds. The clouds began to thin, and you could see patches of night sky here and there. I would have liked to have sat on a bench and continued talking, but everything was wet from the rain. So we just kept walking, with Pino beside us, though he didn't have much to add to the conversation.

"Then things changed."

"What happened?"

"One night, as we were leaving his pied-à-terre, Vito asked me if I'd do him a favor."

"What favor?"

"He asked me if I'd go out with a man he knew. He was a businessman, and Vito was discussing a number of important deals with him. He was scheduled to come to town the following day. Vito told me he was a very distinguished, impeccable gentleman, and handsome, too. Vito wanted him to be in a good mood so he'd sign a big contract. I can't remember if I said anything or not. In the next image in my mind, he's smiling, pulling out his wallet, and counting out ten hundred-thousand-lire bills. He handed them to me, and then he pinched my cheek affectionately, like I'd been a good girl and behaved nicely."

I was about to tell her I didn't want to hear the rest. Then I realized that I didn't want to hear it, and yet, at the same time, I did. I get that feeling sometimes with books or movies when they're about subjects I find disturbing, things I'd prefer to ignore.

"After that, from time to time Vito would ask me if I felt

like going out with some friend of his, but he wouldn't pay. From there I started building a client list of my own. Word of mouth. There were a couple of judges on that list. One of them is dead now; the other is very prominent. Sometimes I see his picture in the newspaper. He always has a very serious expression on his face."

She let that hang in the air for a moment, clearly implying that the judge in question wasn't always as serious as he appeared to be in those photographs. She didn't say his name, and I appreciated that, though it took a certain amount of self-control to keep myself from asking who it was.

"I know this all sounds depressing, and it probably is. But—how can I put this—it was hard to see that at the time. It was hard to tell the difference between my dates and real dates. Lots of my clients took me out to dinner, to the movies, to see shows, and lots of them wanted someone to talk to. As time went by, I realized that for some of them those other things were at least as important as the sex.

"One thing that you often hear prostitutes say is that many men want a woman they can fuck in peace and talk to in peace. Without being judged for one thing or the other. And from my own experience, I can say that's true. But that's always where the problems lie."

"What problems?"

"Sometimes, a client got confused and mistook fiction for reality. In other words, he'd fall in love. When that happened, I cut them off immediately. It seemed like the fair thing to do, the ethical thing. Okay, I know it might seem odd to hear a whore talking about professional ethics, but I think everyone clings to a system of rules to keep things clear, no matter what profession they practice. Ethics aside, it was just smart to put a quick end to those relationships. You never know what goes on in people's heads. A girlfriend of mine was stalked and practically beaten to death after she rejected a client who'd fallen in love with her."

"Of course, you moved out of your parents' apartment?"

"Of course. I told my parents the money came from a job I'd found selling clothing wholesale. I have no idea whether they actually believed me. In fact, I don't know if my mother and father ever figured out what I really did. By the time I was arrested and the whole thing became a matter of public record, they'd both been dead for years."

"So, how did it end?"

"The rest isn't all that interesting, that is, if what I've told you so far was interesting at all. Anyway, what happened later is pretty unclear in my memory. For a while I made movies, but not for long. The pay was much better for prostitution. Then I started having other girls work for me, and that paid even better. I hadn't worked as a prostitute in quite a while by the time they arrested me. Anyway, you know that part of the story, since you were my lawyer."

She seemed to have finished, and I was about to say something, when she started talking again—as if she'd remembered an important detail.

"But there was something I never told you when you were my lawyer."

"What's that?"

"When they arrested me, I was almost relieved. I couldn't take that life anymore, and things got a lot worse once I started running a prostitution ring. It was much easier for me to maintain my equilibrium when I was just a whore. Once I started to manage other girls, I had a better picture of how depressing it all was. I probably didn't realize it—and in any case I can't remember it clearly—but I think I wanted to find a way out. That wasn't easy, though. The work paid so well, and I had no other skills."

We'd walked a long way, from the waterfront to the neighborhood around the Teatro Petruzzelli. I couldn't quite decipher Nadia's story. I wasn't sure of the emotions behind it. She'd described everything that happened to her in a neutral tone of voice, but it was obvious that there was something boiling just beneath the surface. I couldn't figure out what it was. Pino continued walking close to his mistress's left leg, and it occurred to me how nice it would be to have a silent, discreet companion on my nightly walks. I'd never thought of getting a dog before, but just then I decided I liked the idea.

Nadia's voice broke into my thoughts. There was a slightly different tone in her voice than when she was relating her story.

"Can I tell you something silly?"

"I like silly things."

"After my arrest, I asked a friend—not a customer—for a referral to a lawyer. He gave me your name. He said that you were a very good lawyer and a very respectable person, and from the way he said it, I pictured you as some old, chubby bald guy. Somebody's uncle. But then you showed up in the prison visiting room."

"I showed up, and then what?" Sometimes I can be really good at missing the point.

"Well, you're not that old, and you're not chubby or bald. Though you certainly were very serious and very professional."

"You were very serious, too. An ideal client, actually—no pointless chitchat, no ridiculous demands."

"I had to be serious. I didn't want to seem like what I was, which was a whore, even if I was a high-end whore. I figured that any manifestation of femininity would be taken the wrong way."

She stopped for a moment, as if thinking about what she'd just said.

"Or maybe the right way. Anyway, the only thing that I could figure out to do was to give you a book, after the trial. Do you remember?"

"How could I forget? *The Revolution of Hope* by Erich Fromm."

"I suspected you already had a copy, even though you said you didn't. You thanked me and said how happy you were to have it. You said you'd been thinking about buying it for some time now, and you were going to read it right away."

I smiled. I didn't remember saying any of those things, but it was typical of me, the sort of things I always said in that situation. When someone gives me a book that I've already read, I hate to disappoint the gift giver, so I lie.

"Well, in fact, I had already read it."

She smiled, but there was something in her eyes that caused a pang in my heart, completely out of proportion and unconnected to the episode of the book. As if a door had swung open, for a few moments, and I had glimpsed a terrible pool of sorrow.

"What about afterward?"

"What do you mean, afterward?"

"After the trial."

"Oh, right. I've been smart enough to stay clean since then. I had plenty of savings, and I'd invested them wisely. Low-risk mutual funds with moderate but reliable yields. I own three apartments in good neighborhoods, with good tenants paying reasonably high rents. A fourth apartment that I live in. In other words, I could afford to retire, while I tried to figure out what to do with the second half of my life. I traveled a little. Then I got the bad news I told you about, but I had good doctors, and I think they caught it early enough. I think that's over. So when I got back—from my trips and from my time in the hospital—I decided to enroll in college."

"Studying what?"

"Contemporary literature. I'm taking my exams. Can you believe that? Just another couple of years and I'll have my degree."

"Have you decided on a thesis?"

She smiled again, but this time there were no shadows behind her eyes. If anything, a gleam of gratitude that I had taken her seriously.

"No, not yet. But I'd like to do something related to film history. I love movies."

I said nothing. As we walked, I cast her a sidelong glance. But she was looking straight ahead. That is, she wasn't looking at anything. A few minutes went by.

"Anyway, I had a boyfriend, too. The first, and the last, for now, in my second life. For the first time I didn't have to worry about concealing how I made a living."

"How did it go with him?"

"He was—is—a shithead. So it went the way it always goes with a shithead. After less than a year, it was over."

"And since then?"

"Since then, nothing."

I tried to calculate mentally how long it had been. She understood and spared me the effort.

"I haven't been with a man for close to a year."

It seemed like a good time not to say anything.

"I feel as if I'm living my life backwards, if you know what I mean."

I nodded my head. I don't know if she saw me, because she kept looking straight ahead.

"What about the Chelsea Hotel?"

"That's the last part of the story. I really like going to college, but it's not enough for me. I needed something more. I had too much time to think, which isn't always a good thing."

"It almost never is."

"Exactly. So I figured it was time to find a job, and the idea of opening the Chelsea Hotel came to me while I was talking to a gay friend of mine. I like the hours: We get started around eight in the evening, and we go home around four in the morning, and then I sleep until lunchtime. Plus, having a place to go every night, lots of people to see, makes me feel a little less lonely."

There was a boy walking a dog of indeterminate breed on the sidewalk across the street. The dog started barking ferociously, doing his best to yank his leash from the boy's hand. Pino/Baskerville calmly turned his head in the barking dog's direction, stopped, and gazed across the street at him. He neither barked, nor growled, nor showed any intention of lunging at the dog—though he certainly could have, because he wasn't on a leash. He looked over and did nothing, but I imagined that in those seconds terrible images ran through his head—the sounds of violence, the metallic taste of blood, the pain when his ear was ripped off his head, fangs, claws, life and death. Nadia whispered a command and the huge beast methodically arranged himself horizontally, assuming a sphinx-like position. He didn't even look in the other dog's direction.

At last the boy managed to drag the barking dog—by now in the throes of hysteria—down the street. The nocturnal silence was restored, and we resumed our stroll and our conversation. The gaps between the clouds were bigger now, and the sight of the night sky made me happy.

"Do you think I told you the whole truth? Or do you think I changed things to make it less depressing?"

"No one ever tells the whole truth, especially when they're talking about themselves. But if you ask a question like that, it means that in one way or another, you know that and you've done your best. So, if I had to guess, I'd say you probably told me something pretty close to the so-called truth."

She looked at me with an expression that mixed curiosity and concern, as if she'd just heard something with unexpected consequences.

"Really? No one ever tells the truth?"

"The whole truth, no, no one ever does. The ones who tell you that they're being completely honest—and they may even believe it—are the most dangerous. They don't know that lying is inevitable. They have no self-awareness, and they're prisoners of themselves."

"Prisoners of themselves. I like the sound of that."

"That's right, prisoners of themselves, and incapable of figuring out who they really are. You just go ahead and ask one of those people who claim always to tell the truth how he does his work, what his personal strengths and weaknesses are, how he interacts with other people, or anything else that has to do with his, or her, self-image. You'll discover something interesting."

"What's that?"

"They don't know how to answer. They give rote answers and rely on stereotypes, or they describe the qualities they wish they possessed but don't. Qualities that correspond to the false image that they have of themselves. Have you ever heard of Alan Watts?"

"No."

"He was an English philosopher. He studied eastern cultures, and he wrote a beautiful book about Zen. Watts wrote that an honest person is someone who knows that he is a complete impostor and is nonchalant about it. According to that definition, I'm halfway there. I know that I'm an impostor, but I still can't quite pull off the nonchalant part."

"You are completely crazy."

"I hope I can take that as a compliment."

"You can."

"I think it's time to go to sleep," I said, glancing at my watch.

"That's right, you have a serious person's job. You can't stay in bed until noon like I do."

"I'll walk you back to your car."

"There's no need. That is, unless you need a ride home. I don't know where you live, but if it's far away, let's go back to the car and I'll take you home."

"I live just a short walk from here."

"Then there's no need for you to come all the way back to the car."

"Well, thanks for the talk, and for everything."

"Thank you."

"Baskerville is a good sort of demon after all."

"Right."

After a moment's hesitation she leaned toward me and

gave me a kiss on the cheek. Luckily, Pino chose not to view this as an act of hostility, so he didn't rip me limb from limb.

"See you.

"Bye."

"Well, that's ridiculous."

"What?"

"I'm blushing."

"I hadn't noticed." When I really make an effort, I manage to say some truly idiotic things.

"Well, now I really should go."

"Are you sure you'll be all right walking back by yourself?"

I said the words, and then my eyes met Pino's.

He had the kind of patient expression reserved for those who aren't necessarily bad, but clearly are not very bright.

19.

The next day, I asked Maria Teresa to step into my office. I still relied on her for anything having to do with clients and files that had been archived prior to Pasquale's arrival. She knew exactly and immediately how to find things and she remembered every file that had come through the office.

"Do you remember Quintavalle? He was a member of that little group . . . ."

"Of course I remember him. I'm never happy when we take on drug dealers as clients, but at least he was a well-mannered and likable young man."

"That's right, he was likable. We haven't heard from him in years now."

"Either they never caught him again or he's stopped dealing, which would make me very happy."

"Or else he has a new lawyer."

"Impossible. You literally saved his life that time. Winning a plea bargain with the evidence they had against him . . ."

"Do you remember who the prosecutor was?"

"Of course I do."

"Then you have to admit it wasn't all that amazing an achievement. He'd sell his parents into slavery if it would clear a case off his desk. Anyway, do we have Quintavalle's phone number lying around somewhere? I need to talk to him."

"It's definitely in his file, unless he has a new number." Maria Teresa is perfectly aware of how drug dealers operate. They frequently change their cell phones and SIM cards to elude police monitoring, so their phone numbers tend to be somewhat unstable. That, however, applies to their work phones. Their personal phones tend to have a longer half-life.

I asked her to take a look in the file, and five minutes later there was a piece of paper with his phone number on my desk.

Quintavalle answered on the second ring.

"*Buon giorno*, this is Guido Guerrieri, I'd like—"

"Counselor Guerrieri, *buon giorno*! What a pleasure. What an honor. To what do I owe the pleasure? I didn't forget to pay last time, did I?"

"Damiano, how are you?"

"Doing fine, Counselor. And you?"

I hate it when people say they're doing fine, but from Quintavalle it didn't bother me particularly.

"Doing fine myself, thanks. I need to ask you something, but I don't want to talk about it on the phone. Would you mind terribly dropping by my office?"

"Of course, it's no problem at all. When would you like me to drop by?"

"If you could come by today, you'd be doing me a favor."

"How about seven o'clock?"

"A little later would be better, that way I'll be done with my appointments and we can talk without being interrupted."

"Okay, I'll see you at eight."

"Thanks. And . . . Damiano?"

"Yes?"

"I've moved. We're not at the old address anymore."

"I know, I know. I'll see you there at eight o'clock."

When I talk with someone like Damiano Quintavalle—a professional criminal, who makes a living from his illicit activities—I'm even more doubtful than usual of my ability to decipher the world and distinguish between so-called good and so-called evil.

In the first place, Quintavalle is an intelligent young man. He comes from a normal family. He attended college, though he never got a degree. He reads the newspaper and occasionally reads books. Also, as Maria Teresa said, he's nice. Funny, without being vulgar. Well-mannered. Courteous.

But he earns his living by dealing coke.

He's one of those dealers who operate on their own or with a very small group; they tend to make house calls, like the client whose case I had appealed to the Court of Cassation, unsuccessfully, the week before. Quintavalle gets a call, for instance, about a special party. He shows up at the party as an invited guest, then he fills the order, gets his money (with a substantial bonus for home delivery), and leaves. Or else he travels around Italy making deliveries to wealthy purchasers who are reluctant to dirty their hands by having contact with ordinary drug dealers.

The police and prosecutors have gone after him repeatedly, but he is fanatically cautious, he's very careful about his cell phones, and he's only been caught with drugs in his possession once. The quantity was small, so he got off with a few weeks in jail and a highly advantageous plea bargain.

Quintavalle has a wife who owns and runs a *profumeria* and a son who's in middle school. Quintavalle's son is a great kid; his one shortcoming is that he wants to be a lawyer when he grows up. He thinks his father is a businessman who travels frequently for work. And in a way, he's right.

Quintavalle walked into the office at eight o'clock on the dot. I jumped up to greet him—I'll admit that I don't do this for all my clients—and clasped his hand.

"Counselor, how are you?"

"Fine, and you?"

"Pretty good, though these aren't easy times."

"Why not?"

"Oh, I don't know. Maybe I'm just getting old, but I sense a threat, an imminent danger." That's exactly what he said: "an imminent danger." It's not the sort of expression commonly used by a professional drug dealer.

"As if something terrible might happen any day now. That they might arrest me with ironclad evidence of everything I've done over the years. Or—much more likely—one of the thugs who run the city now might come to tell me that I can't work independently anymore, that I have to work for him."

"What thugs?"

"That's right, you don't take on cases involving organized crime, so you might not know about it, but things are grim here in town. There are new gangs in the city, and they want to take charge of everything. They've formed an alliance to monopolize all the neighborhoods, and in particular they want to control extortion, loan sharking, and, of course, drug dealing. If someone really does come around and tell me that I have to work for them, well, that would be the time that I finally quit this racket and find an honest job."

"That wouldn't be the end of the world, you know. Maybe there's nothing happening. Maybe it's just your subconscious telling you that it's time to quit dealing."

"Right. My wife tells me more or less the same thing. The problem is that with a normal job, you just don't make the kind of money I've gotten used to."

"You have the shop. You wouldn't starve to death. And your son is growing up."

"Right, maybe that's the real reason. I'm not afraid of prison, but I couldn't stand it if my son found out how I make a living. Anyway, I doubt that you asked me to come in so we could chat about my future. What can I do for you?"

"To tell the truth, I'm not even sure what it is that I need. I don't quite know where to start."

"Try starting from the beginning."

It was good advice. I did as he suggested and told him the whole story. I told him that I was trying to figure out what had happened to Manuela—he'd never heard of her—and that the only lead I had involved Michele Cantalupi, who was a regular and fairly heavy user of cocaine. That was why I had called him and wanted his help. Did he know Cantalupi, had he ever had him as a customer, and in general had he ever heard of him in his dealings?

"Michele Cantalupi?"

"Yes. I don't know if this is helpful, but they tell me he's good-looking."

"Michele. It sounds familiar, but after all, it's not an unusual name. Do you have a picture of him?"

"No, I don't. I can try to get my hands on one. But never

mind the photograph. There's something I want you to tell me. If this guy was dealing to people in the upper echelons of society, would you know him?"

"Not necessarily. Of course, I know lots of people in town, but Bari is a big city and there are a lot more people consuming—and therefore selling—cocaine than you might imagine. There are times when I deliver fifty grams of cocaine to a party, and then find out they used it all up. That night, at the party."

"Do you mind if I ask you a few questions about how the system works?"

"No, of course not. You're my lawyer, and anyway, it's for something important. Ask me anything you like."

"Say a young man goes to these kinds of parties. How would he evolve from a mere user to a . . ."

I realized that for some reason I was embarrassed to use the term "drug dealer," as if I might offend Quintavalle, who was in fact in that line of work, by using a slightly distasteful phrase. He noticed my discomfort.

"A drug dealer. Really, Counselor, don't worry about it, I'm not offended. It's a fairly typical process. Let's imagine that there's a group of people who want to buy a certain quantity of drugs, to divide up, or even to use all together, as friends. They take up a collection and then one of them goes and meets with the dealer. By the way, the Italian Court of Cassation has ruled that the purchase of drugs for group personal consumption is not a crime under the law and . . . well, I guess I don't have to tell you that. In other words, this one guy is making the buy for his little group of friends and at a certain point it occurs to him that he could make a little profit on the arrangement. So he starts to buy the drugs on his own and sells them just to his friends at a mark-up.

Then word starts getting around: This guy can get drugs in a hurry. If you need some coke, he's the guy to call. He gradually builds up a network of customers, he gets to know more and more suppliers, maybe he goes out of town to buy the product because it's better or cheaper somewhere else, and anyway, out of town is always better, and that's how someone turns into a drug dealer."

"Is that what happened to you?"

"More or less. There were some other things going on, but they're probably of no interest to you."

I nodded and did my best to put on a knowledgeable expression. I was trying not to look baffled, but after that conversation I knew nothing more than I had before. For a few seconds I felt—with excruciating intensity—like a perfect and inexcusable fake. Then the sensation ebbed, leaving me with nothing more than an underlying wave of nausea, faint but inexorable.

"Okay, Damiano, thanks. I'll try to get my hands on a photograph of this guy, and when I do I'll give you a call."

"Okay, in the meantime I'll see what I can remember, and I'll ask around a little bit."

"Don't put yourself in any danger, please."

Quintavalle gave me a smile, stood up, and said good-bye.

The smile meant that he appreciated my concern, but that it was entirely superfluous. For many years, he'd made it his business and his way of life to stay out of the line of fire.

20.

At that point, I was faced with the problem of how to ask Fornelli for a picture of Cantalupi, and it struck me as absurdly challenging.

The minute I asked him for it, he, very reasonably, would ask me why I wanted it. I didn't feel like answering that question, because I didn't want to explain what I was doing. Not right now, anyway. Maybe I was embarrassed to tell him that I'd started digging around in the world of drug dealers, where I obviously had a number of useful contacts. Maybe I was afraid that my ambitions as a would-be private investigator might blow up in my face with an actionable defamation of someone—Cantalupi—who might have absolutely nothing to do with Manuela's disappearance or with dealing drugs. Or maybe I was uncomfortable with the idea that Fornelli might speak to Manuela's parents and, in order to explain his request, tell them that there was good news—that Guerrieri, that old bloodhound, was on someone's trail. That he might get their hopes up for no good reason. Or maybe it was much simpler. Maybe I just didn't want Quintavalle to take a look at the photograph and say that he had no idea who the guy was, bringing a sudden end to my brilliant investigative lead.

So I let the weekend go by without calling him.

On Monday, I was returning to my office after a hearing that had dragged on longer than expected. It was too late for lunch but also too early for my first appointment, so I went over to the Feltrinelli bookshop, had a cappuccino, and bought a book. It was called *The Mysteries of Bari*, and the flap copy promised that the book revealed a number of the most incredible urban legends of Bari, with descriptions of the unsettling historic events that had engendered those legends.

As I walked out of the bookstore, planning to loaf around for another half an hour or so, I saw Signore Ferraro, Manuela's father, coming toward me.

He was walking briskly, looking straight ahead, directly at me, and for a moment I thought he was coming to tell me something. I put on the expression you use to say hello to someone, and the muscles in my right arm tensed in preparation for a handshake.

But Ferraro literally looked right through me, and a few seconds later he strode past me, without seeing me. His expression—which appeared vigilant but in reality was distracted, remote—gave me the shivers.

I turned and watched him for a few seconds and then, almost against my will, I began to follow him.

At first I followed him cautiously, but before long I saw that he wasn't paying the slightest attention to his surroundings. He never looked behind him, and he never looked to either side. He walked at a good pace, and the gaze that had pierced me without seeing me was directed straight ahead, into the void. Or maybe somewhere even worse.

We reached Via Sparano and he turned right, toward the train station.

I didn't even bother to ask myself just what I thought I was doing, or why. I was in the throes of a feverish instinct that drove me to follow him, without thinking about it.

Once I was sure that he wouldn't have noticed me even if I had jumped in front of him, right into his path—he would simply have walked around me and continued on his way—I became more daring and started following right behind him, practically walking at his side, just a couple of yards away from him.

Someone watching the scene from a certain distance might even have thought that we were walking together.

As we walked, a remarkable thing happened. I felt as if I could envision the entire scene—including myself—from an outside vantage point. It was a strange, dissociated vision, as if I were standing on a balcony on the second or third floor of a building behind us.

I didn't like what I saw. Sometimes you see a photograph that has been manipulated on a computer: Everything is black and white, but in the middle there's a patch of color—an object, a detail, or a person. The scene I was looking at was the other way around. Everything was normal, in full color, except for a weird entity in the middle, in black-and-white, almost glowing, and deeply sad. That entity was Manuela's father.

It only lasted for a few seconds, but it made the blood run ice-cold in my veins, as if I were trapped in a nightmare.

We walked through the gardens of Piazza Umberto, passed the university, and reached Piazza Moro. There he stopped for a moment near the fountain, downwind of it, and it struck me that he wanted the spray to splash him. Then he continued past the fountain, walked into the station, strode confidently over to the underpass, descended the steps, walked around a panhandler, and then went up the stairs to Track 5.

There were people waiting all along the platform. I looked up at the display panels to see which train they were waiting for. Then I knew for sure what I had already guessed to be true.

Ferraro sat down on a bench and lit a cigarette. I felt an urge to go over to him and ask for a cigarette so we could smoke together. He had a pack of Camels, and I really would have loved to smoke a Camel right then, to burn— along with the tobacco and the cigarette paper—the viscous, choking sadness that had infected me like a disease.

Then I thought: I shouldn't be here at all. It's not nice to spy on people in the best of circumstances, but peering into the inner recesses of a human being driven mad with grief is cruel and dangerous. Grief can be contagious. Still, I stayed there. I stood, in my gray suit holding my lawyer's briefcase, and I waited for the train from Lecce, Brindisi, Ostuni, and Monopoli to pull into the station. I waited for Signore Ferraro to walk the length of the platform, examining, one by one, each of the passengers getting off the train. I waited for the doors to close and the train to pull back out of the station, and I had to restrain myself from following him again when he walked back into the yawning shadow of the steps down to the underpass and vanished.

When I emerged from the train station onto the piazza, I turned my cell phone back on. I'd turned it off during the hearing and then forgotten about it. Subconscious self-defense, I guess.

TEMPORARY PERFECTIONS

There were a lot of calls and quite a few text messages. One of the text messages read

Yr tel always off i talked to nicoletta call me & i'll tell u all abt it luv caterina.

21.

I called her back immediately, doing my best to ignore the effect that the "luv" at the end of the message was having on me.

"It's Guido Guerrieri, I got your message . . . ."

"I called and called but your phone is always off."

It was a subtle thing, but she had used the familiar Italian *tu* form. She'd addressed me formally back in the office.

"Well, yes, I was in court for a hearing and I turned it off. Did you want to tell me something?"

"Yes, I managed to talk to Nicoletta."

"Great, did you ask if she's willing to meet with me?"

"I had to call her more than once. At first, she said she didn't want to talk to you."

"Why not?"

"I don't know. She was confused and worried and said she didn't want to get involved."

"Involved in what? I only want to ask her a few questions."

"That's what I told her. But I kept after her, and in the end I got her to agree to meet with you."

"Thank you. So what do I do next?"

"She said that she's only willing to talk to you if I come, too."

I said nothing for a few seconds.

"I told her there's nothing to worry about, that you only want to ask her a few questions about Manuela. But she was nervous about it, so I told her that if she wanted, I could come with you. I thought that might reassure her."

"So, now what should we do?"

"Now we should go to Rome together and meet with her."

That answer had a truly schizophrenic effect on me: annoyance at her trespassing on my professional territory, a slight and mounting excitement at the almost explicit seductiveness in Caterina's words and voice. I didn't know what to say, and as I usually do in situations of this kind, I tried to stall.

"Fine. Do you mind dropping by my office this evening so we can talk it over?"

"What time?"

"If it's all the same to you, later is better."

"What if I come at 8:30?"

"8:30 would be perfect. So, see you later, thanks."

"See you later."

The conversation was over, but I stood there, looking down at the cell phone in my hand. A number of thoughts ran through my mind, and some of them were both unprofessional and unlawful. I felt embarrassed, and I knew that I could slip very quickly from the merely embarrassing to the deeply ridiculous. I quickly stuffed my cell phone into my pocket, with a briskness that verged on rage, and I hurried back to my office.

———

The afternoon was filled with appointments and things to do, and it went by quickly. The next day Consuelo's first trial as sole defense counsel was scheduled in a court in the surrounding province. She'd asked me to go over the case with her.

It was a trial for robbery involving violence after the fact. Three high school students, two of them underage and one an adult, had stolen cookies, chocolate bars, and soft drinks from a supermarket. The security guard spotted them and managed to stop one of them. The other two came back to help their friend, and a fairly violent fight broke out. The kids managed to escape, but plenty of people had seen it all, and in just a few hours the Carabinieri had identified them. The two kids who were under eighteen at the time had been tried as minors in juvenile court. The client Consuelo and I were representing was the adult. He'd only come to see us after he'd already been indicted, when it was already too late to plea-bargain—definitely the best approach in a case of this sort. The defense theory that we had all agreed upon was to put all the blame for the assault on the security guard on one of the two minors—he had already gotten off with a judicial pardon, and therefore no longer risked any legal consequences. Let me point out, by the way, that it may even have been true, since one of the two minors was a rugby player who tipped the scales at well over two hundred pounds.

The following day, I was scheduled to attend a hearing at the appeals court in Lecce, so we decided that the case of the cookie thieves would be Consuelo's first solo trial.

While she was summarizing her notes for the following day, my concentration faltered and I drifted away. As so often happens to me, I pursued a memory.

We were a group of boys, high school freshmen, on a winter afternoon. We roamed aimlessly around the city with nothing to do, bored in a way that is possible only when you have all the time in the world.

At a certain point, one of us—I think his name was Beppe—said that his parents were out of town, and that we could go to his house to listen to music and maybe make prank phone calls. Someone else said that'd be great, but first we needed to get something to eat and something to drink.

"Let's go shoplift stuff from the supermarket," said a third kid.

No objections were raised; in fact, the suggestion was met with an enthusiastic response. At last, an exciting development during that long afternoon of boredom. I had never stolen anything in my life, though I knew that many of my friends did it. This was the first time I'd been involved in anything of the sort. I didn't want to do it, but I was too scared to say anything. I didn't want to prove my friends right when they said that if I had an Indian warrior name, it would be He Who Shits in His Pants.

So I went along with them, though as we got closer to the supermarket we had selected for our raid I felt a growing disquiet, comprised of equal measures of fear that something might go wrong and shame over what we were about to do.

Things only got worse once we were inside the supermarket. My friends scattered down the aisles and began filling pants, jackets, and even knee socks with merchandise. They moved around frenetically, like crazed ants, grabbing groceries and concealing them in their clothing with complete nonchalance. They didn't even bother to look around to make sure they weren't being watched.

While they worked busily, I stood motionless, staring at—I'm just inventing a detail here—the shelves of the candy and snack section. I picked up a bag of malted chocolate bars and hefted it, looking furtively to my right and then to my left. There was no one in sight, and I told myself that this was the perfect moment to slip the bag down my pants and be done with it. But I just couldn't bring myself to do it. I kept thinking that in the exact split second I did, someone would come around the corner from one direction or the other, they'd see me, they'd sound the alarm, the security guards would come running, and before long I'd be handcuffed, waiting to be shipped off to the juvenile detention center, fervently hoping the ground would open up and swallow me in a chasm of humiliation and shame.

I can't say how long we stayed in that supermarket. After a while, Beppe came over to where I stood staring intently—with autistic focus—at a package of jam tarts. In a frantic tone of voice he told me that we had to hurry up and leave the store before things got out of hand. He explained that one member of our group, Lino, was going too far, just as he had on other occasions. He'd stuffed way too much food into his clothes, and there was a good chance he'd be caught and then we'd all be fucked. His exact words. That's when I had a clever and cowardly idea.

"Hey, Beppe, let's do this: I'll buy something, and while I'm paying, I'll distract the checkout girl, so you guys can just stroll out without any problems."

He looked at me for a few seconds with a puzzled expression on his face. He was trying to figure it out. Was I a shrewd son of a bitch or—as must have seemed far more likely—a complete pussy who was trying to pull one over on his friends? He probably couldn't come up with a clear answer, but there was no more time to waste.

"Okay, I'll tell the other guys. In a couple of minutes, you go to the cash register and while you pay, we'll walk out. Then we'll meet up back at my house."

I felt an enormous wave of relief. I'd found the perfect solution: I wouldn't come off as an incompetent fuck-up (a description that my friends had applied to me more than once, and with good reason), yet I was taking practically no risk, and I wasn't committing a crime—or so I thought at the time. At that age, I still hadn't grasped the concept of being an accomplice to a crime, much less the fundamental principals of aiding and abetting someone in the commission of a crime.

Thirty minutes later, we were all at Beppe's house, and the dining room table was literally covered with cookies, cans of Coca-Cola, fruit juice cartons, chocolate bars, hard candies, snack cakes, cheese packs, and even a couple of salamis. In the middle of that cornucopia of junk food, solitary and pathetic, was the chocolate bar with puffed rice that I had bought and paid for with my own money.

I guess it was all pretty ridiculous, but back then I had a hard time seeing the fun in it. Once I got over my sense of relief, I was stuck facing the unpleasant truth: I'd abetted a theft, and I was just as much a thief as the others, just a much more cowardly one.

The other boys were eating, drinking, and recalling their daring deeds. I was terrified that someone might bring up my role in the raid and figure out my underlying motivations. Fortunately, that didn't happen, but I soon became too uncomfortable to stay. I invented an excuse that no one cared about anyway and left with my tail between my legs. I left the chocolate bar I'd bought on the dining room table.

"Guido, are you listening to me?"

"I'm sorry, Consuelo, I just got distracted. I remembered something I had forgotten about and . . ."

"Are you okay?"

"Yes, fine."

"You seemed a little spaced out."

"It happens to me from time to time. Though lately it's been happening a little more often, I have to admit."

She said nothing. It seemed as if she were trying to find the words or work up the courage to ask a question but then couldn't.

"Nothing to worry about, in any case. You can ask Maria Teresa. Every so often I seem like I've lost it, but I'm harmless."

More or less.

22.

I gave no further signs of being mentally unbalanced. We finished going over the file, and Consuelo went back to her office. A short while later, a little earlier than we had agreed, Caterina arrived. Pasquale poked his head into my office and asked if he should send in the young lady now or have her wait until the time scheduled for her appointment. I told him to send her in, of course, even though her failure to be punctual annoyed me ever so slightly.

"I'm a little early. I can wait. By the way, I realized that I"—she hemmed and hawed here, uncertain whether to stick with the informal *tu* or go back to the stiff formal *lei*—"used the informal with you on the phone," she said, as she made herself comfortable in the seat across from my desk. "Maybe that was overly familiar."

"No worries. I'm done with what I was working on, and be as familiar as you like."

No worries? Listen to yourself, Guerrieri. Have you lost your mind? After "no worries," there are just three more steps—"just a sec," "irregardless," and "you and I" as the object of a transitive verb. After that, you're well on your way down the road to hell that's paved with slipshod grammar, where you'll end up in the infernal circle of the murderers of language.

"I had a couple of errands to run, and I got them done earlier than I expected, so I thought I'd drop by. If you were still busy, I figured I could just wait."

I nodded, forcing myself to look at her face and not at the white, menswear-style shirt, extensively unbuttoned, that she was wearing under a black leather jacket. I am inclined to imagine that my expression was not the most intelligent.

"So you told me on the phone that Nicoletta didn't want to get involved. Is that really how she put it?"

"Yes, that's what she said. She was pretty worked up."

"But why? What's she afraid of?"

"That I can't say. I figured it might not be a good idea to press her about it on the phone. It seemed to me that if I wanted to help you, my first job was to convince her to agree to meet with you. Then you could ask her everything directly, yourself."

"And was it her idea for you to be present?"

Before answering, Caterina brushed her hair off her forehead and tilted her head back slightly.

"She didn't ask, and I didn't suggest it. What I mean is, we talked, and I could tell that she was feeling uncomfortable, and the idea just kind of came to me that I should be there when you meet."

There was something about what Caterina was saying and the way she was saying it that I couldn't pin down, something I couldn't quite get into focus, that made me slightly uncomfortable. I felt as if something were out of place in the scene, but I couldn't identify what it was. As if the situation was eluding my control.

"So how did you leave things with her?"

"I told her we'd come down to Rome, that we'd all meet,

that you'd ask her a few questions, and that basically it wouldn't be much of a time commitment."

"Did she ask you what kind of questions I have?"

"I told her what you asked me, because I figured you'd ask her the same things."

Evidently, we'd have to do what she'd already decided and planned out. Almost without realizing it, I decided that I'd have to take care of making the reservations and buying the plane tickets myself. I certainly couldn't ask Pasquale, much less Maria Teresa, to do it. The very idea of the red-faced explanations I'd have to give struck me as intolerable. I decided to use a different travel agency than the one we usually went to, in order to avoid any questions. I was caught up in a whirl of paranoid scheming. Caterina broke into my thoughts.

"So, in the meantime, have you talked to anyone else? Have you uncovered anything?"

"Uncovered might not be exactly the right word. I'm checking out some ideas I have about the role that drugs might have played, though I can't say where that's leading."

"What do you mean, checking out some ideas?"

"Well, I'm a lawyer. I have some contacts, so I'm asking around a little bit."

"You mean you're talking to drug dealers?" asked Caterina, putting both hands on my desk and leaning toward me. I was about to tell her about Quintavalle, when it occurred to me that it might not be a good idea to go into too much detail.

"Like I said, I'm asking around, here and there, to see if anything interesting turns up."

Caterina stayed there for a few seconds, leaning against my desk, looking at me. I thought I saw a gleam in her eye, and I guessed that she was about to press for more information, and in that instant I understood that she had decided to use me. To discover what had happened to her friend, I told myself. That idea gave me an unusual sensation, which I tried to decipher but couldn't. Long seconds tiptoed past before she broke the silence.

"So what are we going to do? I don't have anything scheduled in the next few days, so as far as I'm concerned we can go to Rome tomorrow, if you want."

"I have an important hearing tomorrow that I can't miss. The day after tomorrow, though, we could go."

"How should we get there?"

"Well, I'd say it's best to fly, if we have to go and come back on the same day. We can fly up first thing in the morning, meet with Nicoletta, and then fly back in the evening—we can catch the last flight. Of course, I'll take care of the tickets and any other expenses."

"Well, we don't necessarily have to do the whole trip in one day. I'll call Nicoletta and ask her when we can arrange the meeting. Depending on when she's free, we can decide when to leave and whether we're going to stay overnight in Rome."

Her tone of voice was very calm and relaxed, the tone of someone who's just organizing a routine business trip. And yet the idea that we might have to stay overnight in Rome, together, took my breath away.

Caterina tried calling Nicoletta, but her phone must have been turned off, so she sent her a text message.

"If it's all right with you, as soon as Nicoletta gets back to me, I'll call you and let you know what she says, and then we can decide."

"But don't you have . . . somebody?" I realized that I was struggling to find the right words, and it made me feel suddenly old and somehow inadequate.

"What do you mean, a boyfriend, a guy?"

"Yes."

"Why do you ask?"

"I don't know, it just occurred to me, when I thought about the fact that we're planning a trip, that . . . well, it seemed . . ."

I realized that I was floundering. She noticed it, too, and did nothing to help me out of my difficulties. Quite the contrary. A smile came to her lips that at first glance might have seemed gentle and good-natured, but it really wasn't. Not at all. She lowered her voice imperceptibly.

"Are you thinking of trying to seduce me in Rome? Should I be worried?"

I staggered for a second, the way a boxer does when he incautiously lowers his gloves and a solid right hook catches him full in the face. I even felt a faint blush redden my cheeks, and I realized that after all was said and done, I was still the same incompetent fuck-up I had been thirty years earlier, in that supermarket.

"Why not? We'd be a storybook couple, you and me. In fact, I was thinking of getting a ring and asking you to marry me."

A very weak little routine, but I had to find some way of regaining my footing, and fast.

"I was asking because your boyfriend, if you have one, might not be that happy about you flying somewhere with another man, especially a man much older than you."

"I don't have a boyfriend."

"Ah. Why not?"

She leaned back in her chair and shrugged before answering.

"Well, relationships start and then they end. My last relationship ended a while ago, and for now I'm not looking for a replacement. At least not anything permanent. Let's just say that I'm on hiatus. Though of course that doesn't mean that I spend my evenings at home reading books in bed."

Then, as if she'd just remembered that she had something to do, she gripped both the chair arms and pushed herself to her feet.

"As soon as I hear from Nicoletta and we make an appointment for the day after tomorrow, I'll call you. That way you can make all the arrangements for our trip."

"Okay," I said, standing up myself and walking around my desk to escort her to the door.

I reached out to shake her hand and, with a perfectly timed move, she leaned toward me and gave me a kiss on the cheek. Delicate, innocent. So innocent that it made me shiver.

After she left, I tried to get back to work.

I wasn't very successful, and before I knew it I found myself following a distracting tangent of free—although thoroughly predictable—associations. I wondered which hotel I should choose, if it became necessary to spend the night in Rome. Obviously, I would reserve two separate rooms, that went without saying. Then I decided that—although I would of course act like a perfect gentleman, not like a dirty old man—it might even be fun to spend an evening with a pretty young woman. If my professional obligations happened to offer an evening's entertainment, that was hardly a crime. After all, she was no minor. Maybe I could take her to a nice restaurant, a place with a good selection of wines. That was hardly the same as jumping her bones. Trying to get her into bed hadn't even crossed my mind. "I'm not that kind of guy," I said out loud. I felt a tingling sensation in my legs as my nose quickly began to grow.

23.

The following morning, when I turned my phone back on, I found a message from Caterina. She'd spoken with Nicoletta and made an appointment with her for the following afternoon. So I wouldn't be able to reserve a round-trip flight for the same day; I'd have to arrange overnight accommodations. It was exactly what I expected, but I pretended—to myself, that is, a pretty easy audience as far as simple deceptions were concerned—to be moderately surprised at the news and at the consequences that it entailed.

Then I blocked any potential return of awareness by getting ready to leave my apartment. At eight o'clock Signore De Santis, my client in that morning's trial in Lecce, would be swinging by to pick me up.

Signore De Santis was a builder and developer and, as the phrase goes, he was a self-made man. He'd started working as an assistant bricklayer at age fourteen and, step by step—without letting annoying details like paying taxes, respecting safety regulations on the job site, or complying with city zoning plans and regulations get in the way of his climb to the top—he'd become a very wealthy businessman. He was short, slightly popeyed, with a beard dyed a ridiculous, incongruous black, a head of hair that had all the earmarks of a transplant, and a strong smell of cheap aftershave.

He had been charged—unjustly, he claimed—with building an illegal subdivision in a historic district, after bribing a number of city officials. His interpretation of his indictment was that it was clearly a conspiracy orchestrated by a corrupt ring of Communist magistrates.

My own interpretation was that he was about as innocent as Al Capone and that if I succeeded in winning an acquittal (which struck me as a pretty remote possibility), eventually I'd have to answer to a higher authority for it.

He had insisted on giving me a ride to Lecce, in his car, a Lexus that probably cost as much as a decent-size apartment and was nearly as big. It didn't take long for me to regret bitterly having accepted the offer. De Santis drove with all the caution and care of a Mumbai taxi driver, while blasting a succession of Italian pop hits from the seventies— the kind of stuff the U.S. could have used at Guantánamo to extract confessions from al-Qaeda hardliners.

We pulled onto the highway, and De Santis immediately accelerated to a cruising speed of one hundred five miles per hour. He took over the left-hand passing lane and would not give it up. If a car ahead of us failed to move out of his lane quickly enough, De Santis hit the horn—which sounded like a tugboat foghorn—and flicked his headlights so hard and fast that the car must have looked like an ambulance.

Hey, you psycho, slow it down. I don't want to die this young.

"Signore De Santis, why don't you take your foot off the pedal a little? We have plenty of time."

"I like going fast, Counselor. You're not scared, are you? This old bombshell can hit one hundred forty."

I'll take your word for it. Slow down, you old crackpot.

"I have two great passions in life," he said, and he slapped the steering wheel. "Fast cars and fast women. How old are you, Counselor?"

"Forty-five."

"Lucky man. I'm seventy. At your age, I was wild."

"What do you mean?"

"With women. I never let one get away. A waitress—I hit that. My secretary—I hit that. My friend's wife—I hit that. Once even a nun. I was—what's the word?—relentless."

You're still relentless, I thought to myself, thinking of the road still ahead and the fact that I would be spending at least the next four hours with him.

"It's not like I'm not getting any now. I'm still hitting it regularly, but when I was younger . . ."

That's a cleaned-up version of what he said. He was much more clinical, and he frequently gestured at his personal equipment. I nodded understandingly, with an idiotic, bland expression of tolerance painted on my face, while deep down I did my best to repress a vision of myself in my seventies with a dyed mustache, telling someone about how I still hit that.

"Are you married, Counselor?"

"No. I used to be, but not anymore."

"So you're a free man. Free and easy," he said.

At this point, I was afraid he'd ask me whether I, too, was relentless. Whether I hit it with, say, my cleaning woman. In my case, the cleaning woman in question was Signora Nennella, a stout woman who stood four feet eleven inches in her stocking feet and was in her mid-sixties, to say nothing of sagging breasts that were barely contained by her D-cup bra.

The whole scene was disturbing. I tried to find refuge in a Zen place in the recesses of my mind where I could filter out the disturbing stimuli from the outside world. I told myself that if I found my Zen place, it would all be over before I knew it.

De Santis noticed my silence and assumed it must be due to a health issue. Something that might lead me to consult a urologist.

"What, you have some kind of problem?"

"Problem?" I was thinking the time had come to be a little more selective in choosing my clients.

He turned to look at me, completely ignoring the fact that the highway was hurtling toward us at one hundred ten miles per hour now. He looked down at my lap and winked. The melodic guitar and sappy vocals of the Teppisti dei Sogni filled the interior of the car like a mist of maple syrup.

"So, you're okay down there?"

Pull over at the first rest area and let me out, you old psycho. After that, feel free to drive at top speed into a bridge or an oak tree, as long as you're careful not to involve innocent third parties.

That's not what I said.

"Just fine, thanks."

De Santis didn't seem to consider the answer satisfactory, so he kept up his questioning, pursuing the same line of inquiry.

"What about your prostate? You getting your prostate checked?"

"No, I'm not, to tell you the truth."

"Have a doctor look at it, I'll bet you anything he finds it's enlarged. If you ask me, you don't have it looked at because you're afraid of what they do. The urologist puts on a pair of latex gloves and then he takes his finger—"

"I know what a urologist does."

A few minutes of silence ensued. It seemed that our discussion of a visit to the urologist might have given my client pause. I hoped in vain that the silence would last until we reached Lecce. No such luck.

"Have you ever taken Viagra?"

"No."

"I have some on me at all times, even though my doctor tells me not to overdo it, because it can be bad for the heart. But I say, what better way to die than to have a heart attack right in the middle of a good lay."

And so it went, on and on, as we got to Lecce and entered the courtroom. Only when the trial actually got under-way was De Santis forced to stop talking. We listened to the testimony of the prosecution witnesses. We listened to the analysis of the prosecutor's expert witness, and then the court adjourned for another session to hear the testi-mony of the defense witnesses. By that point, if I had ever had any doubts, I was quite certain that my client would be found guilty. For the sake of my own mental health—we still had the whole return trip ahead of us—I decided that the better part of valor would be to keep that information to myself and not share it with the man who always hit it.

When we finally got back to Bari that afternoon, I asked him to drop me off in front of a travel agency across town from my office. This wasn't the agency our law firm nor-mally employed. I bought two round-trip tickets to Rome and I reserved two rooms in a hotel near Piazza del Popolo. I explained to the agent—and I'm pretty sure she could not have cared less—that I was going on a business trip with a colleague. It finally dawned on me that I was behaving as furtively as a criminal about to go on the lam.

As I was leaving the travel agency, Quintavalle called me.

"Counselor."

"Damiano, any news?"

"I have some information that might be useful to you."

"I'm all ears."

After a couple of seconds of silence, I realized how stupid I had been. I thought back on all the times that I had laughed at the stupidity of people who said things on the phone they shouldn't have, only to wind up in handcuffs.

"Or maybe we should meet to discuss it in person?"

"Shall I come to your office?"

"I'm on the street, over near Corso Sonnino. If it's convenient to you, and you're not too far away, maybe you could swing by and meet me in a café."

"I'm on my Vespa. How about we meet in ten minutes at the Riviera?"

"Okay."

24.

It only took me a few minutes to get to the Bar Riviera, which was virtually empty at that hour of the afternoon. I went upstairs to the terrace and took a table with an unbroken view of the Adriatic Sea. This was exactly where I used to sit when I was in college. I'd come here with my friends and spend endless, crazy, wonderful afternoons talking.

One of those afternoons in particular surfaced from my memory. We had just finished a seminar in political economics, and after wandering around town for half an hour we ended up at the Riviera. I'm pretty sure that, as usual, we started off talking about girls. Somehow, I'm not sure how, we wandered from that topic to characters from novels—with whom did we identify with most, who would we have most liked to be. Andrea said Athos, Emilio said Philip Marlowe, I said Captain Fracasse, and, lastly, Nicola said that he wanted to be Athos, too. There ensued a lively exchange of views as to which of the two—Andrea or Nicola—had a better claim to play the role of the Comte de la Fère. Andrea pointed out that Nicola—who made excessive use of cologne and aftershave—might realistically hope to be Aramis, but if the truth be told he really was perfect for the role of Milady. This piece of advice raised the volume of the debate, and Nicola allowed that expert testimony as to his personal virility could be provided, in considerable detail, by either Andrea's mother or his sister.

If I half-closed my eyes I could still hear our voices, rendered up intact and authentic from the archives of my memory. Emilio's deep tenor, Nicola's nasal voice, the quick cadence of Andrea's, occasionally rising to a shrill pitch, and my own voice—which I have never been able to describe. All those voices were there, hovering in the air of that big empty room, reminding me that ghosts exist and wander among us.

That memory could have triggered a bout of sadness. Instead, it gave me a faint, inexplicable sense of excitement, as if the past were suddenly no longer past and instead formed a sort of extended present, simultaneous and welcoming. Sitting in that café, waiting to meet with a coke dealer, I felt for an instant as if my mind had embraced the synchronic mystery of time and memory.

Then the coke dealer arrived, and that odd enchantment vanished as suddenly as it had arrived.

We ordered two cappuccinos and sat silently until the waiter brought them to our table and vanished down the stairs, leaving us alone. Only then did we begin talking.

"So, Damiano?"

"I asked around, and I may have found something."

"Tell me about it."

"There's a young gay guy I know who sells coke in clubs and discos. Actually, he's sort of a hybrid dealer/user: Basically, he sells coke to pay for his personal use. He told me that he does know a certain Michele who often has plenty of cocaine. He said that sometimes he bought small amounts from him, and that other times he sold coke to Michele. This is fairly normal between small-time dealers: They go back and forth—when one guy has it he'll sell to the other, and vice versa."

"Why do you think this could be the Michele we're looking for?"

"You told me your Michele is handsome, right?"

"That's what they tell me."

"My gay friend said this Michele was a prime hunk of meat. His exact words."

"Let me guess: The problem is that he doesn't know his last name."

"No, he doesn't, but if we could just show him a picture . . ."

Right. If we could just show him a picture. I had to stop wasting time and find a way to get that picture. I'd have to call Fornelli. Or maybe, I thought, maybe Caterina could get me a photograph of Michele. That reminded me that I needed to call her to arrange our departure the following day.

"Counselor?"

"Yes?"

"Can I be sure that this guy isn't going to get in trouble because of the things he's telling me?"

"You mean this gay friend of yours?"

"Well, he's not actually a friend, but yes, I mean him."

"Don't worry, Damiano. The only thing I care about is finding out what happened to Manuela. You and I never even had this conversation, as far as I'm concerned."

Quintavalle seemed relieved.

"Sorry to ask, but—"

I raised my hand to stop him. Of course I understood his concern perfectly. For someone in his line of work, just asking questions could be dangerous. I thanked him, told him that I'd try to find a picture of Michele and I'd call him when I did. Then we both left the bar and went back to our respective—more and less legitimate—jobs.

I called Caterina on my way back to my office. I told her that I'd reserved an 11:00 A.M. flight to Rome the next morning and that I'd come by and pick her up on my way to the airport at 9:30. I asked her if her address was still the same as the one listed in the transcripts of the interviews with the Carabinieri; she said, yes, that was the address, but to make things easier we could just meet in front of the Teatro Petruzzelli. I felt an unmistakable wave of relief at the idea that I wouldn't have to go to her house and risk that her mother or father—who were probably more or less the same age I was—might see me, realize that their daughter was consorting with a middle-aged cradle robber, and decide to take drastic steps, possibly involving pipe wrenches or baseball bats or other instruments of dissuasion.

I remembered the picture of Michele just as I was about to hang up.

"Oh, Caterina?"

"Yes?"

"You wouldn't happen to have a picture of Michele Cantalupi, would you?"

She didn't answer right away, and if silence can have an intonation, her silence was followed by a big question mark.

"What do you need it for?" she said at last.

"I need to show it to someone. Anyway, we'd better not talk about it on the phone. I'll explain tomorrow. You think you can find one?"

"I'll take a look, but I don't think I have one."

"Okay, see you tomorrow, then."

"See you tomorrow."

25.

When I got back to my office, tasks and meetings oozed around me like some kind of amoeba out of a sci-fi film. This slimy, gelatinous creature held me captive until late that evening, when it finally decided I wasn't particularly digestible and expelled me, in the physical and moral state of a half-digested zombie. Moreover, since the trip to Rome the following day wasn't part of my planned workflow, I had to arrange for substitutes to attend my hearings and I had to reschedule my appointments.

When I got home, I was exhausted. I took a few half-hearted jabs at Mister Bag, just to reassure him that we were still friends, but I couldn't bring myself to do a proper workout. I wasted more water than I should have on a long hot shower, with the bathroom door wide open and Bruce Springsteen playing at full volume. At eleven o'clock I was back on the street, riding my bike. I was wearing my old black leather jacket, faded jeans, and a pair of track shoes. All in all, I looked exactly like what I was: a middle-aged man, well into his forties, dressing like a kid, as if that allowed him to thumb his nose at time.

I told myself that I knew perfectly well what I was doing, and that I didn't care a bit. Even if I understood the mechanism behind it, it still put me in a good mood.

When I walked into the Chelsea Hotel, I recognized a number of regular customers. They recognized me, too, and a few even nodded hello. I was that strange guy who wasn't gay but still dropped by frequently to eat, drink, and listen to music. There was a feeling of familiarity that I really liked, as if that place had somehow become partly mine. A sense of safety.

I looked around, but Nadia wasn't there. I was disappointed. I thought of asking the bartender where she was, but her expression—as welcoming as a punch in the nose—dissuaded me.

So I sat down and ordered a plate of orecchiette with wild mushrooms and a glass of Primitivo. I managed to focus only on the food and the wine.

Nadia arrived just as I was leaving.

"Ciao, Guido," she said cheerfully. "I was out at a friend's birthday party. She's a sweet girl, but she has the most amazingly dull friends you can imagine. The catering was ghastly: baked pasta in aluminum foil trays. I swear. One of your fellow lawyers, a guy with a gut and dandruff, tried to get my number. You're not already leaving, are you?"

"Well, yes, it's past midnight." I realized there was a hint of resentment in my voice, as if the fact that she hadn't been there when I arrived was a deliberate act of rudeness on her part. Fortunately, she didn't seem to notice.

"Of course, I always forget that other people have jobs and have to get up in the morning."

"Actually, I can sleep in a little bit tomorrow morning. I'm going to Rome for work, and the flight is at eleven."

"Then stay a little longer. I still have to recover from that party. I'll let you taste something I think you'll like."

"Another type of absinthe?"

"Something better. Give me a minute to see if they need my help. I doubt they do. Then I'll come sit with you."

Five minutes later she was at my table with two glasses and a bottle with an attractive, old-fashioned-looking label.

"You've eaten, right? This isn't something you want to drink on an empty stomach."

"What is it?"

"It's an Irish whiskey called The Knot. Try it and tell me what you think."

It didn't taste like a whiskey. It had the scent of rum and it reminded me of Southern Comfort, without being sticky sweet.

"It's good," I said, after draining my glass. She filled it again and poured herself a generous serving as well.

"Sometimes I think I'm getting a little too fond of this stuff."

"Sometimes I think the same thing myself."

"Okay, we'll hash out that problem some other evening. Agreed?"

"Agreed."

"So, you're going to Rome tomorrow. I've got to get there one of these days. See a couple of old girlfriends and spend a little money."

I was trying to figure out how I could bring up the topic of my investigation and the questions I wanted to ask her, but I couldn't seem to find the words. I pretended to focus on my whiskey, admiring its pale golden hue, but I must have seemed about as authentic as Monopoly money.

"Is there something you wanted to ask me?" she inquired, sparing me at least a little effort. For a moment I wondered if I should tell her a lie, any old lie; I told myself that would be a terrible idea.

"Well, actually, yes, there is."

"Then go ahead and ask."

I told her, as concisely as I could, the whole story, leaving out any details that weren't, in my opinion, absolutely essential. Among the nonessential details I skipped were the details of my trip to Rome. For instance, the fact that I wouldn't be going alone.

But when the time came to ask the question I'd come to ask, I couldn't keep myself from looking around warily.

"And so I was wondering if any of the regulars here at the Chelsea might have anything to do with that world— the world of cocaine and drug dealing, I mean. Let me be clear: I don't have any specific ideas, no suspicions. When my client told me that he'd found out some information from a gay friend of his, it occurred to me that I might ask you and see if anything useful came up."

"I'm sorry, I really don't know what to tell you. If any of my customers uses or buys or sells cocaine—and I'd guess the likelihood is high—I don't know anything about it. Obviously, nobody snorts it here—they'd have some explaining to do to Hans and Pino—and we haven't noticed any suspicious activity, nothing to indicate that anyone is using this place as a base to sell coke. I don't know anything about drugs, these days."

"Why do you say 'these days'?"

"Well, in the first half of my life—in my other life— white powder made an occasional appearance. A number of my clients liked coke, and I knew a few people who sold it, though I never used it, much less bought it. Anyway, I'm talking about a long time ago, years ago. It's a world I had a few brushes with, but it's light-years away now. I'm sorry I can't help you."

"Don't worry. It was a stupid idea, the kind of idea only an amateur investigator would come up with."

We went on chatting while the bar slowly emptied out. Then the staff went home, one by one, and in the end we were sitting there alone, with most of the lights turned off, and the music still playing, turned down low. She went and fetched Pino/Baskerville from the car and let him come in and sit with us. He seemed to remember me, because he came over and let me pet him and then stretched out on the floor under our table.

"I like to sit here, after the place shuts down, with Pino. The bar changes—it becomes a different place. And then I can smoke because when it's closed it's no longer a public place. It's my place, and I can do what I want. Pino doesn't mind cigarette smoke, or at least he never objects."

"Can I say something incredibly stupid?"

"Be my guest."

"It seems incredible to me that until just a couple of years ago it was okay to smoke in bars and restaurants. I have a hard time even picturing it. I have to make an effort to remember that there were cigarettes, and that some places you walked into the air was practically unbreathable. It's as if the regulations against smoking interfered with my memories and manipulated them somehow."

"I'm not sure I follow you on that last part."

"Let me give you an example. This afternoon, I was sitting in a bar waiting for someone. While I was sitting there by myself, I thought back and remembered a time, years and years ago, when I was sitting in that same bar with my friends. It was a memory from my time in college, and for sure at least three people who were there with me were smokers. I'm certain on that afternoon we were smoking.

And yet the scene, as I saw it in my mind, had no cigarettes. It's as if the prohibition of smoking in public places had a sort of retroactive effect on my memories."

"A retroactive effect on your memories. You say some odd things. Nice, though. Why did you happen to remember that particular afternoon?"

"We were talking about novels and characters. Each one of us named the character we identified with most."

"Who did you pick?"

"Captain Fracasse."

"Would you say the same thing today?"

"No, I doubt it. Captain Fracasse is still one of my favorite characters from literature, but if I had to play the same game today, I'd pick someone else."

"Who would you pick?"

"Charlie Brown."

She burst into laughter, a short, sharp explosion.

"Come on, really."

"Charlie Brown, really."

She stopped laughing and looked me in the eye to see if I was joking or not. She decided I wasn't joking.

"But you said characters from literature."

"You know what Umberto Eco said about Charles Schulz?"

"What?"

"I'm not sure if I remember it word for word, but I'm pretty sure this was the concept: 'If poetry means the capacity of carrying tenderness, pity, and wickedness to moments of extreme transparence, as if things passed through a light and there were no telling any more what substance they are made of, then Schulz is a poet.' And I would add to that: Schulz was a genius."

"Why Charlie Brown, though?"

"Well, as you probably know, Charlie Brown is a proto-typical loser. His baseball team always loses. The other kids make fun of him, and he's hopelessly in love with a little girl—the Little Red-Haired Girl—even though he's never been able to talk to her. She doesn't even know Charlie Brown exists."

"But what does a loser like Charlie Brown have to do with someone like you? I don't get it."

"Wait, let me finish. Have you read the one where he goes to summer camp with a paper bag over his head, with holes cut out for his eyes?"

"No."

"When Charlie Brown puts the paper bag with eye holes over his head, suddenly, inexplicably, he becomes popular. All the kids at the camp go to him for advice and help. He becomes another person. I haven't read many books that I identified with so intensely as that series of *Peanuts* comic strips. The Charlie Brown who became someone only when his head was covered with a paper bag is me."

She sat in silence, looking at me. Underneath the table the dog wriggled on his back, making low sounds of pleasure like a giant purring cat. Keith Carradine was softly singing "I'm Easy."

"I like to read, but it's always been easier for me to iden-tify with characters in movies. I think I like movies more than anything in the world. I like everything about going to the movies, and the moment I like best is when they turn off the house lights and the film is about to begin."

She was right. It's a perfect moment when the lights go down and everything's about to begin. For a little while neither of us spoke. I let my eyes roam over the film posters hanging on the walls.

"Where do you get these posters?" I asked after a couple of minutes.

"They're almost all originals. Only a few of the oldest ones are reproductions. I started collecting them years ago, and back then to find them you had to go around to junk shops, old film distribution companies, and bookstores that specialized in cinema. Now you can find anything you want on the Internet. But I still prefer going around to dusty old shops to look for posters."

There were posters from every era: from *La Dolce Vita* to *Manhattan*, from *Cinema Paradiso* to *Dead Poets Society*, with a picture of Robin Williams being lifted in triumph by his students, against a yellow background that looked like embossed gold.

"Call me corny, but at the end of that movie, when the boys climb onto their desks, it was all I could do not to cry," I said, pointing at the poster.

"I'm way cornier than you, then. I sobbed like a little girl. And then, when I saw the movie again, I cried just as hard as the first time."

"There's a line I always remember from that movie—"

"O Captain! My Captain!"

"'Our fearful trip is done.' But that's not the part I meant."

"Which one, then?"

"Something that Robin Williams as Keating says to his students: 'No matter what anybody tells you, words and ideas can change the world.'"

"It would be nice if it were true."

"Maybe it is true."

She gave me a serious look, the look of someone hearing something she liked.

"I like movies that make you cry."

"So do I."

"I can name more than you can."

"Want to have a contest?"

"Sure. You go first."

"*Il Postino* with Massimo Troisi and Philippe Noiret."

"Benigni's *Life Is Beautiful*. My favorite scene is the one that echoes Chaplin's *The Great Dictator*."

"If we're talking about Chaplin, then *City Lights*."

"*Beau Geste*."

"With Gary Cooper?"

"Yes."

"You're right. It's the classic melodrama."

"Now it's your turn."

"*Chariots of Fire*. My favorite scene is when the trainer, Mussabini, can't bring himself to go to the stadium. He looks out his hotel window, sees the Union Jack going up the flagpole, and realizes that Abrahams has won. He starts crying with joy and punches his fist through his straw hat."

"*Million Dollar Baby*. Clint Eastwood is a genius. Plus, he's definitely my type."

"*Braveheart* with Mel Gibson. The execution scene. He's on the scaffold, and he yells 'Freedom!' while the executioner stands by with his axe at the ready. Just a few seconds before he's executed, he sees the woman he loves moving through the crowd. She looks at him from a distance and smiles at him, and he smiles back, just as the axe is falling."

"*Ghost*."

"*Gladiator*."

"*The Green Mile*."

"*Schindler's List.*"

"You're rolling out the big guns. *The Way We Were*, the whole movie, especially the final scene, and the soundtrack."

"*Cinema Paradiso.* The scene with the reel of censored kisses."

"It's true, it's wonderful. I think that movie won an Oscar for that scene alone. It's just the kind of thing Americans go crazy over. What about the final scene of *Thelma and Louise?*"

"Spectacular. There's a line in that movie that I've always dreamed of getting a chance to say, someday."

"What line?"

"Harvey Keitel is questioning Brad Pitt, and to get him to talk, he says: 'Son, your misery is gonna be my goddamn mission in life.' Now that's the way you threaten someone."

"It's your turn."

"*Jesus Christ Superstar.* Mary Magdalene singing by Jesus' tent while he's sleeping."

"'I Don't Know How to Love Him.'" As she said the title of the song sung by Mary Magdalene, the prostitute who was in love with Jesus Christ, I realized I'd said the wrong thing.

She didn't notice. Or rather, she noticed so openly that it didn't matter.

"As you can imagine, I really identify with that scene."

At that point, inevitably, there was a pause.

"Okay, fine, I identified with Mary Magdalene. What about you?" Nadia said at last.

"I actually identified with both of the protagonists of *Philadelphia*, Denzel Washington and Tom Hanks."

"My God, that final sequence with the Super 8 home movies of Tom Hanks's character, Andrew, as a child! I remember it as if I were watching the movie right now. The swing, the children playing on the beach, the mother dressed in those sixties clothes with a scarf on her head, the dog, Andrew dressed as a cowboy . . . the music by Neil Young. It's so heartbreaking."

"The final scene is the most moving one, but my favorite is during the trial, when Denzel Washington does that direct examination of Tom Hanks."

"Why is that your favorite scene?"

"If you like, I can recite it for you, and then you'll see why."

"Recite it for me? You know the whole scene by heart?"

"More or less."

"I don't believe it."

"You remember the story, of course?"

She looked at me as if she were a Grand Slam tennis champion and I'd just asked whether she remembered how to hit a backhand. I raised both hands in a sign of surrender.

"Okay, okay, forgive me. So it's a crucial point in the trial, and Denzel Washington is questioning Tom Hanks, who plays a lawyer named Andrew. He's in the advanced stages of the disease and he doesn't have long to live:

"Are you a good lawyer, Andrew?

"I'm an excellent lawyer.

"What makes you an excellent lawyer?

"I love the law. I know the law. I excel at practicing.

"What do you love about the law, Andrew?

"I . . . many things. What do I love the most about the law?

"Yes.

"It's that every now and again, not often, but occasionally, you get to be a part of justice being done. That really is quite a thrill when that happens.

"Thank you, Andrew."

After a few instants of breathless silence, Nadia started clapping slowly.

I hadn't played that game in a long time. Years and years ago, I'd had a strange facility for repeating from memory the words of movies, songs, books, and poems. Then, for a number of reasons, I began to find it increasingly difficult.

There is nothing that evokes the disquieting idea of the passage of time as much as observing the deterioration of an ability that you had always taken for granted. It's more or less the same thing that happens in the gym. You're sparring with someone and you see—to give an example—that he's leading with a straight right punch. You know exactly what you need to do in this case: duck, feint, straighten up, and hit back, all in a single, fluid movement. Your brain issues the order to your back and your arms, but the order arrives just a fraction of a second too late, the punch hits you, and your counter-attack is slow—it seems to you—and slightly off-kilter. It's not a reassuring sensation.

The fact that the words of the movie came back to me that night so easily, so clearly, made me feel good. As if I'd returned to something fundamental about myself.

"How do you do it?"

"I don't know. I've always had a gift for learning and reciting things that I liked—and I really liked that exchange— but recently I thought that I'd lost that ability. I'm as amazed as you are that I was able to pull it off. Though, of course, it might be more impressive if we checked the actual words of the movie to find out if I got it right."

She looked at me, and it seemed as if she were searching for the right words. Or the right question.

"Do you like it so much because you see yourself in it?"

"I think so. It's not something I talk about much. I became a lawyer pretty much by accident. I always thought of this work as something I settled for. I was a little ashamed of it. And it's always been hard for me to admit—to myself, much less to others—how much I've ended up liking it."

She flashed me a beautiful smile, the kind that tells you the other person really is listening to what you're saying. She didn't speak; she didn't need to. She was telling me to go on.

"The truth is that I've always looked upon my work with an element of condescension. In college I enrolled in law because I didn't know what else to do. I've always had an ideological and stereotypical vision of the work that lawyers do, and I've almost always denied myself the right to be proud of being one. I never had the moral courage to revise my slightly childish idea of practicing law being an ethically unacceptable profession. The work of shysters and hair-splitters."

"Isn't that true, though? I've never had a good experience with any lawyer except you."

"Sure, it's often true. The profession is full of scoundrels, shysters, virtual illiterates, and even a few genuine criminals. For that matter, the same is true of the magistrate, or any other profession you care to name. The issue, though, isn't whether there are bad or incompetent people practicing law, or whether the work tends to exaggerate some of the worst qualities of the human mind, and of human beings in general."

"So what is the issue?"

"The issue is that this is a profession in which you can be a free man. It's a line of work that can offer you certain things . . . well, I don't think there are many things in life that rank with the feeling of winning an acquittal for a defendant you know is innocent, especially when he was facing hard time or even life in prison."

"But I wasn't innocent," Nadia said with a smile.

True. Technically, she hadn't been innocent. She had committed the crime of abetting prostitution, that is, she had introduced pretty girls to wealthy men and had received a substantial fee for her intermediation. No one had been forced into it; no one had been blackmailed; no one had been hurt. The idea that we send people to prison—that we deprive people of their freedom—for actions of this sort becomes increasingly inconceivable to me the more time passes.

"It would have been an injustice if you had been convicted. You never harmed anyone."

I was about to say too much. Something along the lines of, if anything, you did good. Which, when you're talking to a former prostitute, a madam who recruited and employed other prostitutes, is not exactly the right thing to say. Those words left the neurons of my brain, hurtled at top speed through my nervous system, and were teetering on my lips, about to spring into the air, when I managed to snatch them back.

"You're a good lawyer."

It was hard to tell from her intonation whether it was a question or a statement. It seemed to hover halfway between the two.

"Is that a question?"

"It is and it isn't. That is, I know you're a good lawyer. I remember when the judge emerged from his chambers into the courtroom and read out the verdict. Never in my life, would I have believed that with the things they had on those wiretaps I could have been acquitted."

"The wiretaps were inadmissible as evidence. There had been a procedural flaw that—"

"Yes, I know, I know, I remember word for word what you said in your summation. But at the time, I just assumed you were posturing to prove you were earning your fee. I was positive they would find me guilty, and I was completely astonished when I was acquitted instead. It was an unexpected gift."

"Well, yeah, that went well, it's true."

"And you want to know something?"

"What?"

"I was ready to throw my arms around you, at that moment. I was about to do it, and then I decided it would be crazy and I would have embarrassed you. So I did nothing."

Then, after a pause: "Anyway, it was a statement, but it was also a question."

"What?"

"Do you consider yourself a good lawyer?"

I didn't answer right away. I took a deep breath.

"Sometimes. Sometimes it seems to me that the words and the concepts and my own actions all fit together perfectly. Compared to most other lawyers, I think I'm pretty good. But if I measure myself against some abstract standard of good practice of law, then I see things very differently. I'm disorganized. I'm inefficient. Often I don't feel like working, and I rely upon improvisation far more frequently and extensively than wisdom or caution would recommend.

"I imagine a good lawyer is one who is capable of great self-discipline. When a good lawyer needs to write something—an appeal, for example, or a brief—he sits down at his desk and doesn't get up again until he is done. What I do is I sit down and I write a few sentences. Then I decide that I've completely taken the wrong tack, and I start getting upset. So then I do something else, obviously less important and less urgent. Sometimes I even leave the office, go to a bookstore, and buy a book. Then I come back and sit at my desk and write, but without much interest or determination. And then finally, when the pressure is on, I focus on the task at hand and I write and I do it. Every time I do it though, I have the impression I've just dashed it off at the last minute, that I've cheated my client. In general, I feel I'm pulling the wool over the eyes of the world."

Nadia scratched the side of her head. She looked at me as if I were a deeply strange individual. Then she shrugged.

"You're crazy. I can't think of any other way to put it."

It wasn't a question. It was a statement that shut down discussion of the topic. I was crazy, and there was no other way to put it.

"And what are you good at?"

I don't know why I kept putting my foot in my mouth. Even I know better than to ask a woman who has been a porn star and a prostitute what special talents she possesses.

"I really would like to be good at something. Let's just say I'm still looking. I know how to sketch and I know how to paint, too, but I wouldn't say I'm really good at either. I know how to sing. I have a good voice and a good ear, though I can't really belt it out. But when I hear a song, I can reproduce it immediately, either by singing it or playing it on a keyboard. I have a great ear, and I've let it go to waste." She experienced a visible twinge of self-pity but suppressed it immediately.

"And I'm good at listening to people. Everyone says so."

"Yeah, you told me you had clients who came mostly to talk with you. They wanted to be able to tell you about themselves without feeling judged."

"Exactly. If you pay someone for her time, you don't have to worry about your performance. When you talk or when you fuck. I had one client who was a stunningly handsome man, about fifty—wealthy, successful, and powerful. He could have had all the women he wanted, for free, and instead he came to see me, to pay me money."

"Because when he was with you, he was free of anxiety."

"He was free of anxiety, that's right. Since he was paying me, he didn't have to worry about whether his performance was up to expectations, in terms of both conversation and sex. He wasn't afraid to be himself."

She paused, smiling, then continued.

"We might say he could take the paper bag off his head."

Those words hung in the air, dissolving slowly into a fine, drifting dust.

Our glasses were empty and it was very late.

"Shall we drink one last glass and then go home and get some sleep?"

I nodded slowly, my vision slightly blurred. She filled two glasses but didn't hand me mine. She kept both on the table in front of her, as if there were a ritual to be completed, before we could drink.

"You know something?"

"What?"

"I notice that when I talk to you I try to choose my words carefully."

"What do you mean?"

"It's as if I want to sound intelligent. As if I'm trying to choose the right words, so I say something smart."

I didn't reply. All the answers that came to my mind were—in fact—unintelligent. So I said nothing.

"I noticed that because I was sitting here and trying to think of a clever, original toast, but I couldn't."

I took my glass and touched it against hers, which still sat on the table.

"Let's forget about words," I said.

After a moment's hesitation, she picked up her glass and raised it while looking at me with a shy smile. Then, at last, we both drank.

From the darkness outside came the muffled, muddled sounds of a moment out of time.

26.

The next morning, I slept a little later than usual. Yet when I woke up, I could still feel the whiskey from the night before coursing through me. To exorcise the remaining fumes, I decided to have an extra healthy breakfast of yogurt and cereal with my usual big cup of coffee. I broke the metal band of pain around my forehead with an aspirin, took a shower, shaved, brushed my teeth a little too vigorously, threw some clothes into an overnight bag, said good-bye to Mister Bag, doing my best to ignore the quizzical look he gave me, and went to get my car.

I showed up at our agreed-upon location a few minutes late. Caterina was there, waiting. We were dressed identically. Jeans, dark-blue blazers, white shirts. Even our luggage was similar. We seemed to be wearing a uniform. I wondered if that would make us more or less conspicuous at the airport.

"Cool car," she said, after fastening her seat belt. We began heading north toward the airport.

"I hardly ever drive it. It's always in the garage. I walk everywhere, or ride my bike."

"That's a shame. When we get back from Rome, you'll have to take me somewhere fun and let me drive."

"What time is our appointment with Nicoletta?"

"I'm supposed to call her when we get to Rome. By the way, do you have anywhere to stay tonight?"

"I reserved two rooms in a hotel near Piazza del Popolo."

"Then we'll have to take a taxi to Nicoletta's apartment. She lives over by Via Ostiense."

She paused, then said, "Why did you reserve two rooms? You could have saved some money and just reserved one room. Are you afraid to be alone with me?"

We had just turned onto the highway, and the traffic was heavy, but I couldn't keep from turning to look at her. She burst into laughter.

"Come on, don't make that face. I was just kidding."

I tried to think of a witticism to defuse the situation, but I couldn't come up with anything. So I concentrated on driving. There was a huge semi right ahead of me, in the right lane. I pulled out to pass the truck when it veered sharply left into the passing lane to pass yet another truck ahead of it, cutting me off. I stomped on the brakes and hit the horn hard. Caterina screamed. I glanced into my rearview mirror, hoping I wouldn't see someone chatting on their cell phone while coming up fast behind me. I managed to avoid hitting the behemoth in front of us by a few inches, but it was so close that I felt the terrifying virtual impact of the accident I'd been sure was coming.

When the huge truck pulled back into the right lane I accelerated and passed it. Caterina lowered her window and gave the driver the finger, holding her hand out until distance must have made it completely invisible. As a rule, I'm opposed to this method of manifesting one's dissent, especially when the guy driving the other vehicle easily weighs over two hundred pounds. But in this case, his driving had been so insanely homicidal that I couldn't really blame Caterina. In fact, I almost did the same.

"What an asshole. I hate those fucking trucks. The drivers would kill you as soon as look at you," she said.

I nodded, waiting for the adrenaline surging through me to ebb. As often happens in these cases, an idiotic thought had come to mind. If we had been involved in an accident and the police had come, they would have discovered that I was about to fly to Rome with a twenty-three-year-old girl, unbeknownst to anyone. They would have assumed questionable intentions. If I had died in the crash, I would have been unable to tell anyone about the real reasons for that trip, and—in the world's recollections of me—my death would forever be linked with a tawdry trip with a young woman more than twenty years my junior.

That demented thought brought up an old memory from years earlier.

One of my friends from the eighties and nineties was getting married. He was the first of our group to tie the knot, so we decided to organize a big bachelor party for him. Since it was our first bachelor party, we had no idea how squalid and unseemly the whole business is. Somebody said we should get some hookers or at least some strippers, or it wouldn't really be a bachelor party worth holding. All—or nearly all—of us agreed, but it turned out that none of us had the contacts, the knowledge, or even the self-confidence to contact hookers or strippers. After further consultation, we changed plans. We'd get some porn films and show them at the party. It was much easier to get porn flicks—and much less awkward. Each of the organizers managed to get at least one videotape. For reasons that now elude me, I was appointed to transport the batch of pornography to the party location.

I was driving alone in the dark to the restaurant out in the country where the party was going to be held, and it suddenly dawned on me that if I was involved in a crash, I would be found dead in a car full of videocassettes with titles like *Clockwork Orgy*, *Ejacula*, *The Sexorcist*, *Edward Penishands*, *Breast Side Story*, *Free My Willy*, and *Sperminator*.

I realize that I may give the impression of being completely mentally unbalanced, but I had a sudden powerful urge—that I was barely able to resist—to toss out all the porn tapes so it wouldn't happen. I imagined my mother and father learning in one fell swoop not only that their son was dead, but that he'd been a professional pervert. I imagined my girlfriend— who would become my wife, and later my ex-wife—learning in a single tragic moment that she had loved a compulsive porn addict. I wouldn't even be able to apologize, as I'd be dead. The best I could hope for was to end up in purgatory. From there, I'd be forced to watch their suffering, yet unable to do anything to alleviate it.

I swear, every one of these stupid thoughts went through my mind. In the end, I didn't throw all the porn movies into a ditch, but I did drive the whole way to the restaurant with the speed and caution you might expect from an eighty-year-old nun.

We got to the airport, made it through check-in and security, and found ourselves at the gate with plenty of time to spare. There was no place to hide, so I started to look around for familiar faces, especially fellow practitioners of the law, who might notice me traveling with a girl half my age and turn it into a prize piece of gossip.

I figured I could reduce the risk by strolling around to look at the shops by myself. Caterina remained seated near the gate, listening to music on her iPod, with an expression that looked like a vacant gaze into a deep void.

I drank an espresso I didn't really need. With exaggerated interest I examined all the articles in a leather goods store. I bought a couple of newspapers. Finally, I heard the announcement that our flight was boarding, and I walked back unhurriedly.

Caterina was where I had left her, and her expression remained unchanged. When she saw me, though, she smiled, removed her earbuds, and told me to sit down next to her.

"The flight is boarding," I said, remaining on my feet and picking up my overnight bag.

"Why should we stand in line and wait with everyone else? Let everyone else get seated, and we can just be the last to board."

No thanks. My natural anxiety keeps me from doing anything so perfectly rational. I prefer to stand in line, for fifteen minutes or even more, ready to catch and scold disapprovingly anyone who tries to slip ahead of me. Lest all the seats fill up, for fear the plane might leave without me.

That's not what I said, though. I sat down and started leafing through one of the newspapers I'd bought. After a couple of minutes, during which time the line of passengers boarding had not budged an inch, Caterina tapped me on the shoulder. I looked over.

"Do you like hip-hop?"

As she said it, she plucked one of the earbuds from her ear and handed it to me, leaning her head very close to mine. I put the earbud next to my ear, so that my cheek was almost grazing hers. Then the music exploded. It took me about ten seconds to recognize it.

"It's Mike Patton doing 'We're Not Alone,' if I'm not mistaken."

She looked at me with an expression of genuine astonishment. The idea that I might know that music, and in fact that song, clearly didn't fit into her worldview. She was about to say something when someone nearby called my name.

"Guerrieri!"

I looked up and saw, right in front of me—make that right in front of us—the uniform of a policeman, and above that uniform, the face of a man who knew me but whose name I couldn't conjure up.

I awkwardly got the earbud out of my ear and stood up, grasping the proffered hand and shaking it.

"Are you going to Rome, Counselor?" he asked, looking at Caterina, who had remained seated.

"Yes, apparently they're boarding the plane now," I said in the most nonchalant tone of voice I could muster, as I wondered whether I should introduce Caterina and, if so, how I should introduce her. I couldn't think of a good solution. What could I say? Let me introduce my daughter? Let me introduce my colleague? Let me introduce my latest steamy affair?

"I'm working here at the airport now. I'm with the border police. I left the judicial police. I was exhausted. You can't work like that your whole life," said the policeman, continuing to look over at Caterina, who just kept listening to her music and ignoring him, me, and everything that was happening around her.

"That was a wise decision," I said, struggling to remember the policeman's name, but without success.

"Are you traveling for business, Counselor?"

Maybe you should mind your own fucking business, friend. It's great that we said hello. It's wonderful that we had a short, polite chat. I'm delighted that you updated me on the latest developments in your career, unasked I might point out, and okay, I can see you eyeing Caterina as if you wanted to have sex with her right here in the airport, but now do you think you could get the hell out of here? Please?

That's not what I said, however. I told him that, yes, in fact, I was going to Rome on business, and I hoped he would excuse me, but it was time to get in line. Otherwise I might not find room to stow my bag; it looked like this flight was going to be pretty full. I was happy to have run into him, congratulations on his new job, best of luck. I turned and walked over to the boarding line. Unhurriedly, with a smile, Caterina joined me.

27.

The plane was taxiing onto the runway and Caterina finally was obliged to turn off her iPod.

"How do you know about Mike Patton?"

"Why, is that confidential information?"

"Come on, you know what I mean."

"You mean I'm too old to know about that kind of music."

"No, but you have to admit it's not the kind of music people your age listen to. It's pretty hardcore hip-hop. My parents listen to the Pooh and Claudio Baglioni."

"How old is your dad?"

"Fifty-two. My mom is forty-nine."

"Do you have brothers or sisters?"

"I have a younger brother. He's seventeen."

That information stirred up a series of vague and unsettling thoughts that I rapidly suppressed.

"What did you tell your parents?"

"What do you mean?"

"About this trip."

"I said I was going to Rome because there was a party tonight. Sometimes I go to Rome for things like that. I decided that it would just be too complicated to explain everything, so it might be best to avoid a lot of questions. Do you think I did the right thing?"

I ignored the question.

"Tell me about Nicoletta. What's she like?"

"Anxious and insecure. She's very pretty, as I told you, but that's not enough to make her confident. And she can't seem to make a decision, even about something that's not important."

"She's not like you."

She was about to say something but then changed her mind and—I'm certain of this—said something else instead.

"Why did you ask me for a picture of Michele yesterday?"

"Did you find one?"

"I found a few group pictures, but none of them are close-ups. You can't really make out the faces. Why do you need a picture of Michele?"

I hesitated for a moment, but then I realized I couldn't conceal the reason from her.

"I talked to an old client of mine. He's a coke dealer, and he works the so-called respectable circles of Bari. I asked him if he had ever heard of someone named Michele in his milieu. He doesn't know him, but he asked around a little bit, and he found a small-time dealer who might know a guy by that name. To be certain, he needs to show him a photograph."

"And who are these two coke dealers?"

"Why do you care? I can't imagine their names will mean anything to you. The important thing is the information they can give us. That is, if it turns out there's a link to Manuela's disappearance, of course."

I realized that I'd answered her sharply, with irritation, more or less the way a policeman answers when someone—

a prosecutor, a lawyer, or a judge—tries to pry the name of a confidential informant out of him. It just isn't done. Caterina looked at me with a mixture of astonishment and resentment.

"Why are you getting mad?"

"I'm not getting mad. It's just that there's no reason for you to know the names of professional criminals. Among other things, I'm a lawyer, and I can always claim attorney-client privilege, but you don't have that option."

"What does that mean?"

"It means that if for any reason, which we can't even imagine right now, we were questioned about what we're doing, by the police, by the Carabinieri, or by a prosecutor, I could refuse to answer by invoking attorney-client privilege. But you would have to answer their questions, and you'd have to tell the truth about anything you know concerning crimes and people who may have committed them. Believe me, the less you know, the better."

I paused for a moment, then added, "And I'm sorry if I sounded a little harsh."

She seemed about to say something, but then she decided against it and just shrugged.

A short while later, the plane began its descent toward Rome.

We finally got a taxi after standing in a long line. While we were in line, Caterina started talking to me again. She'd been giving me the silent treatment to let me know she was offended, I guess. If she wanted to make me feel guilty for what I'd said to her on the plane, she had succeeded brilliantly.

There were no books in that taxi. Instead, there were decals with Fascist double-headed axes and silhouettes of Il Duce. The taxi driver was a twenty-something with a soul patch, a shaved head, an imperial Roman eagle tattooed on his neck, and a dangling lower lip. I felt a sudden, intense desire to land a few hard punches to his head and face and wipe away his dull-eyed, arrogant expression.

I told Caterina about the taxi driver I had the last time I was in Rome and how he'd learned to love reading. It didn't seem to make any particular impression on her.

"I don't really like reading. I rarely find a book that I care much about."

"Have you read anything lately that you liked?"

"No, nothing recently."

I was about to push a little further and ask about the last book she had read, even if it wasn't very recent. Then I realized that I probably wouldn't like the answer, and decided to drop the subject of reading entirely.

"What do you do in your free time?"

"I really like listening to music. I listen whenever I can, especially on the Internet. I like to go to concerts when I can, and I like to go to the movies. Then I work out at the gym, I see my friends and . . . oh, I almost forgot the most important one of all: I love to cook. I'm a good cook. I'll cook for you sometime. Cooking relaxes me. The best thing is if there's someone else who cleans up after me. But I haven't asked you anything about yourself. Are you married, do you live with someone, do you have a girlfriend?"

"I could be gay and have a boyfriend or even be living with a guy."

"That's impossible."

"What makes you think that's impossible?"

"The way you look at me."

That hit me like a straight-armed slap to the face, a fast one that I hadn't seen coming. I had difficulty swallowing as I tried to come up with a clever answer. Of course, I couldn't think of one, so I just pretended I hadn't heard her.

"No, I'm not married. I used to be, but that ended a long time ago. I don't have a girlfriend, either; haven't for a while."

"What a waste. You don't have children, either, do you?"

"No."

"Well, here's what we'll do. One evening when we're back in Bari, you invite me over for dinner. You'll do the shopping—I'll tell you what to get, but you're free to pick the wine—and I'll cook, but I won't wash up. Are you in?"

I said that would be fine, I was in. She looked satisfied. She put her earbuds back in and went back to her music.

28.

This hotel was much nicer than the one I usually used when I had business in Rome that required an overnight stay.

We decided to change and go eat something in a nearby restaurant. Then Caterina would call Nicoletta and make a time for us to meet.

My room was inviting, and it faced a courtyard that was showing the fresh and dazzling signs of an early spring. As I was undressing to take a shower, I realized that it had been years since I'd been in a hotel with a woman. The last time, the woman was Margherita.

Part of me objected indignantly. It was wrong to draw any comparison between two such radically different situations. Margherita and I came as a couple on vacation. Caterina and I were in Rome on business. Not only were we not a couple, but she was half my age and we were sleeping in separate rooms.

It was an impeccably logical argument, so I ignored it. If there is one thing that I'm good at doing, it's ignoring logic when it comes to my private life.

The last time I was in a hotel with Margherita had been three years earlier. We'd gone to Berlin on vacation with two friends of hers. I was crazy about Berlin. If there'd been no such thing as winter, I would have moved there. I even considered taking a German class when I got back. It was one of the best vacations of my life, and I came home bubbling with enthusiasm.

A few weeks after we returned, Margherita told me that she had accepted a job offer in New York. A job offer that she had been considering for months, and therefore even when she was vacationing in Berlin with the clueless, unsuspecting Guido Guerrieri, who was obviously dumb as a post. In Berlin, I'd been walking around like a happy idiot, while she was already in New York in her mind, leading a new life that didn't include me.

A few weeks after that she left, telling me she'd only be gone for a year. I didn't believe her for a second, and in fact she hadn't come back. Not to stay, anyway.

I half-closed my eyes and saw—as if in a theater of my memory—her slender, muscular, self-aware figure in white underwear, in the dim light of that hotel room in Berlin, on the Oranienburger Strasse. It was a picture that was both tragic and, at the same time, pervaded with serenity. The image included both the perfection of that moment and the awareness, visible in hindsight, that it would not last.

I wondered where Margherita was in that moment. It had been a long time since that thought had crossed my mind.

What had happened to me in the years since she'd left? I couldn't remember much at all, aside from my dangerous encounter with Natsu, who happened to be the wife of one of my former clients, and my adopting a series of daily rituals. Leaning out over this void of memory gave me a sense of vertigo, the exact same way you feel when you lean over an actual abyss.

I thought back to the letter that Margherita wrote to me from New York to say she wouldn't be coming back. It was a kind letter. It was clear she was trying not to hurt me and to make that good-bye as painless as possible. So, of course, it was intolerable, I thought to myself as I read it for the third or fourth time, before crumpling it into a ball and tossing it into the trash.

Thinking of Margherita's letter triggered a terrifying plunge down sheer slopes of memory. Those mountainsides became increasingly populated as I tumbled ever further into the distant past. At last, I ended up at the bottom of that deep gorge of memory.

It was the late seventies. Change was afoot in Italy. It was a period of reaction, of backlash. Someone wrote a letter to the newspaper *Il Corriere della Sera*, announcing his intention to kill himself over a love affair, beginning months of interminable, intolerable public debate. And you couldn't turn around without running into John Travolta. Everyone was trying to imitate him—some successfully, others, including myself, much less so.

I went to see *Grease* with a girl I was crazy about named Barbara.

We had met at a party and as we chatted she told me that all her friends had already seen the movie. Now she was stuck: Who would go see it with her? Well, how about that! What a coincidence, I hadn't seen it either and I'd been wondering the same thing, I lied. We could go together. How about the next afternoon? After all it was Sunday.

She accepted my invitation, and the following afternoon, blissfully incredulous at my luck, I was sitting beside her in a theater filled with kids watching and listening to John Travolta, Olivia Newton-John, and their friends—some of them far too old for their roles, unrealistic and even grotesque as they tried to play eighteen-year-old high school seniors—sing, dance, and recite dialogue that stretched the limits of the improbable.

I walked Barbara home and, when it came time to say good-bye, she planted a quick kiss on my lips and then, just as she was vanishing behind the heavy door, she turned and flashed a smile full of promise. Or rather, a smile that I interpreted as being full of promise.

That night, I didn't sleep a wink. I lay there, overjoyed, and when morning came I made up my mind to surprise Barbara by going to meet her after school, since I had cleverly asked her when she got out on Monday afternoons and we had more or less the same schedule.

As I strode briskly and happily toward the Liceo Scientifico Scacchi—Barbara's high school—my mind was racing with fantasies about our future together.

I was about to learn a valuable lesson: It's never a good idea to spring a surprise on someone when you don't have a clear idea of how things stand.

The school bell rang, furious and cheerful, and moments later a clamorous flood of boys and girls surged out into the street. I spotted her almost immediately in that chaotic rush of sweaters, jackets, scarves, backpacks, wool caps, and dark hair, but looking back, I can't remember her face. If I force myself to focus on the face, all I can come up with is a visual cliché of adolescent beauty—blonde, blue-eyed, high cheekbones, a luminous complexion, and fine features.

I was about fifty yards from her. I started smiling, and then the smile faded from my face, like in a cartoon. Pushing his way upstream through the crowd of students pouring out of the school, and ahead of me—in every sense of the word—another boy was moving toward her, then reached her, then kissed her, and finally took her by the hand.

I don't know what happened after that, because I instinctively darted into the nearest apartment building lobby with an open door, my cheeks burning from the shame of that visual slap, my stomach churning with despair.

I stood in the lobby for a good ten minutes and ventured out only once I was certain that Barbara, together with someone who all evidence suggested was her boyfriend, had disappeared, and there was no longer any risk that someone—anyone—might see me in that state.

Because in the meantime, I had begun crying, silently, with a swarm of words and questions buzzing around in my head. Why had she gone to the movies with me the day before? Why had she kissed me? How can anyone be so cruel?

I was terribly unhappy for many weeks. After I started to recover, I ran into her, on the Via Sparano. I saw her from a distance. She was with two girlfriends, while I was alone, standing in front of the display window of the Laterza bookshop.

I straightened up, squared my shoulders, and did my best to look proud and unconcerned.

I told myself to be strong, act like I didn't care, and barely nod to her as we passed. Not scornfully—I had to do better than that. Indifferently. She would probably turn and slow down, but I wouldn't stop. I'd keep walking, dignified and detached.

What the hell.

We'd gone to the movies one time and exchanged a kiss. So what? That certainly didn't mean we were married. It was the sort of thing that happened all the time, between modern, freethinking young women and men. We went out, saw a movie, kissed, said good-bye, and went on with our lives. No problem.

By this point we were quite close to each other, but she hadn't seen me yet. She was deep in conversation with her friends and talking animatedly and suddenly, for no good reason, I assumed that meant she and that boy had broken up. In that case—I said to myself—maybe I shouldn't be too harsh, too pitiless. After all, she'd treated me badly, but it was the kind of thing that happened. Maybe I should give her a second chance. The best thing to do, in that case, was to assume an expression that was dignified, but not hostile. Maybe I could even let the beginnings of a smile form on my lips. She must have realized what a mistake she'd made, and I could be magnanimous and give her a second chance.

She only noticed me as we were about to cross paths. "Ciao," she said distractedly as we passed, and then she plunged back into the conversation with her friends. I was miserable for weeks—again—after that chance encounter. I decided that I'd never look at another girl as long as I lived and that I'd be unhappy forever.

I heard someone knocking on my hotel room door, and I realized I hadn't even changed out of my bathrobe yet.

"Yes?"

"It's me. Are you ready?"

"No, sorry. I had a few phone calls to make. I'm running a little late."

"Why don't you let me in?"

"Because I'm not dressed. Go down to the lobby and I'll catch up with you in five minutes."

"It doesn't bother me. What, are you shy?"

"That's right, I'm shy. Go on down to the lobby and I'll catch up with you in a minute."

As I was tossing my robe onto the bed, I thought I heard a burst of laughter moving away down the hotel corridor.

But maybe it was my imagination.

29.

I was down in the lobby five minutes later, as promised.
Caterina was on the phone, and she snapped her phone
shut as I walked toward her.

"I just spoke to Nicoletta. She's waiting for us at her
house. She said she canceled all her appointments this
afternoon. We can drop by whenever we like."

"Did you say that she lives over near Via Ostiense?"

"That's right, right next to the Pyramid of Cestius. So
let's go get a bite to eat, then we'll get a cab and go to her
house. Sound okay?"

"That's fine."

"You decide where to eat for lunch. I'll pick the place for
dinner, okay?"

That was okay, so we went to a restaurant that I knew,
near the Court of Cassation. We agreed that even though
we were working that afternoon, we could have a glass of
wine—just one glass. Then we agreed that drinking just one
glass of wine is sort of depressing, so we should order a
whole bottle. After all, we didn't have to drink the whole
thing. The restaurant was crowded, no one was paying any
attention to us, and before we knew it we'd drunk the whole
bottle. I was starting to relax.

Caterina said, "I'm ditzy sometimes, I know. I say things I shouldn't and I only realize afterwards what I've done."

She looked at me, evidently expecting a response of some kind, and I had the distinct impression that her meek confession was just one more component of a perfectly calibrated game of seduction.

After she realized I wasn't going to answer her half-asked question, she decided she needed to provoke me further. So she ran a finger over the back of the hand I was resting on the tabletop. It would not be accurate to say that this met with absolute indifference on my part.

"But in a way it's your fault."

I took the bait.

"Why is it my fault?"

"All the men I know try to get me into bed, but you seem completely uninterested. I can't say that I like it."

"I'm glad that you broached this topic. It gives me a chance to provide some clarification," I began, in a ridiculously condescending tone of voice.

"Go ahead, clarify away," she said with a smile. She continued stroking the back of my hand. Although I tried, I didn't have the mental fortitude to pull my hand away.

"You're very beautiful, but for a variety of reasons I cannot even take into consideration the idea of . . . how should I put this . . ."

"Say it in your own words."

"Well, that is, I cannot even take into consideration the idea of courting you, much less allow the prospect that something might happen between us."

The prospect that something might happen between us?

Guerrieri, listen to the ridiculous fucking way you speak. The next time you take a girl out on a date, are you going to ask her if she would be inclined to take into consideration the prospect of establishing a relationship that might entail intermittent sexual congress? With that exact wording, of course, and reserving the right to cancel that contract by providing notice in writing.

"Why not?"

"Well, first and foremost, I'm working on a case, and it's never a good idea to mix professional and private matters."

Well put. A profound truth. Unfortunately, I happen to know that in the not-too-distant past, Guerrieri, you've been pretty flexible on that point.

"And second?"

"And second, aside from the work aspect, I'm twenty years older than you are."

"So?"

"So, it's wrong. There's a vast gap in both age and experience, and there's a risk that someone could get hurt."

"You mean I could get hurt?"

"That's a possibility."

"Well, you're pretty full of yourself. Pompous ass. Maybe you're the one who could get hurt."

"That's another possibility that I would just as soon avoid. So in either case, I see a number of excellent reasons to let matters drop. And now I would say it's time for us to get going."

I thought I'd emerged with my dignity intact, that I'd acquitted myself graciously and well. As she stood up, however, she stuck her tongue out at me, and once again I had the feeling that I was playing a game that was slipping out of my control.

It took Nicoletta more than a minute to come to the door.

She was a tall, skinny young woman, pale and attractive, but dull looking. The kind who always looks much better with the right clothing and the right makeup. She had an expression that was neither amiable nor particularly intelligent. Caterina gave her a hug, wrapping her arms around her and holding her tight for what seemed like a long time. Then she introduced us. Nicoletta's handshake was limp. The apartment smelled faintly of mothballs. There was no sign of anyone living there besides Nicoletta.

We walked down a dimly lit hallway to the kitchen and sat down around an old Formica kitchen table. There was something impersonal and a little stale about the apartment. There was something disagreeable—though hard to pin down—about its tenant. I thought a good investigator would ask to take a look at Manuela's bedroom, even though all her things had probably been removed some time ago and there was probably a new roommate living in it now.

"Would you like a cup of coffee?" Nicoletta offered in the tone of someone who is obliged to provide the minimum required level of hospitality—but no more. We accepted, and she served us coffee in a mismatched set of old chipped demitasses and saucers. After finishing her espresso, Caterina lit a cigarette, leaving her cigarette case on the table. Nicoletta took one, too, and lit it with a series of overly feminine gestures entirely in keeping with her feeble handshake.

"All right, Nico. Counselor Guerrieri is going to ask you a few questions. Don't worry, and answer them to the best of your ability. You're not in any trouble. Like I told you, Counselor Guerrieri is a lawyer hired by Manu's parents to find out if there are any leads that the prosecutors or the

Carabinieri might have overlooked. That's why he needs to talk to me, to you, in other words, to anybody who was close to Manu. But I repeat, you have no reason for concern of any kind."

Caterina had taken on the posture and even the tone of voice of a cop with years of experience. It was an amazing thing to see.

"Okay?"

"Okay," said Nicoletta, with a less-than-enthusiastic expression on her face. Now it was my turn.

"First of all, let me thank you for agreeing to meet with me. I'll try not to take up any more of your time than necessary."

She nodded, though it wasn't clear whether she meant it as a gesture of courtesy or to indicate that it was best not to take up too much of her time. I asked her more or less the same questions I had asked Caterina, and she gave me more or less the same answers. Then we came to the point.

"Now, Nicoletta, if you don't mind, I'd like to ask you to tell me a few things about Manuela's ex-boyfriend, Michele Cantalupi."

"What do you want to know about him?"

I wondered for a second if I should circle around a little bit and approach the subject slowly. But I told myself there was no reason to beat around the bush.

"Everything you can tell me about him and drugs. Before you say anything more, let me remind you that this conversation is completely confidential, and that I won't repeat anything you're about to tell me to anyone—least of all, to the police. I'm just trying to figure out whether and how Michele Cantalupi might have had anything to do, directly or indirectly, with Manuela's disappearance."

"I have no idea whether Michele had anything to do with Manuela's disappearance."

"Tell me about the cocaine."

Nicoletta hesitated, then she looked over at Caterina, who nodded her head as if giving permission. Nicoletta sighed and answered.

"Well, let me begin by saying that I only know what happened while Manuela and Michele were dating."

"Are you talking about what happened with cocaine?"

"That's right."

"Go ahead."

"He always had cocaine."

"Did he have a lot?"

"I never saw how much he had, but he always had it."

Something about the way she answered that question told me that she wasn't telling the truth. I felt sure that Nicoletta had seen the cocaine, and she'd seen that there was a lot of it.

"Did he bring it here, to your apartment?"

She hesitated again, then nodded.

"Was Manuela using?"

"I think so."

"You only think so?"

"She used it sometimes."

"Here?"

"Once or twice."

"Together with Michele?"

"That's right."

Based on the way she answered me and the growing tension I could sense, I decided to change the subject, for a few minutes anyway.

"After she broke up with Michele, Manuela was dating someone else here in Rome, wasn't she?"

She relaxed visibly.

"She went out with a guy for a few weeks, but she wasn't serious about him."

"Did you meet this guy?"

"I only met him once. He came over for dinner one evening."

"How long did they date?"

"They stopped seeing each other before the summer. Manuela didn't really like him. She just went out with him a few times because she was bored. It was a way of passing the time."

"Were there any repercussions to that relationship?"

"What do you mean?"

"Was it an easy breakup, or was there a lot of conflict, the way there was with Michele?"

"The two of them were never even together. They went out a few times, that's all. It wasn't a relationship, just a few dates. I think that after a few weeks Manuela told him that she didn't want to see him again. It just ended. No conflict at all."

"When you and Caterina spoke, you both theorized that Michele might have had something to do with Manuela's disappearance. Is that right?"

Nicoletta looked over at Caterina, who once again nodded, giving her permission to answer.

"Yes, but that was just something we said. Michele is a violent guy, and their relationship ended on an ugly note . . . ."

"Is he a drug dealer?"

"I don't know, I swear."

I had a sudden idea.

"Did Manuela ever have cocaine of her own, independent of Cantalupi? Did she ever bring coke here, even when he wasn't in Rome?"

Caterina shifted in her chair, changing position, and out of the corner of my eye I could see that she seemed less at ease. Nicoletta slouched and the expression on her face was unmistakable: She knew she should never have agreed to talk with me. It had been a mistake, and she was already regretting it.

"Let me ask you again: Did Manuela have a way of getting cocaine, independent of Cantalupi? This information could be very important."

Still no answer.

"She brought some here, and you both used it, on more than one occasion. Isn't that right?"

After another long pause, she finally spoke.

"Once or twice," she said in a voice I could barely hear.

"Did that happen after she broke up with Cantalupi?"

"Yes."

"So Manuela knew how to get cocaine without having to rely on Cantalupi. Did she get it in Rome or Bari?"

"I don't know how or where she got it, I swear."

She was starting to make me mad. If the things she was telling me—and everything that she was still keeping from me—had been reported to the Carabinieri months ago, maybe the investigation would have gone differently. I didn't like this one bit.

"I swear I have no idea where she got the coke," she said again.

"And you didn't say a word to the Carabinieri about all this. Didn't it occur to you that this information could have been helpful to their investigation? It could have made a difference."

"I didn't know who she was getting her coke from. Even if I'd said something to the Carabinieri, it wouldn't have changed anything."

It took all my self-control to suppress a growing wave of anger inside me. I wanted so badly to tell her what an idiot she was. If the Carabinieri had known that Manuela was involved in drug dealing, however tangentially, they would have shifted their investigation in that direction. Maybe that wouldn't have changed anything, but at least there might have been a chance to find out what happened to her.

"You didn't say anything because you didn't want to admit that you'd used cocaine. You didn't want your parents to know, isn't that right?"

She nodded. Now that I thought about it, I decided that stupidity had nothing to do with her behavior. Nicoletta was a small-minded, selfish coward, and the only reason she said nothing to the Carabinieri was to avoid any inconvenience to herself. That her close friend, roommate, companion in studies and everyday life, had vanished into thin air meant less to her than the mere risk that she might have to do some explaining to her parents about doing a line or two—was it a line or two?—of cocaine.

"I need to understand something, Nicoletta, and I'm going to ask you to tell me the truth, without holding anything back. I need to know if Manuela continued to get cocaine from the same people after she and Michele broke up. By 'same people,' I mean the people she met through Michele."

"I swear that I don't know how she got it. I asked once, and she told me to mind my own business."

"What did she say?"

"She was kind of mean about it. She let me know it was none of my business and asking could be dangerous."

"Is that what you understood her to mean, or is that what Manuela actually said to you?"

"I don't remember her exact words, but that was certainly how she made it sound."

A few minutes of complete silence followed. Caterina lit another cigarette. Nicoletta rubbed a hand over her face and sighed deeply. For a minute I thought she was about to burst into tears, but she didn't. I was trying to think of anything else I might be able to get out of her. Nothing came to mind, so I asked if I could see Manuela's bedroom.

"There's nothing of hers left in the room," Nicoletta said.

"Does another girl live in the room now?"

"No, the landlady hasn't found another tenant yet, so I'm living here alone."

"Then you won't mind if I take a look."

Nicoletta shrugged and stood up without a word. Manuela's bedroom was halfway down the hall and, I noticed, the door was locked; Nicoletta turned the key in the lock before opening the door. As I walked into the room, I felt my pulse quicken, as if the information that would solve the case was hidden in that room, and I was about to find it.

But I wasn't. It was just as Nicoletta had said. Nothing in the room was connected with Manuela. There was a single bed. There was a desk with empty drawers. There was an armoire, which was also empty. A series of small, bad watercolors hung on the walls. They appeared to have been part of the original furnishings of the bedroom and of the apartment.

"What happened to Manuela's things?"

"The Carabinieri came and searched the room and then, a few weeks later, Manuela's mother took all her things away."

I decided that the Carabinieri hadn't, technically, performed a search. Among other things, there was no mention of a search in the file. They had gone to the apartment and, as so often happens in these cases, they had taken a look around, found nothing useful, and left.

"Why were her parents in such a hurry to get her stuff out of the room?"

"The landlady asked them if they wanted to keep paying the rent on the room, and of course they didn't. So Manuela's mother, with one of Manuela's aunts, or maybe just a friend, came and took all her things away."

When Nicoletta was done talking, I walked over to the window and looked out. I saw that it overlooked a dirty gray courtyard. I half-closed my eyes and tried to sense Manuela's presence, her voice. Perhaps, in that slightly dreary seventies-style bedroom, I might receive a message from the missing girl.

Fortunately, I acted the fool for a few seconds only, and neither Caterina nor Nicoletta noticed anything. Is your brain turning to mush, Guerrieri? Who do you think you are, Dylan Dog, paranormal investigator? I berated myself loudly, albeit internally, as I left the room, upset with myself.

Ten minutes later, Caterina and I were back out on the street, as darkness fell.

30.

"Did you know all of that already?"

"More or less, though not the details," Caterina replied.

"So why didn't you tell me any of it?"

We were already in a taxi on our way back to the hotel. Rome's traffic was at its spectacular worst. Caterina took a deep breath before answering.

"Try to see it from my point of view. These were things that concerned Nicoletta, and she is a friend of mine, even if we don't hang out anymore. I did what I could so the two of you could meet and she could be the one to tell you about it. It seemed to me like the best solution."

"What if Nicoletta hadn't told me anything?"

"I don't believe that would have happened, but if it had, I would have stepped in."

There wasn't a thing wrong with what Caterina was saying. She'd behaved impeccably. She'd helped me without betraying the trust of a friend.

So why was I feeling so annoyed, as if we were playing a game and I wasn't privy to the rules?

I should have asked her if she had ever tried cocaine herself and if there was anything that she had forgotten to tell me. I was trying to find the words when her cell phone rang. She pulled it out of her pocket but didn't answer.

"Go ahead and answer if you like," I said.

"It's a friend of mine. I don't want to talk to her. I don't want to tell her I'm in Rome. I'll text her later," she said, shrugging as she pushed a button that silenced the phone. I decided I was uncomfortable asking that question, and that it probably wasn't important. I could ask her some other time.

"In your opinion, did Nicoletta tell me everything she knows?"

"Probably not, but she told you what you wanted to know, and I doubt very much that she knows anything specific about Manuela's disappearance."

She was right, I thought, as I looked at her.

She also had beautiful skin, I thought, as I continued to look at her, until I realized that I had become, shall we say, somewhat distracted.

"What do you think? Do you think Manuela's disappearance might have something to do with cocaine?"

Even though the cabbie seemed to be completely absorbed in a soccer game on the radio and completely uninterested in us, I instinctively lowered my voice.

"I don't know. If Michele hadn't been out of the country the day she disappeared, I'd probably think there was some connection. But since he was, it's a mystery."

She began squeezing the bridge of her nose between her thumb and two fingers. She seemed to be staring at something off in the distance. Then, it looked as if she'd located what she'd been looking for, and she spoke.

"Can I say something?"

"Of course," I replied.

"Why are we sure that Manuela disappeared in Puglia? Who says that she didn't come to Rome, that afternoon, that evening, or that night? Why are we ruling that out?"

Right.

We had all taken it for granted that Manuela never left for Rome. And we had excellent grounds for doing so, of course. It was the most credible hypothesis. The ticket clerk remembered selling her a ticket to Bari; Manuela had told Anita that she was going to Bari and would leave for Rome from there. So it was reasonable to theorize that the point and moment of her disappearance was somewhere and sometime along the journey from Ostuni to Bari, or else subsequent to her arrival in Bari. Still, there was no evidence that would allow us to exclude categorically that Manuela might have left for and even arrived in Rome. Whatever had caused her disappearance might have happened in Rome.

Of course, I thought to myself, if Manuela left Bari and then arrived—and later disappeared—in Rome, my entire so-called investigation meant less than zero. Most important: I wouldn't have the slightest idea of where or how to begin again.

Caterina must have sensed what I was thinking.

"Well, we're not going to solve the mystery tonight. We've done what we could. You got all the information from Nicoletta that she could give you. Now it's a matter of thinking about what we know and seeing if we come up with anything. But we should do that after we've had a chance to let it settle, don't you think?"

I nodded, but with a dubious air.

"Have you ever tried Ethiopian food?"

"Excuse me?"

"I asked if you've ever tried Ethiopian food."

"A few years ago in Milan. Why?"

"Did you like it?"

"Sure, it was fun. You eat with your hands and wrap the food up in a sort of soft flatbread, like a crêpe, right?"

"*Injera*—that's what it's called. So tonight we'll go to an Ethiopian restaurant and then we'll think about all of this tomorrow."

We'll think it over? You and me? What are we now, partners?

The Ethiopian restaurant was near the main station. The place was crowded with African customers, which gave me the impression the food would be authentic. The waiters knew Caterina. They greeted her warmly and brought us menus immediately.

"Is there anything you don't eat?"

"No, I eat everything. I was in the army," I said.

"Okay, I'll order for both of us. You can choose the wine."

Picking a wine wasn't an especially challenging job, considering the selection. There were four possibilities and none of them was particularly alluring. I ordered a Sicilian Syrah that struck me as the only acceptable choice.

"You're a regular here, I see."

"When I lived in Rome I came here a lot."

"Did Manuela come here, too?"

"Sure."

It occurred to me that I could ask her to take me to the places that Manuela liked to go when she was in Rome. I could ask around and maybe I'd uncover something. Then it occurred to me that I'd gotten the idea from TV detectives. I changed the subject.

"So, you don't have a boyfriend."

"No," she said, shaking her head.

"Has it been a long time?"

"A few months."

"And why not?"

"What do you mean, why not?"

"Okay, that's not what I meant to ask. You had a relationship that ended a couple of months ago. Was it a long relationship?"

"Fairly long. It lasted a couple of years."

"And when Manuela disappeared, were you still together or was it already over?"

"We were still together, but it was as good as over."

"Then you must have discussed Manuela's disappearance with him."

"Of course."

"Am I bothering you with these questions?"

"You're not bothering me. Or maybe talking about him does bother me a little. But that's my problem. Feel free to ask me anything. Don't worry about it."

"What's his name?"

"Duilio."

"Duilio. That's not a very common name."

"No, and it's not a very nice name either. I don't think I've ever called him by his real name."

"Do you think it would be worth my time to have a talk with him, to see if he can tell me anything about Manuela?"

"I don't think so. They didn't know each other at all, except through me. I mean, the only reason they spent time together was because they both knew me."

"How long were you together after Manuela's disappearance?"

Caterina didn't answer right away. She rested her face on her right hand and her right elbow on the table. She was thinking.

"Maybe a month. More or less a month," she said after a little while.

I figured Manuela's disappearance might have accelerated the end of their relationship. I was about to ask her, but then I didn't. Clearly, she didn't like talking about it, and I had no reason to insist.

Just then, the waiter brought our food, a huge tray covered with a sort of soft and spongy crêpe, upon which was arranged a variety of dishes. Vegetables of all kinds, meat, chicken, sauces, spices—especially hot spices. There were more crêpes on another dish. We used those to scoop up the food and eat it.

For a while we devoted ourselves to the food and the wine, without talking. The bottle was emptying quickly, and it occurred to me that it was our second bottle of wine of the day, and that maybe I should be careful not to overdo it. Then I decided that I'd spent my whole life warning myself not to overdo it and that I was beginning to get sick and tired of my cautious, sensible self.

"So, are you going to take me on at your law firm as an intern when I get my degree?"

"Sure," I said, unable to think of a witty response.

"I'd really like that."

I was about to say something paternalistic and pathetic about the profession of the law, and the sacrifices that it entails, and that you have to be sure it's for you before you get involved in it. Instead, I tore off another piece of *injera* and wrapped it around all that remained of an unidentified—but very spicy—meat dish.

"You took the last of the tibs," Caterina said in a scolding tone.

"Oh, I'm sorry, did you want it?"

"Yes," she said, with the expression of a little girl used to getting her way.

I extended the handful of food to her. She didn't reach for it. Instead, she shook her head. I looked at her quizzically.

"You were doing something very rude and now, to make up for it, you have to do something extra nice for me."

As she spoke these words, she leaned her head toward me and opened her mouth. I looked at her incredulously, gulped, and then extended my fingers toward her mouth. She took the food in her mouth and clamped her lips down on my fingers, looking me right in the eye, with an amused and pitiless expression.

Part of me was still trying to put up some token resistance.

Don't do it, Guerrieri. It's not right: This girl could be your daughter. And not just biologically. Her mother is only a few years older than you; when you were twenty-one, twenty-two years old, you went out with a few girls older than you. For instance, Giusi was twenty-three and you were twenty. A little accident back then, and right now you'd have a daughter exactly Caterina's age, with a mother roughly the age of Caterina's mother.

That is one of the most demented arguments I've heard out of you to date, Guerrieri, replied the other part of me. Biologically, you could have had a daughter at age fifteen. If we apply this line of reasoning and this nonsensical rule— you can't go out with a girl who could biologically be your daughter—you, my dear Guerrieri, at the age of forty-five, are only allowed to socialize with women over thirty. Have you ever heard anything so ridiculous in your life?

We told the taxi driver to drop us off in the Piazza di Spagna, which wasn't far from our hotel. I hadn't been to the Piazza di Spagna in so many years that I couldn't even remember how long it had been. As I got out of the car, I experienced a surge of simple, childish joy. We sat down among the crowd of tourists near the fountain, listening to the voices and the water. Then we climbed up the Spanish Steps and I—aware of what a cliché it was and yet cheered by it at the same time—thought how few places there are on earth where you can feel spring arrive the way you do in the Piazza di Spagna and at the Trinità dei Monti.

We were almost all the way up to the church when a Filipino flower vendor offered me a bunch of roses. I said no thanks and stepped aside to avoid him. Caterina stopped, took one of the roses, and handed it to me.

A little later we went into a small bar with a sign out front advertising a BLAST FROM THE PAST, a night featuring Italian music from the eighties.

We stayed in that bar long enough to hear four or five songs, none of which were particularly memorable. Then Caterina asked me if I wanted to go back to the hotel. I felt a slight electric shock run through my body and decided that I was tired of resisting the impulse—if what I had been doing up till now could be described as resistance. I said yes. We got up and left the bar, and ten minutes later we were at the hotel.

We got the keys to our rooms and I walked her to her

room, which was on the floor below mine. She stopped and leaned back against the door.

She was going to invite me in. I'd accept, and what was about to happen would happen, and who the hell cared, because I was sick of not being able to make a single move in my life without calling up logic and reason and critiquing it in advance.

"Thanks, Gigi, *buona notte*," she said, giving me a kiss on the cheek.

Gigi? *Buona notte?* Have you lost your mind?

I didn't say that. Actually, I didn't say a word. I stood there, stock-still, with an expression on my face that I would have found amusing to look at, if it had been on someone else's face.

"I call people I like by their initials. G.G. for Guido Guerrieri. Ciao, Gi-Gi, *buona notte*, and thanks for a wonderful evening."

And before I could say a word, she had vanished into her room.

I quickly got ready for bed. An emotional storm cloud was massing around me, consisting of equal parts embarrassment, annoyance, relief, and other feelings that were more difficult to decipher. I was reluctant, however, to delve too deeply into that combination of factors and their individual measures, so I decided to read my book—a collection of short stories by Grace Paley—until sleep came. That would be a while, I feared.

For ten minutes or so I read a story that didn't bowl me over. Then I heard a knock at the door.

"Who is it?"

"It's me. Are you going to open the door?"

"Just a second," I called. I was in such a hurry to pull on my pants that I tripped on them.

"Aren't you going to step aside and let me in?"

I did as she asked, and she walked into the room. As she passed by me, I caught a whiff of leather-scented perfume that she hadn't been wearing when we were out together earlier. It was a strangely familiar scent, reassuring and unsettling at the same time. I tried to figure out what it reminded me of, without success.

"Nice t-shirt you have there," she said, sitting on the edge of the bed. I was wearing a silly t-shirt featuring Lupo Alberto from the comics. The wolf was drawn in a ridiculous kung-fu pose.

"Well, yeah, I wasn't expecting visitors . . . ."

"You're terrible, do you know that?"

"I beg your pardon?"

"You're terrible."

"Why am I terrible?"

"At first I thought you'd ask to come into my room. Then I waited for you to knock on my door. Finally, I figured maybe you'd call me. But you didn't. You're a hardass, aren't you, Gigi? I knew from the beginning that you weren't like other guys."

I didn't have the slightest idea what to say, and my face must have shown it. At least I was confirming her theory that I was different from other guys.

"Why are you standing there? Come sit down. Make yourself at home."

I did as I was told. To keep from coming across as a hardass, of course.

As I sat down on the bed, I caught another whiff of her perfume.

And then, her lips, which were warm and fresh and soft and tasted of cherry and invincible youth and summer and lots of wonderful things from years gone by. Things that were there, present and alive.

Before I let myself go, I heard a line of verse echo through my head.

Who is she that looketh forth as the morning,
fair as the moon, clear as the sun,
and terrible as an army with banners?

31.

When I opened my eyes and looked at the clock, it was past nine.

Caterina was sleeping deeply, face down, embracing a pillow. Her bare back was exposed, and it rose and fell gently, rhythmically.

I got out of bed without making a sound, got washed, got dressed, and wrote her a note saying I was out for a walk and I'd be back soon. A few minutes later I was on the Via del Corso.

It was a warm, lovely day. Everyone was wearing spring attire and, as I looked around to decide where I should go for an espresso, I saw a corpulent, almost completely bald man wearing a rumpled suit and a tie hanging loosely around his neck. He was walking toward me with a big smile. Who the hell was that?

"Guido Guerrieri! What a nice surprise. Don't you recognize me? It's me, Enrico. Enrico De Bellis."

When I heard his name, I had a singular experience. The folds and wrinkles that had deformed his face melted away, and the features of the stunningly beautiful but vapid face of a young man I'd known twenty-five years earlier emerged from the sands of time.

The man I now recognized as De Bellis threw his arms

around me and gave me a kiss on the cheek. He reeked of cheap aftershave, cigarettes, a suit that hadn't been cleaned in far too long, and alcohol. At the corner of his mouth was a trace of the espresso he'd recently thrown back. What little hair that remained on his head dangled, in need of a trim, over his ears and the back of his neck.

"Enrico, ciao," I said, once he released me from his embrace. I tried to remember the last time we'd seen one another and to reconstruct his life based on the information in my possession. He'd gone to college—law of course, the refuge of the crooked—but he'd dropped out after taking two or three exams. For years he'd indulged in a variety of pastimes, some more dangerous than others, and some less lawful than others. Businesses and companies were created and then conveniently made to disappear. Check kiting. Questionable operations with his credit cards. A marriage to a homely but wealthy young woman that went sour— very sour—in the wake of a series of legal accusations, police reports, and trials. A guilty verdict for bankruptcy fraud, and additional criminal prosecutions for further fraud and for receiving stolen goods.

He'd disappeared from Bari, with a host of creditors eager to track him down on his back, some of them exceedingly unsavory. Individuals with nicknames like Pierino the Criminal, Mbacola the Shark, and Tyson. That last name succinctly described the methods this character employed to recover debts that were not exactly out in the open.

De Bellis had vanished into thin air, the way only people in that world can. And now he had reappeared out of the void, materializing right in front of me, with his rumpled clothes and the stench of tobacco smoke, his air of slovenliness, and a grim, poorly disguised desperation.

"It's been forever since I've seen you! What are you doing in Rome?"

I decided that it might be best not to tell him exactly what I was doing—what I had just finished doing—in Rome.

"The usual. An appeals case, a hearing at the Court of Cassation."

"Oh, of course—an appeals case, a hearing at the Court of Cassation. You're a big-time lawyer now. I read about your cases. I've kept up with you through our friends."

I preferred not to think too carefully about what mutual friends Enrico De Bellis and I might have. He slapped me on the shoulder.

"Shit, you look great. You haven't changed a bit. I've had some tough times, but things are starting to look up for me. In fact, things already are looking up. Things are going great. If I can get this one project I have in mind off the ground, I'll be all set."

He spoke hurriedly, his words tumbling out with such forced cheerfulness that it verged on the grotesque.

"Come with me. Let me buy you a coffee," he said, taking me by the arm and steering me into a nearby café.

"Two espressos," he said to the barista.

And then, turning to me with a conspiratorial air, he said, "Should we ask for a drop of sambuca in our coffee, Guido?"

No thanks. Sambuca at ten in the morning isn't part of a healthy diet.

I gave him a tight smile and shook my head. So he decided to go ahead and add my dose of sambuca to his coffee. He nodded to the barista, who clearly knew him well. He poured sambuca into Enrico's cup and stopped just before it spilled over the brim.

Technically, that was a glass of sambuca with a little espresso to top it off. De Bellis drank it quickly and immediately afterward—I'm sure of it—decided he'd like another. He got a grip on himself, though, and refrained from ordering the second sambuca with a drop of coffee.

Then he pretended to check his pockets and discover, with mock chagrin, that he'd forgotten his wallet.

"Oh, damn, Guido. I'm sorry. I offered to buy you a cup of coffee and here I am without any money. So sorry."

I paid. We left the bar, and De Bellis extracted an MS cigarette from a packet that was as rumpled as his suit. Healthy living, no question about it. He took my arm as we started walking toward the Piazza del Popolo. Along the way, he decided to brief me on all the options that modern medicine offered in terms of therapy for erectile dysfunction. He was—to his credit—impressively well-informed on the topic.

After explaining to me the various options available— from pills of all sorts and injections worthy of a horror film, up to and including a hydraulic apparatus that would have intrigued Doctor Frankenstein—he added that when it came right down to it, the best thing for us was whores or, even better, DIY. A nice free porn video on the Internet, five minutes of effort, and it's taken care of. No problem, no worries about performance. Because that medicine isn't so good for you. I mean, Guido, you're in good shape, but I'm a few pounds overweight. I'll start a diet one of these days. Anyway, afterward there's no need to make nice and have a smoke together and make plans to see each other again. It's all hydraulics. Prostate maintenance.

I felt like throwing up. I bent down to tie a shoelace that didn't need tying, just to get free of his grasp.

"Can I ask you a favor, Guido? We've always been good friends, and that means a lot to me."

Actually, we hadn't ever been good friends. I knew he was going to ask for money.

"I need to make a payment today. As I told you, I've been through some tough times, but I'm getting back on my feet. I have an incredible project I'd love to tell you about one day when you have time. Maybe we can go out for a drink next time you're in Rome and I'll tell you all about it. Here, take my card."

His business card was the type you print on cheap paper at a vending machine. It read ENRICO DE BELLIS, FINANCIAL AND CORPORATE CONSULTING. No address, just a cell phone number. Financial and corporate consulting? What did that mean? I guess he had to put something on the business card, and he couldn't write ENRICO DE BELLIS, CON ARTIST, GRIFTER, AND EXTORTIONIST.

"If you could make me a small loan, I'd pay it back within a week. It's money that I owe to some people who . . . well, let's just say, it's not a good idea to make them angry. I don't have to tell you, you're a big criminal lawyer. By the way, I haven't congratulated you on your brilliant career. But it was obvious when we were boys that you'd do whatever you set your mind to. I remember that you always said you wanted to be a criminal lawyer, that you were going to grow up to be someone. You're a big success, and you've earned it."

I'd never said I wanted to be a criminal lawyer when I grew up. Certainly not when De Bellis and I knew each other, back when we were kids.

"I need a thousand Euros. Like I said, I'd pay you back in a few days. I can mail you a check, or if you give me your account number, I'll wire the money to you."

Why of course. I'll just give you my account number, and I'm sure I'll receive full payment, with a little extra for interest, in just a day or two.

"I'm sorry, Enrico, but as you can imagine, I don't walk around with that much cash in my pocket."

"Maybe you could write me a check."

"I hardly ever use checks anymore. I put everything on a credit card."

"Of course. You probably have one of those platinum cards with unlimited credit. I'm sure you have no use for cash or checks. Then maybe we could swing by an ATM—there's one on every corner—and you could withdraw a thousand Euros. You can rest assured that in a week, ten days at the most, I'll pay it all back. What do you say?"

What I said was nothing. I pulled out my wallet, opened it, extracted three fifty-Euro banknotes, and handed them to him.

"I'm sorry, Enrico, I'm really in a hurry. As I told you, I'm here in Rome on business."

He took the money without a word and slipped it quickly into the pocket of his rumpled jacket. We stood there face to face in silence for a few seconds. He was weighing the odds of getting anything more out of me. At last, when he had resigned himself to the fact that I wasn't going to give him another cent, the light went out of his eyes and his face went blank. I no longer had anything to offer him, so he could turn and go now.

"All right then, if you really have to go I won't keep you."

He barely bothered to say good-bye as he turned and left, without thanking me and without promising to pay me back. He walked off with a lumbering gait, lighting another cigarette as he went. I imagined him searching for someone else to give him money. It was part of his daily struggle for survival, as well as his never-ending attempt to fend off the desperation that nipped at his heels, ready to catch him by the ankles and swallow him whole.

A few hours later, Caterina and I were on a plane back to Bari.

Just as she had been the night before, during the flight she was perfectly at ease—comfortable, spontaneous, and relaxed. She acted as if nothing had happened or, rather, as if we were a long-standing couple. I, on the other hand, felt increasingly confused and awkward. I kept having the feeling—simultaneously vague and sharp—that there was something obvious that I was overlooking.

When I left her outside her apartment building on Rione Madonnella, near the Cinema Esedra, she gave me a kiss and told me to call her soon, because she was eager to see me again.

32.

My disorientation didn't get any better that afternoon in the office. I turned off my cell phone, asked Pasquale not to put through any calls. Then I sat at my desk and put my nose to the grindstone. I worked my way through all the problems and annoyances that had sprung up in the two days I'd been away. Still, I couldn't really focus on what I was doing. The same thing happened that sometimes keeps me from sleeping at night: I thought I could hear a faint noise—a rustling or a dripping—but I couldn't pin down the source.

When I finally took a break, I decided to identify what I knew for sure, since I was apparently incapable of identifying the metaphorical noises inside me.

I took a notepad and began writing.

1) Manuela likely arrived in Bari but never left for Rome. But we can't say that with any certainty. There is a slim chance that she continued on to Rome, though there is no evidence to support that idea.

How to check this out further?

2) Manuela used cocaine. In all likelihood, Michele got her started, but after they broke up, she continued using. She knew how to get it. She was in contact with circles that she described, in response to a question from her friend Nicoletta, as "dangerous."

I paused for a good long while before I wrote the next sentence.

Is it possible that Manuela was a drug dealer?
How to check this out further?
3) Michele is violent, an idiot, and in all probability a drug dealer.
As soon as possible, get a photograph of him and show it to Quintavalle's friend.
Michele would be the obvious suspect (both Nicoletta and Caterina thought of him immediately when they heard Manuela had disappeared), but he was out of the country on the day that Manuela vanished.
Was he really out of the country? He probably was, but what can we do to establish that fact beyond a shadow of a doubt?
Can we identify the friends with whom he left the country?
What to do next?

It would almost have been better if I hadn't found out anything at all, I told myself. If I hadn't discovered anything, I wouldn't be upset. Everything would be the way it was supposed to be. I wasn't cut out to be an investigator. I would return the Ferraros' money. I'd tell them that I was very sorry but there was nothing to be done—at least, nothing that I could do—and I would be free of that whole situation.

Instead, I had discovered some things, and I thought I could intuit some others, even if I couldn't yet seem to make them all fit together. I couldn't walk away.

I had been turning this concept over and looking at it from different angles for at least a half an hour when Pasquale walked into my room.

"Counselor, there's a young woman who wants to talk to you. She's phoned a number of times, but you told us not to put any calls through. Now she's here, in the office. What should I do?"

Caterina, I assumed. And I felt embarrassed at the idea that she was here, in the office, after everything that had happened. It struck me as an intrusion—yet another intrusion—and I didn't know how to react.

"It's Signorina Salvemini, concerning the Ferraro case."

Salvemini? Anita. What could Anita want?

"That's fine, Pasquale. Please send her in. Thank you."

Anita was dressed exactly the same as the last time I'd seen her. That clothing seemed to be a sort of uniform for her.

"I tried to call you on the cell number you gave me, but it was always turned off."

"Sorry. I've had an incredibly busy afternoon, so I turned it off."

"Sorry if I'm bothering you, but I remembered something and I wanted to tell you. It's probably nothing, but you said to call you if I remembered anything, anything at all."

"You're not bothering me, absolutely not. And I'm glad you came by. I really appreciate it. What did you remember?"

"Manuela had two phones."

"Excuse me?"

"I remembered that Manuela had two cell phones, not just one."

"Two cell phones."

I processed this piece of information. It seemed like it could be important. The call records in the prosecuting attorney's official file were for only one phone number.

"What made you remember that?"

"I told you that during the drive from the *trulli* to Ostuni, Manuela kept fooling around with her cell phone, and that at a certain point I thought she might have received a message."

"Yes, I remember."

"When she received the message, she was holding a phone in her hand, but then she rummaged through her purse to find another phone. The scene came back clearly to me because this morning I happened to hear a cell phone that had the same message alert tone as Manuela's phone— the sound I heard that afternoon in the car."

"What sound was it?"

"It was a strange noise. Like a small glass object—a light bulb or a tiny bottle—breaking. I had forgotten that sound, but it came back to me when I heard it again. It was as if hearing the sound allowed me to recover the rest of the memory."

She said the last few words almost apologetically. Either apologizing for giving me a piece of unimportant information, or apologizing because she was coming up with an important piece of information too late.

"Do you think you could describe the two cell phones?"

"No, I can't. I was driving. But she was definitely doing something with one of the phones, then I heard this sound of breaking glass, and then she pulled out another phone. Out of the corner of my eye, I saw that she was holding two cell phones. But I couldn't tell you what kind of phones they were."

My mind was racing. Then I realized I'd been sitting across the desk from her for a long time without saying a word, and I must have had a pretty strange expression on my face.

"Anything else you want to tell me?"

"No, I don't think so."

"Thank you, Anita. Thank you so much."

"Do you think it will help?"

"Yes, I think it very well might."

I walked her to the door of the office. I shook her hand very warmly and said good-bye, doing my best to control the excitement that was starting to sweep over me.

Why had no one mentioned this other phone to me?

No, that was the wrong question. I hadn't asked any specific questions about the possibility of a second cell phone, and so it was understandable that no one mentioned it to me. The real question was why the Carabinieri and the district attorney didn't know anything about it, and why they hadn't gotten the call records for Manuela's second cell phone.

Then there was a more urgent question: What was I going to do with this information?

The most natural and normal thing would have been for me to call Navarra immediately and tell him. Of course, I realized that would mean I'd be cut out of the rest of the investigation. So then I told myself, of course, I ought to hand the information over to the Carabinieri, but first maybe I should investigate a little myself. A stupid idea. The Carabinieri could easily find out whether Manuela had another cell phone in her name by simply making a blanket request to all the providers. I couldn't. Still, I felt it was my investigation, and I didn't want to hand it over to someone else now that I was finally on to something.

The first thing to do was to call Caterina and ask her if she knew Manuela had had a second phone. I called her repeatedly, but I couldn't get through to her phone. For a moment, I considered looking up her home number in the phone book—I knew her address—and trying to call her there, but I discarded the idea when it occurred to me that her mother or her father might answer.

Then it occurred to me that I could call Manuela's mother. Call her directly, without talking to Fornelli. I was feeling energized, and I wanted to move quickly.

Her cell phone number—hers, not her husband's— was written in the file and I called her immediately, without stopping to think about it. Her phone rang several times, and just as I was about to hang up, she answered.

"*Buona sera*, Signora, it's Counselor Guerrieri."

There was a moment's hesitation, a brief silence. Then she remembered who I was.

"Counselor, *buona sera!*"

For an instant, I was on the verge of asking her how she was doing.

"I'm sorry to bother you. I just wanted to ask you a question."

"Yes?" Suddenly she sounded both hopeful and nervous. I wondered if it had been a good idea to give in to the impulse to call her.

"I wanted to ask you whether Manuela might have had more than one cell phone."

There was a long pause. So long that I finally checked that she was still on the line.

"Yes, forgive me. I was thinking. Manuela likes phones. She's always getting new ones. She likes to play with them, you know, photographs, videos, music, video games."

"But you don't know if she had a second phone number."

"Well, that's why I was trying to think. She certainly had a number of different cell phones, and over the years she'd had a lot of different phone numbers, too. But when she disappeared, she only had one. She'd only had one number for quite a while, at least as far as I know. Why are you asking? Have you found out something?"

It had definitely been a bad idea to call her. I should have waited until Caterina was reachable.

"It's only a theory. Only a theory. And almost certainly a theory that won't lead anywhere. I don't want you to get—" I was going to say that I didn't want her to get her hopes up, but I caught myself just in time. "I don't want you to get any expectations that we're about to discover anything. I'm working on a few leads that I still have to check out. I'll let you know."

There was another pause. A long and painful one.

"Is Manuela alive, Counselor?"

"I don't know, Signora. I'm very sorry, but I have no way of answering that question."

Then I said a hasty good-bye, as if I were eager to escape from a dangerous situation. I closed my eyes and ran my fingers through my hair. Then I ran them lightly over the surface of my face, feeling my eyelids, the ridge of my nose, the whiskers that had sprouted on my face since I'd shaved that morning. The friction made a prickly sound.

At last, I opened my eyes again.

A second telephone. Christ, a second telephone. There could be anything on the call records for that phone. A second telephone was such an obvious possibility that no one had even thought of it. It was like Poe's purloined letter.

I left the office telling myself that I needed to talk it over with Tancredi. He would have known what to do, but he was still in America.

I felt like going to see Nadia, telling her everything, and asking her what she thought, but I immediately discarded that idea. I wasn't sure why, but after what had happened in Rome, the idea of going to see Nadia made me faintly uncomfortable, as if I'd somehow betrayed her.

Absurd, I told myself.

It's all absurd.

I tried calling Caterina again, but her phone was still unreachable.

So I went home, laced up my boxing gloves, and punched Mister Bag over and over again. As I paused between one round and the next, I talked to him, asking his opinion about the latest developments in the case. He didn't say much that evening. He just swung there lazily. Then, finally, he let me know I ought to have something to eat, drink a glass of good wine, and sleep on it. Maybe I'd come up with an idea the following day.

Maybe.

33.

I slept badly and had nightmares. When I woke up, I still didn't have any bright ideas. I got out of bed feeling grumpy, and things only got worse when I remembered what was on the schedule that morning.

I had an appointment at the district attorney's office with a client, a physician and a university professor, not to mention an academic power broker, who was charged with fixing a job search and assigning the position to one of his assistants. The other candidate was an internationally respected researcher who had worked for years in the United States at major universities and medical research centers. At a certain point, he had decided to move back to Italy.

When the search for a chair in his field was announced, he applied, unaware that the position had already been assigned and the job search was a farce. The chosen recipient of the chair was a young researcher, a brainless wonder who was lucky enough to be the son of another professor in the same department. He was known in academic circles for his rigorous lack of morals and nicknamed Little Piero the Greedy.

The vastly disproportionate difference in the two candidates' scientific qualifications—obviously, entirely in favor of the candidate who lacked the inside track—was fairly ludicrous. But that detail was of no interest to the hiring panel, and the brainless wonder was given the position. The better qualified researcher smelled a rat. He took legal action: He appealed to the regional administrative court, won the appeal, and filed a criminal complaint against the professor with the district attorney's office.

So my client received a summons to appear at the district attorney's office, on charges of malfeasance and falsification, and I recommended that he invoke his right not to answer their questions. The evidence against him was minimal, and if he agreed to answer the questions of the prosecutor—who was a very smart young woman, unquestionably much more intelligent than he was—he would likely only make matters worse.

In this case, as in many others that I found myself handling, I had the distinct impression that I was on the wrong side. And in this case, as in many others, I wondered if I really wanted to defend my client. I told myself that I didn't want to, and then I accepted the case anyway. It was something I really should have discussed with my psychiatrist, if only I'd had one.

As I rode my bike over to the court building, I decided that this was the worst possible morning to see my client: He was clearly guilty of a crime that I considered particularly heinous. He was an unctuous windbag, and worst of all, he wore tasseled loafers.

There are only a few matters on which I am unforgiving. These include tasseled loafers, but also cords for sunglasses, Cartier pens, money clips, fake leather shoulder bags, cable-knit cardigans, solid-gold bracelets for men, and breath sprays.

Given these convictions of mine, when we met as arranged outside the office of the prosecuting attorney, a few minutes before the interview was scheduled to begin, I wasn't in the cheeriest of spirits. After the conventional hellos and other conversational boilerplate—devoid of any genuine warmth (at least on my part)—he told me that he had serious doubts about the tactic of choosing to avail himself of his right not to answer any questions. He thought that he could explain everything, and that it struck him that refusing to answer was tantamount to an admission of guilt and in any case the behavior of a criminal, hardly in keeping with his prestigious position.

Your prestigious position as a windbag and a sticky-fingered academic who's slimed his way to the top, I hissed at him in my mind, while somewhere inside me a totally misplaced wave of anger was rising. After all, my client was simply expressing a legitimate doubt about our tactics. Unfortunately for him, he was the wrong person, on the wrong morning, and, worst of all, wearing the wrong shoes.

"I thought we'd already talked this over, Professor. Knowing the prosecutor and considering the current status of the case, I would reiterate my advice: you should take full advantage of your legal right not to respond to questions. Of course, that is entirely your decision, so if you decide not to act accordingly I can hardly interfere. If you do so, however, let me state here and now that I believe you would be committing a grave mistake, and I would certainly reserve the right to resign from the case immediately."

After I was done talking, I was as surprised as he was at how aggressive I'd been. He stood there for a moment without speaking, taken aback, almost frightened, unsure what to do now. Under different circumstances, his arrogance and pomposity would have come into play, and he would have given me a large and indignant piece of his mind. But we were in the district attorney's office, one of the most intimidating places in the world. He was the accused, and I was his attorney. He wasn't in a very good position to take a hard line with me. So he just took a deep breath.

"All right, Counselor, we'll do as you recommend."

At that point, since I'm no paragon of consistency, I felt guilty. I'd mistreated him, abusing my position of power: something no one should ever do. I spoke in a more gentle voice, as if he and I were on the same side.

"It's the right thing, Professor. Then we'll see what the prosecutor decides to do next, and if we need time to draw up a long and detailed written statement and submit it as a response, we'll have it."

A short while later we entered the prosecutor's office and declared that we were availing ourselves of the right not to answer. Five minutes after that I was back out on the street, heading for my office.

I was locking my bike to a lamp post near the front door of my building when I noticed a large black dog with a daunting but very familiar silhouette trotting down the sidewalk.

When I recognized him, I felt a surge of happiness. Baskerville. Nadia couldn't be far behind, I assumed, and I whistled to the dog as I looked around for his owner.

The huge beast loped over to me and when he was close enough, reared up on his hind legs, placing both forepaws on my chest. His tail was wagging frantically and I

beamed—proud of my unexpected popularity with a dog—
at what good friends Baskerville and I had become in such
a short time. To return his cordial greeting, I reached up and
scratched him on the head, behind both ears, the way I had
the night we first met.

Behind *both* ears?

Baskerville only has one ear, I said to myself. And so
that tail-wagging behemoth with both paws planted on my
chest and his nose just inches from my face wasn't Baskerville. I gulped uncomfortably, struggling to read the dog's
expression and figure out whether, having greeted me joy-
fully, he was now ready to rip me limb from limb. But the
monster did seem friendly, and he was licking my hands. I
was wondering how I could disengage from my new friend's
embrace without hurting his feelings when a skinny young
man hurried around the corner and came toward us. When
he reached us, the first thing he did was to snap a leash onto
the dog's collar and pull him away. Then, as he struggled to
catch his breath, he spoke to me.

"I'm so sorry, forgive me. We let him off the leash in the
store, and a customer left the door open, and he got out.
He's always trying to get out. He's just a puppy. He's not
even a year old yet. I hope he didn't scare you."

"No, not a bit," I said, which was a half truth. When it
dawned on me that this dog wasn't Baskerville, I have to
admit an icy shiver ran down my spine, but I didn't think it
was necessary to give this young man all the details.

"Rocco's a gentle dog. He loves children. We got a Corso
because we wanted a guard dog, but I'm afraid he's a big
softie."

I gave him a knowing smile but said nothing more. The
young man seemed a little too chatty and I didn't want to

encourage him; the next thing you know he'd be telling me the story of his life, starting with his first pet hamster. So I said good-bye to him and to Rocco, and as they headed off down the sidewalk I leaned down to snap my bicycle lock shut.

The little padlock made its usual reassuring click. I stood up, and a thought popped into my brain. This new thought was buzzing around, from one side of my head to the other. It was just out of reach, though, and I couldn't quite articulate it.

I tried to reconstruct the last few minutes.

The dog had trotted toward me. I'd whistled for him, expecting Nadia to come around the corner any minute. The dog greeted me enthusiastically. I scratched the dog's ears, and that was when I'd realized it wasn't Baskerville. A second later the dog's owner appeared and . . . wait, wait, back up, Guerrieri.

I'd scratched the dog behind its ears and that was when I realized it wasn't Baskerville. That was exactly when this new thought occurred to me. I frantically tried to put the idea into words.

Pino, also known (to me) as Baskerville, was identified by the fact that he was missing an ear. So he was identified by an absence. A non-presence.

Deep thoughts, I said to myself in an attempt at sarcastic wit. The barb fell flat. There really was something important there that I couldn't quite grasp.

Baskerville. A missing ear. Something that's missing explains everything. What? Something missing.

Baskerville.

Sherlock Holmes.

The dog didn't bark.

The phrase formed in my head, suddenly, and began blinking like a neon sign in the desert.

A dog failing to bark was the famous "curious incident of the dog in the night-time" in the Sherlock Holmes story *The Hound of the Baskervilles.* Or maybe it was another book. I needed to check immediately, even though I wasn't yet sure why.

I went upstairs to the office; no one was there. They were all out visiting court clerks and taking care of business. I was glad to be alone. I made myself an espresso, turned on my computer and Googled "Holmes" and "the dog did nothing."

The phrase wasn't in *The Hound of the Baskervilles*; it was in "Silver Blaze." As I read, I remembered. The short story was about the theft of a thoroughbred racehorse that Holmes solved by observing "the curious incident of the dog in the night-time." The curious incident in question was the fact that the dog had not barked. Therefore, the horse thief was someone the dog knew well.

The key to the mystery was something that didn't happen. Something that should have been there but wasn't.

What did all this have to do with my investigation?

What was missing, that should have been there?

When the answer began to take shape, a bout of nausea came along with it, like a sudden wave of seasickness.

I picked up the file, pulled out Manuela's phone records, and examined them again. I paged through them, and I found clear confirmation of my hypothesis—that is, I failed to find what ought to have been there. I noticed an absence I'd failed to notice until that instant. The nausea grew and spread, becoming so intense that I was sure I'd vomit any minute.

The dog didn't bark. And I knew that dog very well.

I turned on my cell phone and found four calls from Caterina's number.

34.

I wondered if it would be best to wait. Then I immediately decided it would not.

So I called Caterina. She answered on the second ring, sounding cheerful.

"Ciao, Gigi. How nice to see your name on my cell phone."

"Ciao, how are you?"

"Fine. In fact, now that you've called me, I feel wonderful. I saw that you called me last night, but I turned off my phone. I was exhausted." She paused, giggled, then resumed speaking. "I went right to bed like a five-year-old girl. This morning I tried to call you several times, but I couldn't get through."

"I was in court. I just got back to my office. Listen, I was thinking . . ."

"Yes?"

"What do you say if I come by and pick you up and we go get something to eat somewhere along the coast?"

"I'd say yes, what a fantastic idea. I'll run and get ready. I'll see you in twenty minutes. I'll wait for you downstairs, in front of my building."

I pulled up exactly twenty minutes later, the time it took

to get the car out of the garage and drive to her house. I was just double parking to wait for her when she emerged from the apartment building. She was all smiles as she climbed into the car. She leaned over, kissed me, then fastened her seat belt. She seemed to be in an excellent mood, even happy. She was truly beautiful. Mental images of our night in Rome flickered before my eyes for a moment, like still images edited for subliminal effect into a feature film about something else—a movie that did not have a happy ending. It took my breath away, sadness and desire mixing cruelly.

"Where are you taking me?"

"Where would you like to go?"

"How about we go to La Forcatella and eat some sea urchin?"

La Forcatella is a little fishing village on the coast to the south of the city, just beyond the line between the provinces of Bari and Brindisi. It's famous for its excellent sea urchin.

The car ran with silent precision along a highway surrounded by fields. The clouds were magnificent and clean; the scene looked like an Ansel Adams photograph. Spring was bursting out all around us, and it communicated a thrilling, dangerous euphoria. I did my best to focus on my driving and on the individual acts involved—shifting up and down, gently hugging the curves, glancing up at my rearview mirror—and I tried not to think.

There weren't a lot of people in the restaurant, so we were able to get a table overlooking the water. Just a few feet from us, the waves lapped delicately at the rocks. The air was fragrant, and on the horizon a clear and perfect boundary was visible where the deep blue of the sea pressed up against the light blue of the sky.

Damn, I thought to myself as I sat across the table from her.

We ordered fifty sea urchins and a carafe of ice-cold wine. A little later, we ordered another fifty and another carafe. The sea urchins were plump and delicious, their orange flesh offering up their mysterious taste. Between the sea urchins and that cold, light wine, my head began to spin slightly.

Caterina was talking, but I paid no attention to her words. I listened to the sound of her voice. I watched the expressions on her face. I looked at her mouth. I wished I could have a photograph to remember her by.

An absurd thought—but it set a chain of other thoughts in motion, including the idea of just dropping everything. For a few minutes, in fact, I thought that was what I'd do. I'd forget what I'd figured out. For those few minutes, I experienced a feeling of complete mastery, a perfect, unstable equilibrium. The kind of perfection that belongs only to things that are temporary, destined to end shortly.

I remembered a holiday road trip in France, many years earlier, with Sara and some friends. We arrived in Biarritz and fell in love with the beach town's timeless atmosphere, so we decided to stay. That was where I first took a few surfing lessons. After trying countless times, I finally managed to stand up on the board and ride a wave for three, maybe four seconds. In that instant I understood why surfers—real surfers—are obsessed, why the only thing they care about is getting up on a wave and riding it for as long as possible. To hell with everything else. Nothing could be more perfect than that temporary experience.

As I sat listening to the sound of Caterina's voice and savoring the sweet and salty taste of the last few sea urchins, I felt as if I were on a surfboard, riding the wave of time, for an endless, perfect instant.

I wondered what it would be like to remember that moment. That's when I fell off the wave and remembered why I was there.

Soon after that, we got up from the table.

"What have you decided to do next?" she asked, as we were walking toward the car.

"About what?"

"About your investigation. You mentioned that you wanted to show pictures of Michele to a drug dealer."

"Oh, right. I was thinking of doing that, but I'm still trying to figure everything out. Turns out, it might not be necessary. I thought of something else."

"What?"

"Let's get in the car and I'll tell you about it."

The car was parked facing the beach, in a gravel lot that's always packed with cars in the summer. That afternoon, it was deserted.

"First I want to smoke a cigarette," she said, pulling her colorful cigarette case out of her purse.

"You can smoke in the car, if you want."

"No, I hate the smell of cigarette smoke in my own car, so I can only imagine how gross it must be for someone who doesn't even smoke."

I was about to tell her that I'd been a smoker for years, and that I hated the smell of smoke in the car, too, even back then. Then I decided that the time had come to deal with things.

"I need to ask you something."

"Go on," she said, exhaling her first drag of smoke.

"As far as you know, did Manuela have two cell phones?"

35.

The smoke went down the wrong way and she coughed violently, in shock and confusion. As if she were in a bad play.

"What do you mean, two cell phones?"

"Did Manuela just have one cell phone, or did she have more than one?"

"I . . . I think she only had one. Why do you want to know?"

"Are you sure? Think carefully."

"Why are you asking me this?"

Now her voice took on a note of impatience and grew almost aggressive.

"I was told that Manuela may have had two phones, and I thought you'd probably know."

"Who told you that?"

"What does that matter? Do you know whether or not she had two phone numbers?"

"I don't know. I only called her on one number."

"Do you know that number by heart?"

"No, why would I? It was saved in my cell phone. I didn't need to memorize it."

"Do you still have it?"

"Have what?"

"Manuela's phone number, saved."

She stared at me, wide-eyed. She wasn't sure what was happening, but she knew it wasn't good. She decided to get angry.

"Can I ask what the fuck you're trying to find out? What the fuck is the meaning of these questions?"

"Have you gotten a new cell phone, since Manuela's disappearance?"

"No. Could you tell me . . ."

"Did you erase Manuela from your phone?"

"No, of course not."

"Can I take look at the contacts saved in your cell phone?"

She looked at me with an incredulous expression that rapidly deteriorated into a grimace of rage as she flicked what was left of her cigarette onto the ground.

"Fuck you. Unlock this car, get in, and drive me home."

I punched the remote door lock with my thumb, and the doors clicked open, with a soft and inevitable thunk. She pulled the door open and got in the car immediately. I got in and sat next to her a few seconds later, but I wished I were somewhere else. Somewhere far away.

For a minute, or maybe longer, neither of us spoke.

"May I ask why you're not starting the car?"

"I need you to tell me about Manuela's second cell phone."

"And I need you to leave me alone and take me home. I'm not going to tell you a fucking thing."

"If you want me to, I'll take you home, but the minute I drop you off I have to go to the Carabinieri, you understand that, right?"

"As far as I'm concerned, you can jump off a tall building. That might be the best thing you could do."

Her voice was starting to crack, from anger and emotion, but also because of the fear that was beginning to break through.

"If I go to the Carabinieri, I'll have to tell them that Manuela had a second telephone that no one else knew about. It won't take them long to find the phone number, and then they'll check the phone records. And then there will be plenty of things to explain, in situations much more disagreeable than this one."

She said nothing. She opened the car window, took out a cigarette, and lit it. Without asking if I minded, without apologizing for the stink. She smoked and looked straight ahead, at the sea. I thought how incredible it was that such a pretty face could be so twisted and deformed by rage and fear that it became ugly.

"I think you'd better tell me the things you've been keeping from me. I think it'll be better for you to tell me, rather than being forced to tell the Carabinieri and the prosecutor. There may be a way to limit the damage."

"Why are you so sure that Manuela had another number and that I have it?"

I was about to ask her if she'd ever read that story by Arthur Conan Doyle. I didn't, though, because it struck me as highly unlikely that she had.

"Your number doesn't appear in the call records for Manuela's cell phone that the Carabinieri obtained."

It took her a little while to absorb that information.

"It's inexplicable that there would never be a single call between the two of you, since you were such close friends. And at least one call should appear on the records, because you told me that you called Manuela to meet you for a drink that time. But not even that call shows up."

"I don't remember where I called her. Maybe I called her at her house."

"Caterina, tell me about the other phone. Please."

She lit another cigarette. She smoked half of it, moving her head in an awkward, unnatural manner, as if her balance were suddenly off. Her lovely complexion had drained to a lusterless, sickly gray. Then, suddenly, she began to speak, but her eyes looked straight ahead.

"Manuela had another phone number and another cell phone."

"And that's the phone you called her on."

"Yes."

I hovered for a few seconds in a precarious equilibrium. I had focused entirely on getting her to admit the existence of a second phone number; I wasn't ready for what came next. Then I decided that there was no reason, at that point, to beat around the bush.

"What happened that Sunday?"

"I'm cold," she said. Her face had definitely lost all its color now.

I pushed the button to close the passenger-side window, even though the cold wasn't coming from outside.

Then I waited for her to answer my question.

36.

"It seems impossible that it's come to this point," she said after a long silence, continuing to look away. Her words were dramatic, but her tone of voice was strangely neutral and colorless.

"You had plans to meet, that Sunday afternoon, didn't you?"

She nodded without speaking.

"You'd made those plans the day before."

She nodded again.

"Did you go pick her up at the station, when she arrived from Ostuni?"

"No. I was at Duilio's house, and she was supposed to come meet us there."

"And did she?"

"Yes, she got there around six, maybe a little later. She took a cab there from the train station and asked if she could take a shower."

"Does Duilio live alone?"

"Yes, of course."

"Where?"

"Well, now he's moved. He didn't want to live in that apartment anymore."

"And that apartment would be where?"

"He used to live up by the lighthouse, in one of those new apartment buildings facing the sea. Now he's in the center of town."

"Why had you made plans to meet?"

"Manuela was going back to Rome, and she wanted to stock up."

I swallowed, gulping uncomfortably. It was what I had expected to hear, but I still didn't like it.

"You mean, she wanted to stock up on cocaine?"

"That's right."

"Was the cocaine only for her personal use?"

"No, she sold coke, too, so she could pay for all the coke she was using."

"Did she sell it in Rome?"

"Mostly. But I don't know who her customers were."

"Did Nicoletta know? I mean, did she know that Manuela was dealing drugs?"

"I don't know, but I doubt it. What she told you when we went to see her is all she knows. More or less."

"So she came over to Duilio's apartment to buy some cocaine to take with her to Rome."

"That's right."

"How much was she going to get?"

"I don't know. She bought fifty, even a hundred grams at a time. They had an agreement. If she had the money, she paid right away. Otherwise, Duilio fronted her the money."

"What does Duilio do for a living?"

"He has a car dealership. That is, he works at his father's car dealership, but he's involved in politics, too."

"And he makes a little extra by selling cocaine."

Once again, she nodded.

"And how old is this gentleman?"

"Thirty-two."

I took a few seconds to get my mental bearings, and then I continued questioning her.

"So, Manuela came over to Duilio's house, and you were there, too. She took a shower, and then what happened?"

"The plan had been to go out for dinner, but first Manuela wanted to try some of the coke. It was from a new shipment that Duilio had just received the day before."

"And she had come for that purpose?"

"That's right. She'd been out of coke for a few days. She'd hoped to find some at the *trulli*, but nobody had any that weekend. So when she arrived she had only one thing in mind."

It occurred to me that Anita was a sharp-eyed observer. What was it she had said? *Manuela didn't strike me as an easygoing person. She seemed a little speedy.*

"What are you saying? Was she an addict?"

"Well, she used almost every day. At first, she took other people's coke, just at parties. Then gifts of a gram here and there and lines at parties weren't enough anymore. And that's why she started having to deal coke. She definitely couldn't pay for all the coke she consumed with the money her parents gave her."

"Go on."

"She took a shower and then we decided to do a few lines before going out. That coke was incredible, like the best I've ever had. After two or three lines we were ready to go out, but she wanted more. She snorted more and more, and I told her to stop, that she was overdoing it. But she told me she hadn't had any in days, and that it had been depressing and she needed to make up for lost time. She was laughing and looked a little crazy. At a certain point, Duilio started to get worried too."

"Then what happened?"

"Duilio said that's enough, and he tried to take the bag away from her. She got mad at him, started shouting, and said that unless he gave her some more, she'd start screaming, she'd tear the house apart. I'm telling you, it seemed like she'd lost her mind."

For a few seconds, I stopped listening to Caterina's words and concentrated instead on the sound of her voice. There was no emotion; the cadence was monotonous. It didn't seem like she was telling a story that was rushing ineluctably toward a tragic ending. It didn't sound at all like the voice of a young woman describing the death of her closest friend. I shook my head and shoulders as a shiver ran through me.

"Could you repeat that last part, please? I'm sorry, I got distracted for a second."

"He told her he'd give her one more line and that was it. He was pouring the coke onto the table and his hand must have slipped. Like I said, she'd already had way too much cocaine, and then she took everything that had spilled out. It wasn't the first time she'd gone over the top like that."

"And then?"

"And then, a little while later, she started to feel sick. She was sweating and shaking and her heart was racing. It was like she'd suddenly come down with a fever. Her pupils were so dilated, it was scary to look her in the eye."

"What did you do?"

"I wanted to call 911, but Duilio said we should wait. He'd seen people in that condition before, and after a little while they always got better. He said, 'Come on, let's wait.

It happens sometimes. If you call 911, the police will come and we'll be in deep shit. You'll see. She'll feel better in a minute.' At a certain point, she stopped shaking and closed her eyes. We were so relieved, because it seemed like she'd fallen asleep. We thought it was over."

"But it wasn't?"

"After a few minutes, we realized she'd stopped breathing."

She still had the same neutral, flat tone of voice, no intensity to it. It was frightening.

I had believed from the very outset that Manuela was dead. But now that I knew it, really knew it, now that a person who'd watched her die was telling me that she was dead, I had a hard time believing it. I tried to put my finger on the feeling and I realized that the whole time, even though I was convinced that Manuela was dead, I'd always imagined her alive.

She *was* alive, in one of those parallel worlds where our imaginations create and keep their stories. The stories that we tell other people and the stories, so much more powerful and deceptive, that we tell ourselves.

"So what did you do then?"

"Duilio tried to give her mouth-to-mouth. Then he massaged her heart, but it didn't do any good. So I said that we had to call the police immediately. I was starting to freak out."

I refrained from telling her that I found that difficult to believe, considering the cool, matter-of-fact way that she was relating the horrifying tale.

"But you didn't call."

"Duilio said it would be stupid. He said we'd both wind up in jail for no good reason. He said it had been an accident and that, after all was said and done, it had been Manuela's fault for shoving all that cocaine up her nose. We couldn't bring her back to life, and we'd just destroy our own lives."

"So what did you do next?"

She told me what they did next. She told me how they got rid of Manuela's body. They wrapped her in a carpet, just like in a B movie, took her to an illegal dump, in a distant corner of the Murgia highlands, and burned her with her possessions on a stack of old car tires. Duilio told her that was the best method to get rid of a body. It was what Mafia hit men did. The tires burn completely, down to the smallest particle, and when they're done burning there's nothing left.

As I listened, I was struck with a terrifying, dizzying feeling of unreality.

This can't be happening. This is a nightmare. Any minute now I'll wake up in my own bed, drenched with sweat, and I'll realize that none of this really happened. I'll get out of bed, drink a glass of water, and then I'll very slowly get dressed and go out for a walk, even though it's dark out. The way I used to sometimes when I couldn't sleep.

Then I felt an overwhelming urge to punch her and free myself of her. My right hand formed a fist up on the seat. I thought that if it was unbearable for me to hear these things, for Manuela's parents it would be torture.

I didn't hit her. I kept asking questions, because there were still things that I needed to know. Details. Or maybe not.

"Didn't you think the police would catch up with you eventually?"

"No. Manuela had that second cell phone, the one you found out about. It had a memory card that she asked some guy in Rome to buy for her. That was Duilio's idea. Duilio was really paranoid about wiretaps and eavesdropping, both because of the drugs and because of his political activity. She only used that phone to talk to me, Duilio, and, I think, the people she sold drugs to in Rome. The phone wasn't in her name, and even her parents didn't know about it. So we were pretty sure that no one could ever find the number and trace it back to us by checking the calls. No one knew we were going to see her that afternoon."

There was nothing else to say. It was banal—almost bureaucratic, almost perfect.

Almost.

"Why did you agree to talk to me?"

"What else could I do? Manuela's mother asked me to, and I couldn't refuse. You all would have gotten suspicious, the way you got suspicious when Michele refused to meet with you."

"Then why did you decide to help me? To the extent that you did, of course."

Caterina took a deep breath, pulled out another cigarette, and lit it.

"When I found out that I was going to have to meet with you, I called Duilio. We hadn't talked for months. We got together and planned how I should act. I was supposed to confirm everything I'd already told the Carabinieri, and if by chance you asked me what I'd done that evening, I would tell you that I'd been with Duilio, that we went out to dinner, and that the last time I'd seen Manuela was a few days before that. I didn't expect you to bring up the subject of drugs. When you did, I just kind of lost it. I had no idea you already knew about the cocaine."

And in fact I didn't. I just bluffed, and you fell for it.

I should have felt proud of myself, but I couldn't feel good about anything. My mouth was dry and sour.

"Once you told me that Michele had refused to meet with you, that his lawyer had threatened to take action against you, I thought I could push the whole drug thing onto Michele and keep you from looking any further."

"And, of course, Michele had nothing to do with any of this."

"He had nothing to do with Manuela's death, but he had plenty to do with the cocaine. He got her started on it, and he was in business with Duilio. That's why his lawyer wouldn't let him meet with you, because he has a lot to hide."

"Does he know what happened to Manuela?"

"No. When he got back from his trip, he asked Duilio if he knew what had happened. Duilio told him that he didn't know a thing, and Michele let it go. It's possible he didn't believe him, but Michele is such an asshole that he only cares about his own comfort and convenience. He doesn't give a shit about anybody else. Everything I told you about him is true."

"Why did you persuade Nicoletta to talk to me?"

"One way or another, you would have gotten in touch with her. So Duilio and I thought it would be a good idea for me to convince you I could help. If I pretended to help you in your investigation, it would be easier for me to control what you were doing and maybe I could even feed you false leads. There was the Michele thing, and then my suggesting that Manuela might have disappeared in Rome and not in Puglia."

She suddenly shut her mouth and stopped talking. In fact, I thought, there's nothing left to say.

It was getting dark.

Not just outside.

37.

"What happens now?" she asked after several long minutes of silence, reviving me from the troubled torpor into which I had drifted.

"Excuse me for a moment," I replied, opening my door and getting out of the car.

A wind had sprung up and was gusting the sky clean of clouds. The air was clear, briny, tragic.

I walked back to the restaurant and stepped inside to make sure that she couldn't see or hear me. I called Navarra and he answered almost immediately, on the second or third ring.

"*Buona sera*, Counselor."

"*Buona sera*, Officer."

"You're not calling to tell me you found out what happened to the girl, are you?" he asked jokingly, just to start the conversation. I said nothing. The silence dragged on.

"Counselor?" The playful tone was gone from his voice.

"I'm here. I assume you're at home."

"No, I'm still at the office, but I was about to leave. It's been a brutal day."

"Well, I'm sorry to tell you, you'll have to stay in the office a little longer."

"What happened?"

"In a short while, I'm going to bring someone in to see you. You should get in touch with the public defender currently on duty while you wait for me. We're going to need him."

There was a long, heavy pause.

"So, the girl is dead?"

"Yes."

"The day she disappeared?"

"Yes."

I told him the bare bones of the story and we agreed that in forty-five minutes he would be waiting outside the Carabinieri barracks. Then I hung up and went back out to the car.

Caterina was still there. She hadn't moved an inch. I got back in the car, started the engine, and pulled out. She didn't ask me again what was going to happen next. She didn't say a thing. Neither of us spoke until we were back in the city and I stopped the car a few blocks away from the Carabinieri barracks.

"You're going to have to tell the Carabinieri the things you told me."

Before she said anything, she gave me a long look that I was unable to decipher.

"Will they arrest me?"

"No. First of all, you weren't caught in the act, and the basic elements for arrest are lacking. Second, you're turning yourself in voluntarily, and most importantly, the cocaine wasn't yours. You didn't give it to Manuela. You'll just face charges of being an accomplice to concealing a dead body. You'll get off with a plea bargain and probation."

"What about Duilio?"

"That's up to him. In many ways, Manuela's death was accidental. If he cooperates with the law—and it's entirely in his interest to do so—he can stay out of prison while he awaits trial, and with a good lawyer he might be able to strike a plea bargain, too. Of course, he'll get a stiffer penalty."

I was about to add a few other technical details about the process, describing the steps a good lawyer could take to reduce damage and possibly even keep Duilio What's-His-Name out of prison entirely. But I realized that I had no interest in offering him any help at all. In fact, I was surprised to find myself hoping that his lawyer would turn out to be an incompetent—maybe Schirani—and that the prosecutor would be ill-disposed toward him, and that Duilio would be tossed into prison with the maximum sentence. It was probably a place where he'd thrive, anyway.

"Will he be looking at drug charges?"

"Yes. He'll face charges of concealing a dead body, possession of narcotics with intent to distribute, and Article 586."

"What's Article 586?"

"Article 586 of the penal code: You should have studied that."

She said nothing, so I went on.

"Death during commission of another crime. It's a variation on a manslaughter charge, but less serious. The idea is that if you provide someone with drugs and the person dies from taking the drugs, you're liable."

"Will we have to take them to the place where we . . . will we have to go to the dump?"

"I don't think that'll be necessary," I lied.

She wrung her hands. She scratched the left side of her

neck with her right hand. She sniffed loudly, as if she'd been crying, not seeming to notice that she was making any noise. Then she ran her hand over face and looked up at me. Now her face was filled with sorrow and sincerity and remorse. She was a damned good actress, and she was preparing her last-ditch attempt in the form of a dramatic monologue.

"Guido, do I really have to? Manuela is dead and I'll live with my remorse over what happened for the rest of my life. But it won't bring her back to her family if I go and confess. The only thing I'll succeed in doing is ruining my own life, without benefiting anyone else. What good would that do?"

An excellent question. The first and only answer that came to mind was that maybe that poor miserable soul would stop going to the station to meet trains. Maybe.

I could feel my determination wavering. I wondered if I'd been in too much of a hurry to call Navarra. Maybe she was right. Forcing her to confess would only ravage other lives, without doing anything to repair the lives that were already lying in ruins, irreparably.

What good would that do, indeed?

Then, like a flickering light in great darkness, I remembered something that Hannah Arendt wrote.

"The remedy for unpredictability, for the chaotic uncertainty of the future, is contained in the faculty to make and keep promises."

I'd be keeping a promise. Maybe that's what good it would do. Anyway, it was all I had.

"You have to do it. Unfortunately, I'm going to have to insist."

"What if I refuse?"

"Then I'll go by myself, and it will be a lot worse. For everyone."

"You can't. You're bound by attorney-client privilege to keep everything I told you secret."

It was phrased as a statement, but it was actually a desperate question. And legally speaking, utter nonsense.

"You're not my client."

"What if I tell them you had sex with me? Will they kick you out of the bar association?"

"That would be unpleasant," I admitted. "Unpleasant but nothing more. There would be no consequences for me. Like I said, you're not my client, and you're not even a minor."

Caterina sat there for a minute without speaking, casting around for some final, desperate argument, but she came up empty-handed. She finally realized that this was the end.

"You're a piece of shit. You're giving me up because you want your clients to pay you. You don't give a shit about them, about me, about anybody. The only thing you care about is getting your goddamned money."

I put the car in gear and drove the few remaining blocks to the main gate of the Carabinieri barracks. Navarra was already there, and as I drove past him, we exchanged nods. I stopped about twenty yards up the street and parked the car next to a couple of small dumpsters.

"Before we go to the cops and flush my life down the toilet, there's something I want to say to you."

Her voice was seething with rage and violence. Perhaps she was expecting me to ask what it was she wanted to say. I didn't, and that only stoked her fury.

"The only reason I had sex with you was to control you, to keep you from finding out about what we did."

Well, then, perhaps we should say that it didn't work out the way you planned, I thought as I nodded my head.

"It was a real effort. I was faking it the whole time. You disgust me. You're old, and when you're lying there with Alzheimer's, pissing on yourself, or you're hobbling down the street with a Moldavian caregiver holding you by the elbow, I'll still be young and pretty, and I'll think back with loathing on the day I let you lay your hands on my body."

Now, hold on there a minute. You're taking it a little too far, sweetheart. I'd like to remind you that there are twenty-two years between us, not forty. It's a big difference, sure, but when my caregiver is taking me for a walk, you're not exactly going to be in the first blush of youth yourself.

That's not what I said, but I was seriously considering saying it when she put an end to my dilemma and the whole uncomfortable situation with a final flash of real class.

"Piece of shit," she said, just in case the concept she had explicated a minute earlier hadn't been clear to me. Then she spat in my face, jerked open the car door, and got out.

I sat there motionless, watching her walk down the sidewalk in my rearview mirror.

I saw her go up to Navarra and then vanish with him, once and for all, into the Carabinieri barracks.

Only then did I wipe my face clean and drive away.

38.

For a few minutes, I thought I would give Fornelli a call, tell him what I'd uncovered, and leave it to him to inform Manuela's parents.

After all, I'd done the job they'd hired me to do. In fact, I'd done much more. They had asked me—Fornelli's words were still in my mind—to identify any further lines of investigation to suggest to the prosecutor, to keep him from closing the case. I had gone well beyond that request. I had done the further investigations myself. I had solved the case, and so I had more than fulfilled my responsibility.

It wasn't my job to tell Manuela's parents what had become of their daughter.

Like I said, for a few minutes that was my plan. During the course of those few minutes, I picked up my phone to call Fornelli repeatedly; each time, I put the phone back down. A lot of things went through my mind. And in the end, I remembered the time—it might have been two years ago—that Carmelo Tancredi invited me out for a spin in his inflatable motorboat.

It was a beautiful day in late May. The sea was calm, the light opalescent.

We set out from San Nicola wharf, steered north, and an hour later we were in the ancient port of Giovinazzo. It was a surreal place, almost metaphysical. There was no sign that time had passed over the last two or three centuries. There were no cars in sight, no antennas, no speedboats. Only rowboats, medieval ramparts, little boys in their underwear diving into the water, large seagulls gliding through the air, solitary and elegant.

We ate focaccia and drank beer. We sunbathed. And we talked a lot. As so often happens, we went from idle chit-chat to deep discussion.

"Do you have rules, Guerrieri?" Tancredi asked me at one point.

"Rules? Never gave it much thought. I don't think I have any explicit rules. But I imagine I have some, yes. What about you?"

"Yeah, I have some rules."

"What are your rules?"

"I'm a cop. The first rule for a cop is never to humiliate the people you have to interact with in your job as a policeman. Power over other people is obscene, and the only way to make it tolerable is to show respect. That's the most important rule. It's also the easiest one to break. What about you?"

"Adorno said that the highest form of morality is never to feel at home, not even in one's own home. I agree. You should never get too comfortable. You should always feel a little bit out of place."

"Right. For me, another rule has to do with lies. You should try to tell as few lies as possible to other people. And none to yourself."

He thought for a few seconds, then added, "Which is of course impossible, but you should try at least."

The port, awash in opaque sunlight and unseasonably

muggy heat for May, slowly dissolved as the lights of the city and the frantic chaos of evening traffic reappeared. Tancredi's words shimmered out of that seascape and into my car, where they stayed, hovering in midair.

You're wetting your pants at the idea of meeting the girl's parents and giving them the news. So you look for excuses and you tell lies. To yourself, which—as we were saying—isn't a good thing.

Isn't it up to you to tell the parents? If not, whose job is it?

No one else's job but mine. End of discussion.

I stopped thinking. From then on I did everything as if in a trance, and it all came easily to me. I called Fornelli, explained the bare essentials to him, and told him I'd drive by his office to pick him up so we could go see Manuela's parents together. He might have wanted to say something or raise some objection, but I didn't give him time. I hung up and started the car for what seemed like the thousandth time that day. I was about to experience the worst part of the whole horrible story.

When we got to the Ferraros' house, they were expecting us. Fornelli had called ahead, and when I saw their faces, I knew they already understood what was coming.

For the third time in less than two hours, I told the story of what I had found, and what had happened to Manuela.

I told them almost everything.

I kept a few parts of the story to myself. The fact that Manuela was a coke dealer, and the way the young couple disposed of her corpse. I decided that I had the right to spare myself that agony, at least. Of course, sooner or later they'd find out everything, down to the last cruel detail. Not that evening, though, and not from me.

When I said that Manuela was dead, Rosaria Ferraro rested her head in her hands, and I thought she was going to scream. But she didn't. She just emitted a muffled sob and then remained motionless for a long time, her head in her hands and her mouth half-open, in a still image of mute, infinite, intolerable sadness.

Antonio, aka Tonino, Ferraro was seated slightly behind her, leaning on a table. Tears started running down his face, and then he began to sob. And there I sat, watching and listening, because there was nothing else I could do.

Luckily, it didn't take long. Three quarters of an hour after I walked into the Ferraro's house, I was back in my car. I dropped Fornelli off after helplessly sitting through a long monologue about how amazing it was that I had discovered what I had discovered, and how I would have to tell him all the details in the coming days. And, of course, I should represent the family as civil plaintiffs in the upcoming trial, he said, as we shook hands.

Absolutely not, I replied. He'd need to find another lawyer. Something in my voice, or my face—or both—must have dissuaded him from trying to change my mind, or even asking me why.

I walked into my apartment; I felt enveloped by, and pervaded with, a perfect, throbbing exhaustion.

I greeted Mister Bag and told him that I would be with him in two minutes, no more. I walked into my bedroom, calmly undressed, and carefully and thoroughly taped up my hands. Then I put on my gloves. There are times when you have to do things right.

I boxed for half an hour. I was loose and I was quick, as if the exhaustion and other things that I carried inside me—things much worse than exhaustion—had been transformed into a fluid and mysterious energy.

Then I took a long hot shower, soaping myself with an amber-scented bath foam that I'd bought years earlier but never opened because I was waiting for the right occasion. The right occasion had never arrived.

When I walked back into the living room, in my bathrobe, I said out loud that I didn't want to be alone that evening, and that I intended to go see Nadia and old Baskerville.

"Forgive me, Mister Bag, it's not that I don't enjoy your company. Quite the contrary. It's just that sometimes, you really can be a little too taciturn."

Once I got outside, I realized that the city had turned silent, and the wind had died down, leaving only a slight scent of the sea in the air. The night once again seemed like a tranquil, welcoming place.

So I got on my bike and started pedaling fast down the deserted street.

ABOUT THE AUTHOR

Award-winning, best-selling Italian crime novelist Gianrico Carofiglio is the author of three previous novels featuring the character of defense lawyer Guido Guerrieri: *Involuntary Witness*, *A Walk in the Dark*, and *Reasonable Doubts*. A former prosecutor in Bari, Puglia, Carofiglio is an expert in the investigation of organized crime and related psychology. His other novels include *The Past Is a Foreign Country*. Carofiglio's books have been translated in seventeen languages worldwide.

10112 (4)